I0638183

GABRIEL'S
TRUMPET

Jon Black

GABRIEL'S TRUMPET
An 18thWall Productions book published by
arrangement with Jon Black
verba mea in minibus
desiderium meum
Cover by Barbara Sobczyńska
Design by M.H. Norris
Text Copyright
Gabriel's Trumpet © Jon Black

All rights reserved.
ISBN-13: 978-1-946033-12-3
ISBN-10:1-946033-12-X

PUBLISHER'S NOTE
This is a work of fiction. Names, characters, places, and incidents either are the products of
the author's imagination or used fictitiously. Any resemblance to actual persons, living or
dead, business establishments, events, locales, public figures, private figures, and fictional
characters is entirely coincidental.

The Publisher wishes to extend special thanks to Jordan O'Neal for his assistance as a
historian.

I dedicate this story to the memories of Tom "Pops" Carter, who helped me fall in love with roots music, and of Bob Sullivan, who opened an extraordinary window into its history. I know the music must be great where you both are.

Firstly, I want to thank everyone who made the short story version of "Gabriel's Trumpet" the *Best Short Story Published in 2017 (Other Genres)* in the P&E Readers' Poll. Special gratitude goes to my alpha readers, Reyna Arndorfer, Christopher Harrell, Kendra Harrell, and Matt Parr for your eyes on the working draft and for your feedback that made the short story, and ultimately the novel, a success.

Like most writers, I am constantly weaving stories requiring more knowledge on various topics than I possess. Fortunately, I am blessed with friends and acquaintances whose collective knowledge is as formidable as it is eclectic.

The character of Dr. Marcus Roads would never have gotten off the ground without the medical and pharmacological expertise of Drs. Michelle and Constantine Markides. They went above and beyond the call of duty, doing independent research to provide (often frightening) answers every time I asked "how was it done in the 1920s?" Any of this story's errors or liberties in that regard are mine and not theirs.

Themes of African-American history and culture are intimately interwoven with the narrative of *Gabriel's Trumpet*. Special gratitude goes to historian Jordan O'Neal for ensuring I rendered these elements as accurately, clearly, and sensitively as possible.

As always, thanks to Shaun Tomeff for being my "cars and guns" guy (as a Texan, you'd really think I'd know more about both).

Finally, thanks to Kristin and Eunice Taylor for answering some quirky questions about the birds of New England.

I remain in a state of constant thankfulness (and amazement) to the entire 18thWall Productions team for their ongoing support of whatever crazy thing I'm trying to do at the moment. Love to my parents for always believing in me and encouraging their weird kid who, at the age of 42, finally figured out what he wanted to be when he grew up. And, of course, none of this would have been possible without the support of my lovely wife, Jess, and our two furry "mewses."

TABLE OF CONTENTS

This is a work of fiction. It draws extensively on the tapestry of history and folklore for its narrative but also occasionally fudges, tweaks, or ignores facts in service to that narrative. Readers interested in a scholarly examination of the topics presented in this work are invited to consult the suggested sources provided at the end of the book. Following this list of sources is a brief discussion of some of the history, and some of the fiction, that went into the writing of *Gabriel's Trumpet*.

Chapter One

New York City; September 27, 1929

The Savoy Ballroom was jumping. Fess Williams led his Royal Flush Orchestra through a furious rendition of "Hot Town" as patrons Lindy hopped across the dancefloor. Others listened to the music or were content simply to see and be seen. Women wore fancy dresses. Men wore suits. The Savoy's dress code was stringent.

Even for Harlem's swankest nightclub, the evening was exceptional. Five thousand people crowded the venue. Thousands more stood outside on Lennox Avenue, hoping to get in. All of them came to see a miracle.

Frank Marvin's husky tenor vocals gave way to a clarinet solo, which melted into a glorious crescendo of saxophones. As the sax notes faded away, a slender young man with delicate features and mocha complexion took the spotlight. Raising a gleaming silver trumpet to his lips, the whole of the Savoy waited expectantly. This was what they came for.

Long, sweet, and clear, his opening note rung like a church bell through the venue. The trumpeter began a sonorous melody of rapidly accelerating tempo. Playing notes at lightning speed, his fingers melted into a translucent blur. Shifting tempo up and down, always just before the audience expected it, he kept them hanging on every note.

At its most frenetic, even the stars of the Savoy's dancefloor struggled to keep up. But the trumpeter's slower passages moved the crowd most. The sound was haunting and ethereal. Sweetness and melancholy inseparable from one another. His music beckoned visions of dreamlike landscapes and conjured long-forgotten bittersweet memories. For a moment, even the Lindy hoppers stopped to watch.

At last, he took the silver trumpet from his lips.

"Ladies and Gentlemen," Fess Williams shouted from his bandleader's podium. "Put your hands together for Gabriel 'Resurrection' Gibbs!"

The crowd exploded in applause. It was a remarkable performance. Especially from a man who died two years ago.

Gibbs bowed, a tiny smile on his lips. Raising the trumpet, he played on.

In the crowd, Langston Hughes looked on, scribbling notes on his pad. Moe Gale, the Savoy's owner, nodded approvingly, hearing profit in the trumpeter's every note. Near Hughes, two men watched Gibbs and eyed each other suspiciously. They stood out. Not because they were white, the Savoy had always been proudly integrated, but because they were square. One, younger and tall, nervously cleaned his glasses as if expecting misfortune to fall at any moment. The older man was portly and possessed the pallor of someone recently escaping confinement.

Near the bandstand, another outsider lingered. Motionless and stony-faced, he stood unmoved by the revelry around him. Bald and sturdy framed, the man knocked at the door of middle age. His now threadbare suit epitomized the conservative style of another era, in contrast with Savoy regulars who stood on the cutting edge of Harlem fashion.

Packed as the Savoy was, patrons remained at arm's length from him, heeding warnings of which their conscious minds were unaware. Unobserved amidst the crowd, the interloper produced a revolver and fired, empting the cylinder toward the bandstand.

Crying out in pain and surprise, "Jelly" James dropped his trombone and grasped his shoulder. But all eyes turned toward "Resurrection" Gibbs. Blood plastering his white tuxedo shirt, the trumpeter swooned momentarily before collapsing into the drums.

Chapter Two

Boston; August 27, 1929

"You can judge a man by his library," Marcus thought, pacing along the well-apportioned bookshelves of a mansion in Boston's Beacon Hill neighborhood.

All the titles marking an educated, patrician man were present. So, too, were some curious outliers: bound collections of Madam Blavatsky's correspondence, Capron's *Modern Spiritualism*, the full twelve-volume edition of Frazer's *Golden Bough,* even an alleged unpublished autobiography of Franz Mesmer. What was absent were the Moderns: no Anderson, Fitzgerald, Hemmingway, or Joyce.

He heard the double doors slide open behind him. "Dr. Roads, thank you for coming."

Marcus turned to face Dr. Walter Franklin Prince. The research director of the Boston Society for Psychical Research was old. But the curiosity in his eyes and determination of his lantern jaw testified to age's irrelevance. Prince was, in fact, the BSPR's driving force.

"As I've said, please call me Marcus."

"Very well, Marcus, please be seated."

Reposing in a high-backed leather chair, his profession's signature black bag deposited to one side, Marcus cleaned his glasses. The action had been a nervous habit since childhood. And Prince's secretive phone call, more a summons than a request, had unnerved him. Why did he want to meet away from

11

the society's headquarters? And why was he so tightlipped about the meeting's purpose? It was oddly reminiscent of his first one-on-one encounter with Prince five years ago.

"Do you remember our discussion of Gabriel Gibbs last month?" Prince began.

"The trumpeter. Down in New York, correct?"

Prince nodded.

Marcus recalled something of it. The musician, rumors said, had died somewhere in the South but then returned from the dead …with his musicianship much advanced. Now in Harlem, Gibbs was quite the cause célèbre there.

There had been brief discussion of the BSPR investigating the case. Discussion mixed with laughter. The story was preposterous. Séances were one thing, resurrection quite another. Anyway, how would one even investigate such claims? The idea was quickly shelved. It intrigued Marcus that Prince referenced it again.

"The ASPR is investigating Gibbs," Prince said, his lips curled into a grimace. "I have no choice but to open an investigation as well. If those damned New Yorkers go off half-cocked again, we need to be able to counter it."

Marcus nodded understandingly. Based in New York, the ASPR, American Society for Psychical Research, was the BSPR's rival. Both societies conducted their feud with all the bitterness of the civil war it was. The two groups had once been one. Before a medium named Margery…

In 1924, the ASPR participated in an investigation of the 37 year-old Boston psychic. The society's top leadership actively defended Margery against allegations of fraud. Many of its members, however, felt compelling evidence existed to question Margery's bona fides. That faction, led by Prince, departed the organization and established the Boston Society.

"Even so," Prince continued, "many of our members would be unhappy about our treating this case seriously. That's why I asked to meet at my home. This investigation is unofficial, and secret, unless we need to go against the ASPR report."

"That's reasonable," Marcus acknowledged. "What do you want from me?"

12

"Why, dear boy." Prince smiled drolly. "You're heading the investigation."

Marcus hoped the choking noise he made was only in his head. "You're not serious? Why me? Why not Rhine? He's more experienced. Or Lydia Allison? She's better with people."

"You're every bit as good as those two. Besides, Rhine's down at Duke now," Prince scolded. "More importantly, you're a physician. If anyone is qualified to determine whether a man has returned from the dead, it's you."

That argument made sense. And it offered an opportunity to break the tedium of his recent investigations. But that brought its own difficulties. "This isn't like checking out a séance. It's different from anything I've done," Marcus explained. "I can't just look for wires and cheesecloth. I'm not a Pinkerton. I don't know how to go about this."

"You'll figure it out," Prince smiled. "If in doubt, you can start at the beginning."

"I accept," Marcus grinned. "Do you know who the ASPR has put on the case?"

"Theodore Fenno," Prince replied.

"Oh." This time, it was Marcus who grimaced.

Chapter Three

Mississippi Delta; August 31, 1929

Marcus had never spent so much time on trains. Boston to New York. New York to Chattanooga, where he spent a night at the Read House. The following morning he switched to the Nashville, Chattanooga, and St. Louis Railroad, which carried him as far as Memphis. Overnighting at the Peabody Hotel, he then boarded the Jackson Bell, traveling south along the river, bound for a place called Terraplane.

Riding the rails, Marcus caught up on back issues of the *Journal of the American Medical Association*. Research linked a wave of methyl chloride poisonings to the new electric refrigerators. Conversely, ferric chloride, a related chemical, showed promise in treating varicose veins. At the Jewish Hospital of Brooklyn, Drs. Collen and Grayzel had created new protocols for treating diabetic children. And recently released statistics on silicosis painted a frightening picture of coalminers' lives in West Virginia and around the world.

It was his work as a physician that had led him to the ASPR and then, following the split, to the BSPR. He'd seen things. Not frequently, but often enough. Possible occurrences of astral projection or clairvoyance by unconscious patients. The ubiquitous "tunnel with a bright light" reported by those pulled back from the brink of death…or beyond. Recoveries that could only be called miraculous. Were these tantalizing hints of a life, and afterlife, filled with wonders? Or were they artifacts of prosaic, explainable, and mundane organic processes that people read too much into? Marcus wanted to know.

Now, his hospital shifts had been reassigned. Friendly colleagues temporarily took on Marcus's regular patients. It had required only minimal effort to put his, admittedly rather dilettante, practice on hold to focus on Gabriel Gibbs.

He had been honest in telling Walter Franklin Prince that the Gibbs case was unlike any he had undertaken. Marcus had investigated séances and haunted houses up and down the East Coast. He examined a Key West poltergeist, a serpent-handling faith healer in Appalachia, an automatic writer from Ohio farm country, and even a New England doomsday cult. Along the way, he encountered cheesecloth ectoplasm, cleverly rigged tables, vivid imaginations, cranks, cons, and hysterics. What he had not found was solid evidence for the spirit world or any of the other supernormal phenomena with which the society concerned itself.

After his medical journals, Marcus reviewed the available material on Gibbs. An article from the *New York Sentinel,* one of many papers energizing what was being called the Harlem Renaissance, admirably collated the relevant information. The musician came from Gates County, Mississippi, born in the grandiosely-named Venice and raised near Pilate's Point. Marcus noted the curious spelling, P-I-L-A-T-E, as in Pontius, not P-I-L-O-T, like an aviator or old steamboat navigator. While musically talented from a young age, details of the man's formative years were something of a cipher. Furthering his musical career, he moved to New Orleans, frequenting its infamous Storyville district. Gibbs was murdered there, a death certificate allegedly on file, but the case remained unsolved. He was buried back in Mississippi, in the Gates County Cemetery. But, afterward, sightings of the trumpeter began to be reported in New Orleans and elsewhere in the South. He later turned up in New York where, with its renaissance, Harlem was emerging as America's musical capital.

The headstrong young man in Marcus yearned to go straight to New York and confront the trumpeter. But the scientist in him knew visiting Mississippi and New Orleans to get a baseline for

16

Gibbs was the best way to determine if the man in Harlem was the same person and, allowing the indulgence, whether he had returned from the dead. He would follow Prince's advice. He would begin at the beginning.

Miles clicked away over the rails as Marcus watched the Mississippi Delta pass by. Through his window, small towns and clusters of shacks that were little more than overgrown villages appeared, and vanished almost as quickly, as the Jackson Bell sped by. Such communities stood as lonely milestones between fecund fields still yielding the last of the cotton crop and irregular patches of woodland and wild that had never felt the sting of axe or plow.

In some ways, Marcus had never traveled so far. True, he saw England and France as part of his finishing after school. Had he been a little older, he would have seen them from the trenches. Yet, in their way, London and Paris felt less exotic, less "other" than this land.

The Jackson Bell ran from Memphis, down through its namesake, before terminating in New Orleans. Marcus took his leave of the train long before then. "Terraplane!" The conductor's cry for the only rail stop in rural Gates County rung through the train car. "All out for Terraplane!"

Stepping off the Jackson Bell, even after a night in Memphis, the heat and humidity overwhelmed Marcus. That any work got accomplished here struck Marcus as a herculean feat. But, clearly, it did. Silos of cotton lined one side of the tracks. On the other were hotels, restaurants, shops, and the other infrastructure of country whistle-stops.

Upon being informed that the optimistically named "interurban bus" from Terraplane to Pilate's Point was running late, Marcus decided to stretch his legs and explore the town. Five thousand souls, perhaps, called it home. It had its patches of prosperity. Everything he would expect of a similarly-sized community in the Northeast was here. But churches, mostly smaller than the ones back home, sprung from the ground with a fertility rivaling the cotton. Stranger to him were the town's twin commercial districts. Clark Street served Terraplane's white residents. Jackson Street, its black. Less than a quarter mile apart, they existed in separate worlds.

Returning to the station, Marcus saw the interurban bus idling out front and smelled its diesel fumes even from a distance. Traveling in the smoky metal box through the heat and humidity did not appeal to him in the slightest. Instead, he flagged down the driver of a passing wagon. "Good afternoon. Would you be willing to take a passenger to Pilate's Point?"

"It happens I'm headed there myself," the man said.

"Well, what about it?" Marcus asked. "Can you take one more?"

Quoting a price, the driver appeared disappointed when Marcus didn't haggle and instead agreed immediately to the proposed sum.

"Well, Figaro likes your money," the driver smiled, indicating his horse. "And I like your manners. Hop on in."

Marcus climbed onto the buckboard beside the driver. Once underway, they began talking in earnest. Bartholomew Jenkins made his living delivering goods around Gates County and, apparently, giving rides to the occasional passenger. In the process, he'd become something of an expert on the area, sharing interesting tidbits with Marcus as they drove along.

At one crossroads, the driver indicated an abandoned house standing amidst fields as nature quickly reclaimed by it. There, in the dark hours of Christmas Eve, 1911, all nine members of the Carroll family were killed with a machete. While the police held a tramp for about a week following the incident, no arrests were ever made.

Later, passing over a rickety wooden bridge, Bartholomew identified the creek below as a place where fossils, arrowheads, and pottery shards far older than those of the Quapaw could be found. "One time, a bunch of kids pulled a skull out of its banks," he commented. "Looked like a gator's skull. But bigger than any gator you've ever seen."

Marcus didn't mention that, other than on visits to the zoos in Boston and New York, he had never seen an alligator of any size.

"Some of the more religious types around here claim it was a dragon skull from back before the Flood," the driver continued.

"Bartholomew, can you explain something to me?" Marcus asked. "I'm guessing Terraplane is the county's biggest city and the commercial center. It's the place the railroad runs through. So, why is the county seat in Pilate's Point rather than Terraplane?"

"You're a smart man," Bartholomew said with an approving look. "Lots of folks spend their whole lives here without wondering that.

"Pilate's Point was here long before king cotton. In fact, seems like nobody really knows how long. But, even way back, some farmers, trappers, and hermits lived here, scattered across the county. Even a few villages of Quapaw still hung on. Pilate's Point is at a place in the river where there's a natural port, so boats would put in there to trade with all those folks. A village grew up there. When the plantations came and cotton started shipping out, it grew into a town. By the time the Johnny-come-lately railroad ran through, even though moving the county seat to Terraplane might have made sense, Pilate's Point had the weight of history on its side. You know how those old money folks are."

Marcus certainly did. While he came from money, few in his part of the country would have called it old.

From Bartholomew's tales, Marcus had learned quite a bit about the region he now visited. In return, he shared stories of some of the things he'd seen or heard about in his investigations.

"You'd be here about Gabriel Gibbs, then?" Bartholomew asked, putting two and two together.

The driver wasn't just smart, Marcus realized as he answered in the affirmative, he was also quick.

"I know the Gibbs family," he responded. "They're good people. Their spread is a couple miles northeast of Pilate's Point on the Lula Pike," with that answer Bartholomew probably saved Marcus at least a day's worth of time and effort.

Marcus knew Pilate's Point the moment he glimpsed it. Sitting high on a bluff over the Mississippi, buildings stretched from its peak down to the base and spilled outward onto the surrounding Delta flatland. Near the peak, its mansions and churches proclaimed opulence. The buildings further down, less so.

In town, they drove up the bluff to Marcus's hotel, located in part of town Bartholomew called "The Point."

Marcus thanked him for the ride. And the conversation.

"Welcome. Figaro enjoyed it, too. If you need to get about while you're here, just find me in Underbluff," he responded. Marcus had no idea where or what Underbluff was but he committed it to memory. Bartholomew was a useful contact in more ways than one.

Only after the driver departed did Marcus curse his forgetfulness, failing to ask the one question not related to the trumpet player which he was really curious about: the reason behind the curious spelling of the town's name.

Chapter Four

Drained by heat and travel, Marcus was indifferent to the Mississippian Hotel's commanding view over the river. Still, it was a fine hotel and he had been fortunate to find it. Before departing Boston, he had wired a classmate from Harvard who came from Mississippi to see if he could offer any useful insights for the trip. It was serendipitous decision.

While his classmate currently resided in Jackson, he had an older cousin in Pilate's Point. A cousin who was, of all things, the longtime sheriff of Gates County. Though Marcus now felt obligated to pay a courtesy call on the cousin, it seemed a fair price to pay for the name of the community's only lodging of distinction. He was grateful to be staying at the Mississippian Hotel rather than the more dubious establishments he'd seen along the way.

Intending to rest for a minute, Marcus sunk into a deep sleep. It was twilight when he woke, his stomach loudly proclaiming its vacant state. Fortunately, from downstairs, welcome aromas informed him the hotel's dining room remained open.

At the doorway to the dining room, he heard an unwelcome voice.

"Hello, fishmonger."

Even before the schism between ASPR and BSPR, Theodore Fenno had no love for Marcus. Never mind Marcus's hometown of Marblehead had long been a respectable community of suburban Boston elites. Never mind he was a physician graduating with honors from Harvard Medical School, as were his father and grandfather before him. At some point in the distant past, Marcus's people had been Cornish fisherfolk. That was enough to earn scorn from the portly Knickerbocker, whose family name appeared prominently on New York City's social register.

"So, Boston finally decided to pay attention to the Gibbs case," Fenno jibed. "A day late and a dollar short, as usual."

"If the ASPR is doing so well, why are you still here?" Marcus retorted.

Theodore's pug-like face drew uncomfortably close to his. "It's of no matter. Our investigation is almost complete."

Marcus wondered if it was true or if the New Yorker bluffed.

"Even if you had a head start, your minds are too closed to appreciate this case," Fenno continued.

"Glad to see you're not rushing to conclusions," the sarcasm in Marcus's voice was subtle but unmistakable.

Their exchange typified dialogue between the ASPR and BSPR. Since the split over the Margery case, to the Boston Society, their New York counterparts grew dangerously credulous. From the ASPR's perspective, the Bostonians became increasingly ossified and reactionary, little better than Houdini. Or, perhaps, worse than Houdini. The escape artist, at least, openly declared his hostility to spiritualism and the paranormal. Each society waged a constant war of words against the other to dominate debate over supernatural phenomena. Both societies wanted to believe. In Marcus's opinion, the ASPR wanted it too much.

"Forget anything as mundane as communicating with discarnate spirits," Fenno elaborated. "We're talking about actual bodily resurrection. No longer losing loved ones. Death abolished forever. Contemplate that. If you can," with that blustery parting shot, his rival departed.

Shaking his head, Marcus sighed. He restrained himself. He always did with Fenno, at least since hearing the gossip around pre-schism ASPR headquarters.

Determined not to allow the man's venom to ruin his meal, Marcus proceeded into the dining room. As he entered, its lone occupant raised his head. "A friend of yours?"

Barking with laughter, Marcus considered the man. Something about the stranger's bearing and demeanor bespoke education while his expression implied an invitation. "May I join you?" Marcus asked.

"Please," he replied. "Dining alone is sometimes a necessity but rarely a welcome one."

"Are you a guest here?" Marcus inquired.

"I am not, but Chef Fleury sets the finest table in town and so I prefer to dine here at least once weekly." His new companion introduced himself as William Blackmon, president of the Gates County Historical Society.

"From an old local family, then?" Marcus presumed.

"Hardly. I just happen to love history," he replied. "My grandfather followed opportunities down here from Pennsylvania after the war. What you'd call a carpetbagger. Three generations later and our family is considered almost respectable."

They continued with small talk until Marcus's dinner of bacon-wrapped bourbon-glazed chicken and cheesy grits appeared. "So, I've got a question and you would seem to be the person to ask," Marcus said before beginning his meal. "The town's name. Or rather its spelling, Pilate's Point, is…unusual. What's the story?"

Laughing, William glanced around the dining room as if to confirm its emptiness and gave his companion a rather conspiratorial grin. "I'm glad you asked me. Some of the locals, especially those from old families, are still quite touchy about it." As Marcus ate, the historian relayed the tale.

"Originally, yes, the town was 'Pilot's Point,' with the conventional spelling you would expect. The name referred to this bluff which, from the earliest days of boat traffic on the Mississippi, served as a reference point for boat navigators, pilots. When a settlement developed here, it naturally took its name from the landform. After the Delta economy began growing, this was a natural point for loading cotton. And the community became the county's commercial and political center.

"That's the backstory. The answer to your question starts very late in the war, as Union efforts to secure the Mississippi River neared their climax. One day, it started raining. And didn't stop. When the waters began rising, Chapel Bar, a small religious community a few miles downriver from Pilot's Point, prepared to evacuate. But the city fathers of Pilot's Point told them to stay put, promising they'd rescue them if the weather became truly dangerous.

"By the time it was clear the storm would be remembered as the Great Gates County Flood, those same city fathers decided conditions were too risky and kept Pilot's Point's ships in port. The rising waters swallowed Chapel Bar and its 300 or so residents. History passed judgment on those who washed their hands of them. Forever after, this community's name has been written 'Pilate's Point.'"

The heady tale, told with macabre relish by William Blackmon, lasted through dinner and past desert and coffee. Now quite dark, if Marcus wished to get an early start the next morning, it was time to turn in. He politely excused himself.

"If you have the opportunity during your visit," William said as they parted ways, "you are most welcome at the historical society."

Thanking the historian, Marcus didn't expect to have time to follow up on that invitation but appreciated it all the same.

Perhaps troubled by his exchange with the ASPR investigator before dinner, that night Marcus dreamed of an earlier encounter with Theodore Fenno.

FIRST

INTERLUDE

New York; June 1924

As it would turn out, it was all Scientific American's *fault.*

Marcus's part in the matter began as he sat in the ASPR headquarters reading room in New York, absorbed in a folder provided by another investigator. The case involved an alleged poltergeist in rural Maryland. His colleague's file overflowed with accounts of dramatic nocturnal activity: chairs sliding across the floor, pots and vases flying from cabinets, and even heavy bookcases tipping over.

He carefully scrutinized photographs of the property owner, one of the most ardent believers in the poltergeist, taken by the investigator. Most of the photos offered little of note, showing a typical middle-aged man who had done a mediocre job taking care of himself. Then something caught Marcus's eye. Thin, discolored marks encircled the man's wrists and ankles. To a trained observer, the abrasions and mild burns indicated where rope or twine had bitten into flesh.

Taking his pen, Marcus circled the marks in the photos and made a simple note at the top of each, "Fraud." With unscrupulous individuals all over America seeking to cash in on the spiritualist craze, this was not the first time Marcus discovered this simple but effective ruse behind "poltergeists" moving objects at a distance. He suspected it would not be the last.

The sound of laughter disturbed Marcus as he formulated a

25

more expansive note to add to the file. Glancing up, he saw three society members whispering among themselves at the opposite end of the room. One, a well-bred Knickerbocker named Theodore Fenno, had initially served as a mentor to Marcus when he joined the ASPR. Taking the younger fellow Ivy-Leaguer and presumed society man in hand, he showed him the ropes. In the following weeks though, Fenno had cooled, put off by a certain seaport flatness to Marcus's vowels and proletarian family origins which Marcus did not advertise but did not deny either.

Not actively seeking to eavesdrop, Marcus could not avoid overhearing bits of their conversation, picking out phrases like "Yankee Farmer," "Scribbler," and "Immigrant Showman." He heard Fenno comment "Too many of that sort of person," before the men furtively glanced at Marcus. "And, of course, fishmongers," Fenno added in a stage whisper, sending his companions back into laughter.

There could be no mistaking the meaning of their statements. The men were discussing the Margery investigation.

Throughout the early 1920s, Scientific American *had covered spiritualist phenomenon within its pages. Officially, the magazine took an agnostic editorial line: not validating spiritualism but remaining open to the possibility such validation might be forthcoming. In truth, it was little different from the publication's handling of relativity and quantum mechanics.*

Early in 1924, to drive up readership, the magazine offered a $2,500 prize to anyone who could demonstrate physical mediumship under scientific controls. The contest required candidates to demonstrate telekinesis, the moving of objects, or other material manifestations; not merely ESP, believed to be too subjective for evaluation. Scientific American *appointed a board of experts to judge prospective mediums. While not an ASPR investigation per se, its judges included several highly regarded members of the society, thus thoroughly entangling the ASPR in the matter.*

After judges had refuted several other candidates, their attention now focused on a purported medium named Mina

Crandon, the wife of Dr. Le Roi Crandon, a prominent Boston physician. To protect the family's privacy during the investigation, the rest of the world knew Mina Crandon simply as "Margery."

As the investigation progressed, cleavages appeared within the society between members predisposed to sympathy toward mediums and those who, to Marcus's way of thinking, brought the rigors of the scientific method to such questions. The issue involved class as well. Coincidently or not, the most skeptical of the judges were self-made men.

Walter Franklin Prince, the ASPR's research director, was the "Yankee Farmer." Born to a Maine agricultural family, Prince progressed through careers as an Episcopal minister and psychologist before landing in parapsychology. The "immigrant showman," escape artist and professional debunker Harry Houdini, supplied the magazine's investigation with star power. Though, in deference to the man's rigorous schedule, Houdini would not be brought in until the other judges completed preliminary investigations. The "scribbler," Malcolm Bird, was an employee of the magazine. Not formally part of the committee, Bird served as liaison between the publication and the judges and was considered to have sway over their opinions.

Three judges of more privileged origins rounded out the committee. William McDougal, a British psychologist, currently chaired that department at Harvard and had previously been president of the ASPR. The physicist and engineer Daniel Comstock hailed from blue-blooded Newport. Another Englishman, Hereward Carrington was a honey-tongued and debonair psychic researcher with a sideline in stage magic.

It had been less than a year since the "deceased" Antonio Silvano had sprung off Marcus's operating table, the final straw in a series of unusual experiences bringing Marcus to the American Society for Psychical Research. In that short time, he had found a niche. Within a society dominated by psychologists and parapsychologists, with a healthy sprinkling of journalists, clergy, and physicists, Marcus's expertise as a physician offered an invaluable perspective on investigations.

In addition to several poltergeist debunks like the one just *concluded, he had spotted patterns of bruising explaining how alleged physical mediums moved tables or other large objects with knees, legs, or forearms. Familiarity with the physical indications of mental illness occasionally allowed him to assess cases of so-called possession missed by the psychologists.*

Sometimes, his role involved debunking his colleague's attempts at debunking. In particular, many of his fellow investigators, some of whom were married and presumably should have known better, had unrealistic notions about the sort of equipment a fraudulent medium might conceal within her anatomy to aid in trickery.

"Dr. Prince will see you now," one of the society's secretaries informed Marcus. For all the value of his medical expertise, he remained a small player in a much larger organization. So it came as a surprise when the society's research director had asked to meet with him at headquarters.

The secretary led him into an office where Walter Franklin Prince sat behind his desk. The man reminded Marcus of a silver-haired tree trunk. His eyes blended intellectual agility with the solid pragmatism of the Maine farmer he'd once been. Marcus squirmed uncomfortably, feeling awkward in the presence of a giant in in the field of paranormal research. In his long career, Prince accrued a reputation not only for resourcefulness and determination but personal bravery, the celebrated debunker of the "Antigonish Hoax."

In 1922, already in his late 50s, Prince journeyed to a remote farmhouse in Antigonish County, Nova Scotia. Traveling the last 20 miles by sled, he intended to confront an especially angry poltergeist. In addition to violence, the alleged spirit's proclivities including starting fires and terrorizing people. Having already chased away a long list of investigators, it was claimed no one could successfully spend a night in the farmhouse. Some of the fleeing investigators, rumors said, had required recuperation at sanitariums following the experience.

After rigging the farmhouse with devices which would indicate any human agency behind the haunting, Prince spent the night there with only a revolver and camera for companionship. The following morning, Prince emerged unscathed and with his sanity intact, pointing a finger at the family's troubled daughter as the true Antigonish poltergeist.

"Dr. Roads," Prince began, "it is a pleasure to meet you finally. I hear very good things about your contributions to the society. I understand you are a physician?"

"Yes, sir. And, please, call me Marcus."

"And you reside in Boston, Marcus?"

"Yes. In addition to having a private practice there, I am a surgeon at Massachusetts General."

"What do you know of Dr. Le Roi Crandon?" Prince asked, inquiring of Margery's or, more properly, Mina's, husband.

"He has a reputation as a solid physician. He's generally well liked by colleagues." For a moment Marcus's inclination toward privacy, and to respect the privacy of others, warred with his desire to please Prince. "But that are stories the man is something of a playboy."

"The serial marriages, you mean?"

Figuring in for a penny, in for a pound, Marcus continued passing on hearsay. "More than that. If you believe some people, he works a lot of late hours that have nothing to do with medicine. If you take my meaning."

"I do," Prince replied. "Do you know why I'm asking?"

"The Margery Case and the Scientific American *investigation. But what does her husband's private life matter?"*

"Perhaps nothing. Hopefully nothing," Prince clarified. "But if there is willful fraud, understanding what the motives might be can give you an idea of what to look for.

"Marcus, I'm going to level with you. I have serious concerns regarding how this investigation is being conducted. Several of the other judges, including members of our society, are lodging with the Crandons when they are in Boston to investigate Margery and have become quite friendly with them socially. In any other kind of scientific or legal endeavor, that would constitute a clear conflict of interest. Dr. Roads, if we want to be treated as a science, we have to act like a science.

"As someone who lives in Boston and has entre to Dr. Crandon's professional circles, I want you to be an extra set of eyes and ears for me. If you hear anything of interest, I want you

to pass it along to me."

Marcus did not relish the idea of spying, either on a senior colleague in medicine or on his fellow society members. Still, he saw the matter from Prince's perspective. The results of the investigation would reflect directly on the ASPR. If something questionable occurred, Prince had an interest in knowing about it. Hesitantly, Marcus nodded.

"And would you be comfortable, would you be willing, to keep this arrangement private?"

"Comfortable? No. Willing? Yes."

Chapter Five

The next morning, Marcus resolved to get the social call on his classmate's cousin out of the way. Steven Caldwell was not what he had expected from a rural Southern sheriff. If not precisely a man of letters, he was at least well-spoken and somewhat well read. After Marcus explained his errand, the sheriff's reply surprised him.

"Yes, I know the Gibbs. A respectable family. Sam Senior and I go back a ways. His place is out of town, a bit north of here."

"So, you knew Gabriel, then?"

"Of course," he replied. "Fine young man. Polite. Hard working. Good musician. Damn shame what happened. It's sad. But things like that happen a lot down in New Orleans."

"You're familiar with the stories about...after?" Marcus asked, uncertain how best to broach the subject.

"I know them," Sheriff Caldwell replied cautiously. "Most everyone in the county knows them. Even if some only talk about it whispers."

"What do you think?"

"Some people claim to have seen him. I haven't. After two decades in this business, there are precious few things I'll say for certain. But one of them is that people don't come back from the dead."

Both his career as a physician and work with the society had sharpened Marcus's ability to read people. He knew Sheriff

Caldwell had more information than he was sharing. And, law enforcement also being a profession which honed that skill, the sheriff knew he knew. With neither of them willing to acknowledge the elephant in the room, Marcus politely but abruptly ended the interview.

Talking with the Gibbs family was the obvious place to begin. Thinking it a good idea to hire Bartholomew again, the distasteful looks Marcus received when inquiring about Underbluff provided a quick lesson in the geography of Pilate's Point. Far below the patrician Point, where the elite lived, did their business, worshipped, died, and were buried, Underbluff sloped down to the river. There, the community's riffraff and ne'er-do-wells congregated. In between was Midtown, where regular commerce occurred and average people lived out their workaday lives.

Underbluff lived up to its promise. Or, perhaps, "lived down" was more appropriate. Amidst thickly clustered shacks and hovels, an assortment of riverside brothels and barely disguised speakeasies sprouted. As a well-dressed stranger, eyes that Marcus hoped were merely curious followed him as he travelled through the area. Fortunately, he quickly found a familiar face.

"Bartholomew, how are you?"

Unloading crates from his wagon, the driver looked surprised but pleased. "Dr. Roads, how are you this morning?"

"Good, thank you. And please call me Marcus. Are you busy or are you available for hire?"

"You give me a few minutes and I'll be free," he replied. "Where do you want to go?"

"Lula Pike, I think you said. I want to talk to the Gibbs family."

"Sure thing," he replied, quoting Marcus a price. Again, he expected the doctor to haggle and, again, Marcus didn't. As they journeyed out of Pilate's Point along a rural lane, Marcus told the driver of his encounter with William Blackmon and what the historian shared with him about the city's distinctive name.

"That's right," Bartholomew acknowledged. Marcus wasn't surprised when the driver then added a few bits of his own to the tale. "When the river is low, some people say you can see the steeple of the old Chapel Bar church poking out above the waterline. Others claim it's just a big old tree trunk. I've never gotten close to it, so I don't know. There are also stories that before his community slipped below the water, Jeremiah Chapel called down a curse on the old families of the Point. Though, if everyone in Chapel Bar drowned, I don't see how anyone could know that."

Marcus smiled inwardly. The driver had the makings of a fine investigator. While he wasn't sure how some of the BSPR's membership might feel about that, at the very least the man merited cultivation as a valuable contact.

As Figaro pulled the wagon through a cluster of homes too few in number to be called a village, Bartholomew stopped at a two-story wooden house. The home was small but tidy and maintained with obvious pride. Its recent whitewash gleamed like alabaster in the late summer sun. Even at a distance, the smell of freshly baked bread beckoned invitingly from within.

Flowerbeds and lush grass accented the front yard. Two young girls played there, half-heartedly tending the flowers. A vegetable garden dominated the backyard, where a woman of maybe Marcus's age hung washing. On the front porch, an elderly woman sewed in a rocking chair.

"Can I help you, friend?" A robust man also about Marcus's age emerged from the fields. Many people might be wary finding a stranger in their yard. The welcome in the man's smile and, more importantly, his eyes said he meant the "friend" and generally viewed the world in those terms.

"I'm Marcus Roads. I'm looking for the Gibbs place."

"You've found it. I'm Sampson Gibbs, to my folks anyway. Just Sam, or Junior, to everybody else." Looking over Marcus's shoulder, he exchanged nods with Bartholomew, still sitting on his wagon. Sam's nod struck Marcus as bit guarded, more courteous than heartfelt.

"I'd like to talk to you about Gabriel," Marcus asked, returning his focus to the man in front of him. "Your... brother?" he ventured a guess.

The man nodded affirmatively. "Gabe? He's quite popular these days."

While Marcus knew that Theodore Fenno had almost certainly already come calling, Sam's next remark confirmed it. "I don't have answers for what you really want to know. But I'm happy to talk about Gabe's life."

Clearly, the ASPR man had been here. "I'd like that," Marcus responded.

Sam invited Marcus onto the porch, adding "Ma and Pa are in town shopping but let me introduce you to the rest of the family." Two young men coming in from the fields were his younger brothers, Ezekiel and Enoch. Their younger sister, Hannah, was baking inside. The old woman on the rocker was Aunt Mancie, Sam's maternal great aunt. His wife, Henrietta, had been the woman hanging laundry. The two girls playing in the front yard were their children, Mary and Myrna.

"Got tired of the Old Testament names?" Marcus smiled.

Sam laughed, "Yeah. And Henrietta loves the picture shows. We named the girls after her favorite actresses."

As they sat and talked, Henrietta served sweet tea.

"So, that's the family?" Marcus smiled.

"Yep," Sam's face grew solemn. "Well, except for Gabe, of course. You know about him. And my sister, Rebekah. She's not really with us anymore, either."

Wanting to keep conversation light at first, Marcus switched topics. "You've got a beautiful place."

"We've done alright," Sam replied, drinking his tea. "Pa always plants the right crops at the right time. Some folks whisper it's not quite natural. Truth is, he reads three things every day: the Bible, the almanac, and the crop futures. Not necessarily in that order."

"Sheriff Caldwell thinks very highly of your family."

Sam chuckled. "Well, there's a little more to it than that. Ever since we moved here, Pa's been a regular contributor to the sheriff's reelection fund."

Marcus raised an eyebrow. "Really? I don't want to seem impolite but, down here, I wouldn't have thought that…"

"We can't," Sam answered the question before Marcus figured out how to ask it. "Jim Crow sees to that. And, for those same reasons, not everyone around here is happy to see our family doing well. So, Pa figures there's a value in giving the law a solid reason to be on his side. That being said, over the years it seems like he and the sheriff have grown to like each other. They're friends, at least as much as the world lets them be."

"Before I forget," Marcus interjected. "Do you have a photo of Gabriel I could see?"

Sam went inside to fetch a photo. As Marcus awaited his return, a grackle landed on the porch railing beside him. He disliked the creatures. While grackles could be found in Boston, Marcus had never seen the unpleasant birds so numerous as in Mississippi. As it perched, the lean, dark avian eyed him with a look better suited to a bird of prey.

"You best watch out," Aunt Mancie said from her rocker. "Grackles will swallow your soul if you give them the chance." When Marcus was uncertain how to respond, the elderly woman laughed to herself and resumed sewing.

Sam returned, handing Marcus a family photo. The Gibbs' were distinctive. Ma Gibbs and her children had delicate features and dark, expressive eyes. Even the hearty Sam's face seemed better suited to a poet or scholar than a gentleman farmer. "That's Gabe," Sam said, indicating a slender youth. The smallest of the family's boys, Gabriel's eyes possessed a distant, dreamy quality.

"Thank you," Marcus said, returning the photo.

"You can keep it," Sam replied. "We've got a couple."

Marcus slid the photo into the interior pocket of his jacket. "Tell me about Gabriel?"

Looking reflective as he gathered his thoughts, Sam began the story of his brother's life. "I think Gabriel always loved music. He had the colic really badly as a baby. But Ma's singing always put him right to sleep.

"All us kids were born in Venice. Don't let the fancy name fool you. It's a nothing little plantation town way out east in the county. My folks sharecropped then. But with Pa's skill and Ma managing the money, they put by enough to buy this place.

"Gabe was four when we moved. He was an odd kid. Got lost in his own thoughts. He was easygoing, almost pliant. But, every so often, he got a notion. Then he was a mule. Music was like that for him. He'd seek it anywhere he could. Sometimes it was Ma singing around the house or those old songs Pa sung in the fields. But, mostly, he found music in church.

"Being a Northern man, you don't really understand about church. You think you do, but you don't. Down here, church isn't just a place you go on Sunday. It's the center of your life. And the Ascending Glory Tabernacle had a stronger pull than most.

"Actually, its pastor was the pull. Jericho Heulen was larger than life. Broad shouldered, balding, and no end to his energy and enthusiasm. Always spearheading some improvement or addition to the tabernacle. He took an active interest in every member of his flock, exhorting all of us to walk the righteous path. And he had lots of opinions about what that meant. But, I'll tell you; nobody at that church went hungry. And he saw to it that all the children got some schooling, even if it was just reading, writing, and ciphering.

"When we started going there, the tabernacle pulled about 100 families every Sunday from this little hamlet and two others nearby. It was neat, tidy, and always had a fresh coat of paint. A little oasis of prosperity. Some of the poor families out here had never seen anything like it.

"And the tabernacle had music. Only holy music, of course. The choirs. The spirituals. The call and response between the Pastor and flock."

"Call and response?" Marcus asked.

"That's where one person sings a line or two," Sam explained, "and everyone else repeats it. In church music, it'll be the pastor who does the call and the congregation responds. If it's something else, like a field song, the caller will be the person with the best voice, maybe. Or whoever knows the song best. And everybody else responds.

"With his fine baritone voice, Pastor Heulen was a great caller. And he was a trumpeter himself. In fact, that's what started it all.

"My brother heard Pastor playing trumpet at church and his eyes lit up. It captivated him. Not too long after, he started demanding one of his own. By that time, Gabe had grown into a slender and sickly kid. He never was much good in the fields and Ma and Pa were always happy to indulge his whims. For his twelfth birthday, they bought him a brass trumpet from the catalogue store in Terraplane.

"From the moment he got his hands on that thing, Gabe was obsessed. If he was awake, he was playing trumpet…and he never wanted to sleep. He was keeping up the neighbors, to say nothing of his family. Eventually, Pa forbid him to play at night.

"But every evening, he'd play trumpet in the parlor, Rebekah watching him. Those two were inseparable, always together fishing, playing tag, or pinching a bit of sugarcane from the field. Of us all, I think she loved him most. When he died, she died too. At least on the inside.

"Gabe got good fast. He might not get a song perfect the first time, but it never took him too many tries. And he loved showing off. He'd hold those long, perfect notes for a minute at a time just to show he could. One day, making the rounds to check in on his flock, Pastor Heulen heard Gabe working through a piece that Pastor had played at church the Sunday before. Well, his hard face softened like butter. He showed my brother how to play it right. Then they stood in the dining room together playing it as a duet.

"After that, Pastor took Gabe under his wing. Called him his 'Little Lamb.' Pastor never married or had children of his own. I think Gabe became like a surrogate child to him. He had my brother perform in church every chance he got. Picnics. Revivals. The Christmas and Easter services. Whatever it was, Pastor would find a way for Gabe to play.

And whenever my brother did, Pastor Heulen got that warm glow he never had otherwise. During services, they'd play duets of Bosom of Abraham, John the Revelator, Wade in the Water, all those old spirituals. No doubt there was vanity in it, but my brother's favorite was always "Blow Your Trumpet, Gabriel. "I'm biased, of course, but that was always the best part of Sunday services.

"Pastor started talking to my parents about sending Gabe to seminary when he got old enough. Don't quote me but, with no son of his own, I think it was even in his mind to hand the tabernacle over to Gabe one day.

"Everything was unfolding like part of some bigger plan. Then Pa brought home that Crosley radio…"

Sam paused, looking up and out into the yard. Following his gaze, Marcus saw a smartly-dressed couple walking toward them, their arms laden with parcels. In age, the pair appeared about halfway between Sam and Aunt Mancie. Ma and Pa Gibbs had returned home.

Spotting Marcus on the porch chatting with Sam, Ma Gibbs' eyes went wide and her jaw dropped. "Oh no you don't! I won't have someone else here who wants to spread lies about my baby. I won't have it!" Oh yes, Theodore Fenno had been here.

Flustered, Marcus stood as he attempted to explain that he was different from Fenno. Deferential, nearly penitent, in his demeanor, he tried to control the damage. "Ma'am, my name is Marcus Roads. I'm not here to tell lies. I just want to learn more about Gabriel."

She was having none of it. "Not in my house, you won't. You get!" she shouted over his protestations.

Pa Gibbs' eyes were apologetic. They were also unyielding. "Son, I think you better leave."

Making a hasty exit, Marcus slunk back to the wagon.

As Bartholomew pulled back onto the road toward Pilate's Point, Marcus touched his jacket. Reassured, he felt the firmness of the photo inside and was glad he had asked for it at the beginning of the conversation. The pair traveled in silence most of the way home.

Chapter Six

Next morning, with information from the Gibbs family cut off, Marcus cast a broader net for informants. Engaging Bartholomew, who was available only for half the day, Marcus talked with residents along Lula Pike. Afterward, he hit the streets of Pilate's Point, making inquiries. In both places he found plenty of people who knew Gabriel Gibbs. Or at least knew of him. Most, however, did not want to talk.

Some could only be persuaded with quarters or half-dollars. Others required a shot of whisky at an Underbluff barrelhouse to loosen their tongues. Marcus was far from certain his expenditures were worth it. He heard his fill of wild tales about crossroad deals with the Devil. Others said witchcraft worked through that silver trumpet of his. And that Gibbs robbed a grave to get it. What grave? Nobody seemed sure. Whenever he dug deeper, the results inevitably disappointed. Informants credited stories to "a friend of a friend" or "everybody knows." Opinions split on whether the trumpet player had, in fact, returned from the dead. But most found something nefarious about him, in life if not death.

One piece of intriguing information did come from the rumormongers. Those he considered more credible recalled Gibbs as an extremely good musician. Not a great one. How could Marcus square that with the musical prowess credited to man currently performing in Harlem?

For hard facts, Marcus realized he needed to somehow mend fences with the musician's family. Fortunately, he caught a break. Trimming his moustache the next morning, a knocking at his door disturbed Marcus. "Sir, there is a man here to see you," one of the hotel staff informed him.

Marcus found Sam Gibbs waiting in the lobby.

"Good morning."

"Good morning, Sam. After yesterday, I admit I'm surprised to see you."

"Can we talk?" Sam asked.

They sat in plush chairs in a remote corner of the lobby. "After you left," he began "we had a big blow up. You don't need to know the details. But, when all the hollering and crying was done, we sat down and had ourselves a serious talk. There are a lot things we don't know about my brother. Especially after he left home. We'd like to know. And you seem in a position to find out. Beyond that, Pa said, unlike that other man, you seemed to be a stand-up fellow. Ma didn't say so, but I think she agrees. We'll help you…on two conditions."

"Name your terms," Marcus replied, "and I'll let you know if I can accept."

"First, share whatever you learn with us. Second, if this person in New York really is Gabe, you tell him to come home. We've all got some guilt about how we treated Gabe before he left. And about how we reacted when he died, especially Ma. Whether he's come back from the dead or not, we want him with us. Between him and Rebekah, we've lost two family members. She's in the hands of God, and the doctors, but maybe you can bring Gabe back to us."

"I can agree to those," Marcus replied after brief reflection. "But, if I'm going to be the stand-up guy your father thinks I am, you need to know that anything I learn may be put into a report for my associates back in Boston. And that report may be made public. While I don't know this for certain, it's possible that report may say some things about Gabriel your family doesn't want to hear. Are you all going to be okay with that?"

Sam considered the question for a moment. "People already say some terrible things about Gabe. And, to be honest, not many folks around here are likely ever to see that report. Or much care even if they did. So, yes, I think we can accept that. We just want Gabe back or, failing that, some closure."

"When would you like to get started?"

"Any time. You want me to give you a lift out to the house?"

"That's very kind. But, if you did that, you'd have to return to Pilate's Point to drop me off and then go back home again. That's asking a lot of you. I'll just see if I can hire Bartholomew again." While true, it represented only part of Marcus's reasoning. He enjoyed his lessons in local lore from the driver…and never knew when something might come from them that would prove pertinent to the investigation.

"As you like," Sam said in neutral tones.

The pair exited the hotel under the watchful eyes of its manager and desk clerk. Clearly, local convention had been flouted. The clerk's expression was a mixture of bafflement and indifference, suggesting that, while he had no idea what a Yankee might do, he also didn't much care. The manager's frosty gaze, on the other hand, clearly indicated that any future chats Marcus and Sam might have should be conducted elsewhere.

Engaging Bartholomew's services, Marcus did not proceed directly to the Gibbs home. Instead, he made two stops before departing Pilate's Point. From the florist, he picked up a bouquet of colorful coneflowers and black-eyed-Susans. At a butcher, he acquired a fine glazed ham.

At the Gibbs place, Marcus presented both items as tokens of his sincerity about making peace with the family. With blooming flowerbeds of their own, reaction to his bouquet was muted. The ham, however, found favor as a conciliatory gesture. The family, in turn, invited him off the porch and into their parlor. If Marcus understood the complicated forms of Southern etiquette correctly, it signified the family's acceptance.

Ma Gibbs dispatched Hannah to stoke the oven and begin cooking. The rest of the family joined Marcus in listening to Sam continue his story where he had left off the day before yesterday.

"Over the years, Pa bought things to make our family's life

easier: a washing machine, the farm truck, a little electric icebox. But I think the first purely vanity purchase he made was that Crossley," Sam said, indicating the fine rosewood radio in the corner. "For the weather reports and crop futures, he said. I think Pa just wanted to listen to baseball. But it was Gabe who got the most out of it. He discovered worldly music and it changed his life."

Marcus's face announced his incomprehension.

"There's a big gulf between church music and worldly music down here," Sam explained. "The worldly folks don't much care if musicians want to sneak off and play church music once in a while. Though, if that's all you're playing, they'll think it's a pity and say you're wasting your talent. The church folks don't see it the same way. The call worldly music 'The Devil's music.' And they're not joking.

"Gabe loved it all: ballads, polkas, dance reels, blues, sometimes even the Opry out of Nashville. But especially jazz. The boy was jazz mad. His favorites were the broadcasts from those swinging Harlem nightclubs.

"One night we listened to Louis Armstrong playing at the Cotton Club. Fingering his trumpet along with Satchmo, Gabe turned to Rebekah and me, saying, 'I swear, someday I'll headline one of those fancy New York clubs. No matter what.'"

Sam's nose twitched as the aroma of baking ham and other smells began wafting from the kitchen into the parlor. Refocusing, he resumed his tale. "Pastor was a firebrand about worldly music. Even more than most. Maybe being a church musician himself, secular music especially appalled him. Or maybe, in his heart, it tempted him and couldn't stand being reminded of that. Either way, he banned secular music for his flock. We weren't even supposed to listen to it at home. We sure weren't supposed to play or sing it. Lots of families flouted that commandment outside Pastor's sight, not just us. But Gabe got careless.

"One day at the tabernacle, Pastor Heulen overheard my brother playing 'Squeeze Me,' that old Fats Waller tune. It looked like the pastor was being called Home right there, having some kind of fit. He dragged Gabriel by the ear to the cane field behind the tabernacle. Pastor took a cane stalk and gave my brother the worst whupping I've ever seen. As he did it, he kept repeating 'Music cannot serve both God and Satan.' When he was done, Pastor told Gabe not to return 'til he decided who he served.

"I'm sure it made it worse for Gabe that Ma and Pa never really whupped us much. It had to be something big, like the time I set a cotton bale on fire and nearly burned up the whole crop. Even then, you could tell their hearts weren't really in it.

"Gabe was beside himself. Hardly spoke for a week. Most folks figured it for embarrassment about being shamed in public. But I knew my brother better than that. He was thinking things over. The Saturday night after it happened, I woke up just before midnight and found Gabe here in the parlor listening to the radio quietly by himself. 'Basin Street Blues' was playing. Seeing the look on his face as heard that horn blow, I knew which way things would go.

"Next morning, Gabe went to the tabernacle one last time. Interrupting the service, he shouted that he was a better trumpeter than Pastor and would keep getting better, no matter who it served. As if to prove it, he pulled out his trumpet and started playing 'Squeeze Me' again.

"When Gabe did that in front of his whole congregation, Pastor Heulen's eyes rolled back in his head and he yelled, 'Get behind me Satan, I cast thee out.' Like he was Jesus himself casting out Legion. Then Pastor chased Gabe from the church.

"As I said, Gabe never went back. Our whole family were pariahs at the tabernacle for a while. Didn't matter too much to Pa and me. But Ma took it hard. Especially the whispering behind our backs. Eventually, Pastor and his flock let the rest of us back. By unspoken agreement nobody mentioned Gabe, at least not openly. But the whispers continued."

Hannah brought out the ham, placing it on the table along with a large gravy boat of dark red-eye gravy, named for the coffee which was a key ingredient. Generous sides of fresh biscuits, okra, and butter beans surrounded the main dish.

Conversation switched to pleasantries and small talk as they ate. Pa Gibbs was hopeful that, with another good harvest or two, the family could purchase a car. It would take some of the load off the rugged but temperamental truck currently doing double duty both as a farm truck and transporting the family to town…to say nothing of being a more comfortable way of getting around.

While Sam's earlier remark indicated that Pa Gibbs was a baseball fan, it seemed the whole family followed the game. They were faithful fans of both the St. Louis Browns, giving Marcus some good-natured ribbing about Boston's unstoppable plummet toward the bottom of the American League, and, in the Negro Leagues, of the Birmingham Black Barons. Most of their baseball talk, however, lionized Babe Ruth who, just the month before, became the only player ever to hit 500 home runs. Pa Gibbs was openly skeptical Ruth's achievement would ever be equaled.

Coffee and chess pie followed the meal; the latter lent a citrusy kick by a sprinkling of orange zest. With the table cleared and Sam poised to resume his tale, a knock at the door interrupted them. Bartholomew stood there, hat in hand. "Very sorry to disturb you folks," he announced "but I've got some deliveries that need making."

Excusing himself, Marcus thanked the family for their hospitality.

"I'll see you out," Sam said. As they walked toward the wagon, he continued talking. "It's probably just as well we stop for now. Some of the next bits of the story are likely too painful for Ma and Pa to hear said as plainly as you need to hear them."

With Sam indicating the tale only grew more uncomfortable from here, Marcus suggested future conversations occur between just the two of them. Perhaps meeting somewhere in town but not the hotel. Sam proposed a session the following day at a certain Underbluff establishment where they could speak easily and not be bothered.

On their way home to Pilate's Point, Bartholomew continued Marcus's education in the unorthodox aspects of Gates County history. This time the driver told two tales certain to appeal to a physician.

A local man named Hero Simms was renowned throughout

the county for being impervious to any kind of pain or discomfort. Indeed, the man once won a $100 bet by picking cotton for 24-hours straight. Congenital analgesia, Marcus knew, was the clinical name for that condition. It was extremely rare, he had never actually seen a case. If time allowed, perhaps he could examine the man during his visit.

Expressing that hope to Bartholomew, Marcus learned he was too late. The condition had also been the man's undoing. Falling into a brush-burn while clearing a field, Simms wasn't aware of the extent of his injuries and died later that night.

From the driver, Marcus also heard about the Gates County Wild Child. Unspeaking, unclothed, and, according to some versions, covered with hair, the young woman was sighted around the county throughout the 1870s. Living off the land, during lean winter months she occasionally pilfered food from isolated homesteads. Eventually, a local planter managed to capture her. Naming her Eve, the planter taught her to wear clothes, respond to her name, and even utter a few, halting words including the Lord's Prayer. About two years later, Eve escaped never to be seen again.

Feral children were another well-documented phenomenon, but unusual in a relatively settled area like Gates County. As far as stories of Eve being covered with hair, hirsutism was also a recognized medical condition, one considerably more common than congenital analgesia. But Marcus wondered if such reports spoke the truth or if they had been added because it fit some primordial myth-pattern documented in sources as ancient as the Epic of Gilgamesh and, perhaps, as far back as Stone Age cave walls.

Chapter Seven

"The Landing" wasn't a fancy name. But it was still too fancy for the rotting riverside warehouse, pressed into service as a speakeasy, which Sam had suggested for their meeting. Where parts of the floor had rotted away, successive layers of hay and sawdust had been haphazardly laid down. After a single sip, Marcus didn't view the filthy rotgut sitting in front of him as drink so much as the price of admission.

In the far corner, a man sat on a chair playing banjo while his twin brother sang and strummed a washboard around his neck. Their repertoire consisted of old folk tunes, blues in the fashion of W.C. Handy or Lead Belly, and last year's jazz hits. But there was no firm distinction between styles. The duo might throw syncopation and improvisation into a traditional ballad or insert archaic vocalizations into their rendition of "Blue Skies."

"Ma and Pa don't like it that I come here sometimes," Sam acknowledged, looking around the dive. "But I work hard. And I'm a good family man. If I want a shot of lightning now and again, that's no one's business but mine. Not Ma and Pa's. Not the church's. Not the politicians'. I'll tell you something, Marcus, all that holier-than-thou bunch in Washington accomplished is forcing hardworking folks to pay more money for worse whisky."

Based on the Landing's stock, Marcus had to agree. He had difficulty focusing on his conversation with Sam, instead transfixed by two men brawling and biting in the mud-splattered sawdust. Nobody else paid them much attention. At least until the knives came out. Then, even the musicians stopped to gawk. From under the bar, sloppily thrown together with slats of green wood, the bartender deftly produced a shotgun and bellowed "You boys put those pig-stickers away."

"Sorry, Horace," one of the men apologized. Mystified, Marcus watched as the two men sat down and resumed talking as if nothing had happened. In his distraction, Marcus forgot and took another sip of moonshine. Making a sour face, he pushed the dirty glass away to ensure he would not make the same mistake again. The excitement over, at least for now, Sam resumed talking.

"After his falling out with Pastor, Gabe devoted himself completely to music. Worldly music. He practiced all day. At night, he made money playing country dances, at Underbluff speakeasies like this, or Colonel Scobie's fancy parties.

"Gabe had no problem talking about any of that with me. But there was something else. He took to wandering. Folks spotted him at odd hours all over the county. And he started disappearing for periods. A couple days at a stretch, sometimes. Between those absences and his strange wanderings, people began saying he'd gone to the crossroads and made a deal. That he was off at the crossroads or some graveyard being taught how to play by Old Scratch.

"Then, one day, after being gone for a good bit, my brother showed up with that silver trumpet. Some folks said there had been one just like it buried with a body up at the Episcopal churchyard. Well, that didn't help Gabe's case. Not at all.

"We knew what folks said. But whenever we asked Gabe, he kept his lips shut. He told us he hadn't gone to the crossroads, but that's all we got from him. Where he went, what he did, and where that trumpet really came from, we hadn't a clue."

Eventually, the time came for Sam to return home. Watching the man leave, Marcus reflected he had no reason to distrust the Gibbs family. Indeed, instinct told him Sam was as forthright as anyone he'd ever met. But they were just one family. And one deeply caught up in the events Marcus investigated. He wanted some outside perspectives.

Wandering back through Underbluff, Marcus detoured down the street where he'd met Bartholomew previously. He found the driver half under his wagon, greasing the axel.

"Afternoon, Marcus. You need to go somewhere?"

"Actually, I wanted to pick your brain about some things," not wishing the driver to feel he was being taken advantage of, Marcus added, "Would you like me to compensate you for your time?"

"That's for free. Though, I'm warning you, you may get what you pay for," Bartholomew grinned at him. After Marcus nodded, the driver asked "What's on your mind?"

"Do you think Gabriel went to the crossroads?"

"I don't rightly know," Bartholomew answered from beneath the wagon. "Does it really matter?"

"What do you mean?"

"It seems to me that the bargains folks make with themselves mean as much to them as ones they make with God or Ol' Scratch."

"I notice people say 'the' crossroad, not 'a' crossroad. Is it a specific place? Or can it be any crossroad?"

"I reckon any crossroad might do…" Bartholomew paused. "But there's one on Old Terraplane Highway. You'd know it if you saw it. But it's not a place for decent folks to linger."

Emerging from under the wagon, Bartholomew wiped his greasy hands on an old rag before joining Marcus in leaning against the vehicle. Making casual conversation, Bartholomew discussed his deliveries for the day. Marcus admired the man's grueling schedule…and felt even more grateful the driver found time to transport him.

"I've got a lady friend. From a respectable family," Bartholomew explained. "Maybe not as well off as the Gibbs are, but awfully close. I want to do right by her. Maybe even move us to Midtown one day. But I need a little nest egg to make that happen. As far as making time to take you around…" He smiled. "It might be that I've been charging you a bit more than local rates. I figured if you minded, you'd haggle some. But that also means, if it's possible, I'll shift things around to accommodate you."

"Do you work every day?"

"Every day except Sunday."

"That's the day after tomorrow?"

"Yep."

"I'd like to relax, see a few sights. Can I hire Figaro and the wagon for Sunday? I'll get him back to you by Monday morning."

Seeing the driver hesitate, Marcus flashed a $20 gold piece. "This help with that nest egg?"

"That would be just fine."

Marcus felt badly for deceiving the man about his intentions.

Bartholomew had given Marcus the Underbluff perspective of events. That was invaluable. But he was also curious what the Point might have to say. Fittingly, the Gates County Historical Society occupied an antebellum mansion high on the Point, only a brief stroll from his hotel. As Marcus passed through its doors, William Blackmon spotted him immediately. Pleased by Marcus's reappearance, the historical society's president insisted on providing his guest a personal tour.

A small, rather disorganized museum occupied the ground floor, painting Gates County's history in broad strokes. A collection of stone projectile points. A Quapaw canoe. A weathered crucifix ascribed to the Jesuit missionaries who once accompanied French voyageurs through the area. The bell from one of the first steamships to regularly stop and trade here. A pyramid of Civil War cannonballs. The battle banner from the Confederate 13th Mississippi Cavalry. An oak barrel that had once served as a raft, saving a resident's life during the Great Gates County Flood. A matched pair of dueling pistols. The uniform of one the county's young men who had served in the Great War. And, everywhere Marcus looked, paintings preserving generations of proud, patrician faces.

The mansion's cellar served as an archives, crammed with boxes as well as cabinets filled with genealogical records and documents chronicling more than a century of matters both mighty and mundane. The tour concluded on the top floor, which housed the historical society's offices.

As they sat in William's office, Marcus summarized what he had seen of Gates County so far. The historian also inquired more fully into the errand which brought Marcus to Mississippi. In response, the physician provided a rather abridged version of the saga of Gabriel Gibbs.

"Now, that is interesting," William commented following Marcus's reference to the musician's distinctive instrument. "There's another silver trumpet connected with Gates County, one which skirts that nebulous line between history and folklore. Follow me." Leading Marcus back to the ground floor, the historian indicated one of the portraits. While the young woman in the frame was certainly fetching, her eyes were shadowy. It was, Marcus reflected, a face with secrets.

"That's Lenora Scobie, nee Wardwell," William began. "Her family moved down here from your part of the country before the Civil War. Her father, Return Wardwell, built a plantation northward near the county line. They were a respectable family. All except Lenora. Though she was a great beauty, people whispered about her. The kind of things you didn't say about the daughter of planter aristocracy. As a Massachusetts man who, I don't doubt, knows all about Salem and its history, you probably realize the kind of things I'm talking about.

"So, it was a scandal when she married Amicus Scobie, scion of one of Gates County's best families. After the marriage Lenora appeared to settle down. That, and the prestige of the Scobie name she now carried, put most of the rumormongering to rest.

At least until the Civil War. Shortly after the fall of Fort Sumter, Amicus Scobie rode from his family home at Eden Plantation all the way down to Jackson to secure authorization from the state legislature for raising a cavalry company from Gates County. The legislators, already debating a motion of secession, were happy to have someone not only give them a cavalry unit but do it on his own dime. So, the newly created Colonel Scobie returned to Gates County, authorization in hand.

Marcus remembered Sam saying that Gabriel had played for a Colonel Scobie. "I've heard that name before," he said. After doing some quick math, he added "You're talking about the grandfather of the current Colonel Scobie?"

"You'd think so, wouldn't you? But you'd be wrong. Same one."

"You're joking. He must be…"

"Ninety-four years old, if he's a day."

Marcus gave a low whistle, the Colonel was a piece of living history. Meanwhile, William continued his narrative. "Before Colonel Scobie led the 13th Mississippi Cavalry out of the state to serve under General Lee, Lenora gave her husband a gift. A trumpet. Keep in mind; valved trumpets had only been around for about 20 years at the time. So, even without the fancy silver plating, it was quite an item. I've never been able to discover anything about where she got it.

"But, supposedly, more exists to the tale. I've heard from multiple people that, when Lenora gifted him the trumpet, she told him as long as he kept it with him the instrument would protect him.

"Keep it with him, he did. The Colonel himself always sounded his company's charge. Remember, almost every unit back then, Yankee or Confederate, used old-fashioned bugles. No valves, you see. So you could recognize the sound of the 13th Mississippi's charge from anywhere on the battlefield. You would have heard it at First Manassas, Shiloh, and Chancellorsville. And you would have heard it on the third day of Gettysburg. The 13th was part of Pickett's Charge on the Union positions at Cemetery Ridge.

"As Scobie sounded the charge, the trumpet caught a Minie ball from Meade's lines. It deflected the projectile, which struck the Colonel's right arm. The limb's never been right since. Still, if he hadn't been playing the trumpet, the ball would have hit him in the face. So, I guess Lenora's promise mostly held good.

"With his injury, Scobie wasn't fit for frontline duty. Eldon Gates, eldest son of the family this county is named after, took over the 13th. The Colonel came back here and commanded the local militia unit for the remainder of the war. As soon as he got home, he fixed up the trumpet and displayed it over his mantle. One day, someone noticed it wasn't there anymore. Lenora died in childbirth in 1865. There were rumors he buried it with her up in the Episcopal churchyard. And people have just kept on telling those stories."

Suddenly moved to stretch his feet in a very specific direction, Marcus thanked the antiquarian for his time. William extended the invitation to return, even if Marcus simply found himself with leisure time and desired to poke around the museum or archives for amusement. Again, the physician thought it unlikely, but expressed gratitude for the offer.

Before returning to the Mississippian Hotel, Marcus visited the Episcopal Church. Exploring the elaborate monuments dominating its churchyard, he soon discovered the Scobie mausoleum. Lenora Scobie, nee Wardwell, had rested within for more than half a century.

A massive granite structure with a locked and bolted iron door, the mausoleum was a fortress in its own right. Assuming he didn't have supernatural aid, Gabriel Gibbs would have needed, at the minimum, a bolt cutter and crowbar to have removed anything from within. A stick of dynamite would have been better. Its iron door looked venerable, not like it had been replaced in the recent years. Still, it might be worth further inquiry.

Chapter Eight

The next day, Marcus again sought out Bartholomew and his wagon. Time had come to pay a call on Gates County's most venerable veteran. There was no guarantee that Gibbs' silver trumpet was the same one folklore tied to the Scobie family. In fact, it was a longshot. Still, Gibbs had performed for the Colonel on several occasions. That alone merited a social call.

The pair traveled north on the River Road. Locals periodically waved to Bartholomew as he and Marcus drove past. Apparently, people along the route knew the driver well.

Prompted by the impending visit with Amicus Scobie, Bartholomew shared a bit of local legend connected with the man. Gates County had its own incarnation of the headless horseman archetype. "It's supposed to be the ghost of old Lieutenant Lightfoot," Bartholomew explained. "He was under Colonel Scobie at Gettysburg when a cannonball took off his head. Folks say he's still trying to make his way home. Only he can't find it 'cause he has no head. Of course, if that's what's stopping him, I wonder how he made it this far."

Marcus liked that last comment. Once again, it showed the man thought things through. He didn't accept folklore uncritically.

On the River Road, with the Mississippi frequently in view, Bartholomew also described the exploits of "Pig Eye" Garrett. The notorious smuggler and river pirate had found redemption, in some eyes at least, as a blockade runner par excellence for the

Confederacy. Pig Eye and his specially built boat, the *Deuceman,* disappeared about the time Union forces showed up in Gates County. Perhaps killed in action. Perhaps relocated to a more hospitable climate.

Five miles north of Pilate's Point, Eden Plantation made Marcus feel like he'd stepped into a painting. Or seventy years back in time. The porch of the vast two-story Greek Revival plantation house was supported by eight massive ionic columns. A well-manicured lawn and carefully-tended arbors spread out in three directions. The fourth ran down to the river, where a large wooden dock stretched over the water.

The display of living history impressed Marcus. "It doesn't seem like Colonel Scobie's allowed this place to age a day since before the war."

Bartholomew laughed. "Not exactly. From what I hear, the Colonel just let the place go after the war. By the time I was a boy, it was a real rattrap. He started fixing things up about ten years ago. First the house. Then the grounds. For the past few years there's no doubt it's the finest home in the county."

A handsomely-attired doorman intercepted Marcus on the plantation house porch. After Marcus explained his errand, the doorman ushered him inside and directed him to a chair in the foyer. The doorman disappeared, returning minutes later with an even more immaculately dressed man in early middle age. "Sir," he introduced himself to Marcus, "I am Colonel Scobie's personal secretary."

"I would be grateful to speak with your employer regarding an entertainer he hired on several occasions, Gabriel Gibbs," Marcus stated after returning the introduction.

"I am afraid the Colonel isn't feeling well and is currently indisposed."

"I'm sorry to hear that. I would only take a few minutes of his time."

"I appreciate that. But it really is impossible, the Colonel has not been well recently. If you'd like to leave a calling card?"

As the man took Marcus's card, he nodded cordially. "I will ensure Colonel Scobie receives this when he feels better."

When Marcus was the better part of the way back to

Bartholomew's wagon, the secretary called after him. He turned around as the man caught up with him, out of breath. "Sir, I presented your card to the Colonel. It seems he is feeling fine enough today to briefly entertain a guest."

The secretary escorted Marcus upstairs to an elegant and tastefully old-fashioned study which precisely matched the venerable man sitting in it. More than nine decades of life had left Amicus Scobie stooped and paper thin, but a pair of keen eyes suggested time had dulled the man's mind little if at all.

The one discrepancy between the man and his study was the latter's clutter. It stood at odds with the tidy finery of the rest of the plantation house. Volumes stuffed its bookshelves. Books and papers piled atop each other on his desk, concentrated on its left side. The arrangement, no doubt, reflected the Colonel's adaption to a right arm crippled since Gettysburg.

After cleaning his glasses, Marcus scanned the shelves. Unsurprisingly, an entire bookcase was given over to works on the Civil War. Elsewhere were the collected papers of Thomas Jefferson and James Madison. Several massive tomes of Biblical exegesis. Works by Cicero and Plutarch. The Colonel's taste in fiction ran toward socially respectable classics, old and new, from Shakespeare to Twain. More surprisingly, tucked away on a corner of his desk where few would likely notice, was Faulkner's *Sartoris,* barely half a year off the press.

When introductions and pleasantries had concluded, Marcus sat and wondered anxiously what was going through the old man's mind. Was he thinking about how the ancestors of Marcus's friends and neighbors had killed his friends and neighbors? And vise versa. Age had not blunted the Colonel's powers of perception. He read Marcus like one of his books.

"You put yourself at ease, young man. Anywhere but the battlefield, I've got a soft spot for Yankees. My first wife was from Massachusetts, you know. God rest her soul. I mean real Yankees, not those counterfeits from places like Ohio, Pennsylvania, and California. I can tell by your speech that you're one of the genuine article. Massachusetts, Connecticut, Maine, and so forth. I tell you, the First Maine Cavalry fought like devils at Chancellorsville.

"You'll find some folks around here that swear Yankees are soft. I'll tell you one thing, Marcus, was it? Anyone who says that Yankees have no fire in their bellies is too young to have fought against 'em in the War Between the States. And too old to have fought beside 'em in the Great War.

"I'm sorry, I'm rambling. Afraid it gets worse with old age. What did you come to see me about?"

"I wanted to ask you about a musician I've been told you employed, Gabriel Gibbs."

"Yes. I often hired Gabriel. God rest his soul. That's the price of getting old, Marcus. You find yourself saying 'God rest his soul' more and more often. Terrible thing. Bless my heart, I'm rambling again, aren't I?" he asked rhetorically, before returning to topic. "I like to entertain. A habit I picked up from dear Lenora. Gabriel came to my attention as one of the finest musicians in the county. And one always available, even on short notice."

"What was he like?"

"Understand that my personal interactions with him were limited. But I remember him as well-mannered, genial, showing initiative, and possessing a quick wit. And a most memorable musician. If there was one area in which he was imperfectly gracious, it was pride in his musicianship. Even I noticed he could be something of a showboat. Not just his playing. He liked showing off how he could take a note and just keep holding it. The man never seemed to run out of air." The Colonel winked conspiratorially at Marcus. "I understand more than a few people lost silver dollars betting against him at that."

"Did you know there are people in Gates County who didn't think particularly well of him?"

"My staff told me there was gossip. I forget the details but, somehow, he had found himself on the wrong side of local superstition. I hope you understand that such things weren't really my concern. And, again, he was always perfectly correct in his dealings with myself and my household."

"What about his trumpet?"

"Oh, yes, a beautiful piece."

"Do you think it had anything to do with his playing?"

"I don't know. Perhaps some. But, I'll tell you something. He didn't have the trumpet when he first started performing at my parties. And he was a fine player even then."

"An interesting point. I hope this isn't indiscrete," Marcus said, "but you once possessed a similar instrument yourself, correct?" He wondered if he imagined a pained look on the Colonel's face.

"I did. A gift from dear, departed Lenora." Colonel Scobie paused. "But a silver-plated trumpet is hardly a unique item."

"That's fair, Colonel. Hardly unique but rather uncommon. Whatever became of yours?"

The Colonel exploded into a fit of hacking coughs. With what appeared to be great difficulty, he reached up and grabbed the ornate rope bell-pull by his desk.

His personal secretary appeared, glancing with concern at the colonel. "As I said, Colonel Scobie has often been indisposed of late," the note of apology in his voice seemed more polite than sincere. "He needs to lie down."

"Of course." Marcus pushed, "I have only a couple more questions."

Continuing his spasmodic coughing, the Colonel waved him off. "I'm sorry, sir," the secretary said, his tone making it plain he was anything but, "that simply is not possible."

Given local custom and deference, Marcus had no doubt such a performance would end most meetings here without question. Marcus wasn't a local. And a physician knew a phony cough when he heard one.

"That was a pretty quick social call." Bartholomew said as Marcus returned to the wagon.

"Colonel's not feeling well," he replied.

Bartholomew chuckled. "At his age, the Colonel's lucky to be feeling anything at all."

Marcus had hoped for a lengthier stay at Eden Plantation. With unexpected time on his hands, he asked Bartholomew how far out of their way the Gibbs place was. When the driver indicated not too terribly, Marcus decided to drop in on the family.

Leaving the River Road, Bartholomew confidently negotiated

backcountry roads as well as old wagon tracks that were little more than parallel ruts running between fields of cut cotton. Occasionally, they passed through one-store hamlets that appeared stuck in the final decade of the last century. When, at last, the driver put the wagon onto Lula Pike, it was less than a quarter mile from the Gibbs spread. Marcus marveled at the driver's knowledge of the obscure byways and corners of Gates County.

They found the Gibbs household busy with preparations to visit family friends for Saturday supper. In spite of the frantic activity, Sam made time to fill Marcus in on the next chapter in his brother's life.

"Everything came to a head when King Oliver came to town," he explained while polishing his good shoes. "As a gimmick to promote his new recordings, Gennett Records sent King Oliver all over the country judging jazz trumpet contests. The prize was $10. But each local contest winner got to play against the King for $100. Of course, nobody won that prize. Well, almost nobody...

"That morning, Gabe showed up at the county fairgrounds where King Oliver was holding his big to-do. And he wasn't alone. Every trumpet blower in Gates County came. Underbluff was a ghost town that day. Even a few white players turned up. And, I'll tell you, some of them weren't half-bad. But one contestant took everyone's breath away just by being there. Pastor Heulen himself, in the flesh. After everything he'd said about worldly music. All I can figure is that his pride couldn't abide it if Gabriel got named Gates County's best trumpeter. No man knows what he's worth 'til he's tested. And it seemed like his pride proved to mean more to Pastor than anything else.

"From the first, the real contest was between Gabe and Pastor. The way the contest was supposed to work, each contestant would play a piece. When everyone had played, King Oliver would dismiss some of them. Then the ones that remained would play another piece. And so on. Until the King declared somebody the winner.

"But Gabe and Pastor couldn't leave each other alone. Each kept barging in while the other one played. Pretty soon, it turned into a cutting contest between the two of them. Both playing back and forth, playing off each other but trying to outdo each other. Those weren't the rules. But, seeing how fired up it got the crowd, King Oliver just let it go.

"In a lot of ways, it was just like when the two of them used to duet in the parlor. Except now, instead of trying to build each other up, each was trying to tear the other down. They played like men possessed, like their lives depended on it. In a way, maybe they did," as Sam spoke, he helped Hannah pack two loaves of bread and a peach pie into a wicker basket, covering it with a checkered cloth. "Both of them were magnificent. But Gabe knew jazz better. Maybe he wanted it more, too. When the last note faded, King Oliver declared my brother the winner."

"Squaring off against King Oliver, Gabe did something risky, playing nothing but the King's own tunes. In most ways, he just matched King Oliver. But everyone thrilled at his long, bold notes. It was like my brother was challenging the King to do the same. Well, Gabe held those notes longer and bolder than he could. Red Allen, King Oliver's junior trumpeter, judged the contest. He had to acknowledge his own bandleader was beaten by Gabe.

"As for Pastor Heulen, he'd staked everything and lost. He knew it. His flock knew it too. He tried to keep the tabernacle going. But folks drifted away. And the ones who had been his most fervent supporters were the first to go." Sam halted his tale as he and Henrietta straightened their daughters' dresses and subjected them to a final inspection. "A year gone by, the tabernacle's doors shut for good. Pastor Heulen became a recluse and eventually disappeared. Rumor says he's preaching somewhere else now: Clarksdale, Panther Burn, Tutwiler, even all the way down in Jackson.

"Gabe took that $100 and made his way to New Orleans. 'The bigtime,' as he said." With that, Sam excused himself. Marcus watched him help the children and Aunt Mancie into the old farm truck. Sliding behind the wheel, Pa Gibbs brought the thing to life and sent it rolling down the pike.

Marcus and Bartholomew returned to Pilate's Point with daylight remaining. While he had received useful information both from Colonel Scobie and Sam Gibbs, the day's general turn of events left Marcus frustrated. Hoping to turn his luck around, after reconfirming their arrangement for him to borrow Figaro and the wagon the following morning, Marcus asked the driver to drop him off at the Gates County Sheriff's office.

He wanted to follow up on things learned at the historical society, Eden Plantation, and, most of all, the Episcopal churchyard. The Scobie Mausoleum stood foremost in his thoughts. It didn't appear to have been broken in to or vandalized. But, if it had been, Sheriff Caldwell would know.

It surprised Marcus to find the congenial, if heavily guarded, demeanor the sheriff displayed on their first meeting replaced with storm clouds. "I know you've got a job to do," Sheriff Caldwell began forcefully, "but leave Colonel Scobie alone. The Scobies are an honorable family and don't deserve rumors circulating because of some outsider poking around. Amicus Scobie has led a good, respectable life. He's an old man now and doesn't need people upsetting him."

Somehow the sheriff knew of his visit to Eden Plantation. Marcus was tempted to argue with him. But the lawman's face suggested his odds weren't good. Based on everything Marcus had heard about Southern tempers, he decided not to press the point.

Despondently, Marcus returned to the Mississippian Hotel. Few things could have further soured his mood at that point. Unfortunately, another exchange with Theodore Fenno was one of them. Entering through the lobby door, the ASPR man carried a variety of cones, bells, and other odd equipment. Marcus also noted the dust and mud coating the New Yorker's boots.

"I thought you said your investigation here was almost complete?" Marcus jibbed. Perhaps it was unseemly, but he enjoyed the sensation of striking the first blow for once.

"Taunt all you want, fishmonger. I've been to the crossroads. I know its secrets," Fenno gloated. "That's the problem with you BSPR people. You're afraid to get your hands dirty."

Laughing at Fenno, Marcus noticed an edge to his laughter that was more manic than mirthful. Hearing the same, his rival instinctively shirked away. As Fenno departed, Marcus wondered how the socially correct Knickerbocker would react if he knew exactly how dirty Marcus's hands would soon become.

Chapter Nine

Shortly after sunup, Marcus paid a call on Bartholomew to pick up Figaro and the wagon. It came as a surprise to find the driver wearing pressed-pants and buttoning up a well-starched shirt. "I wouldn't have figured you for a church goer," Marcus teased lightly but honestly. He remembered the comment Sam Gibbs had made during their first meeting. Maybe Marcus really didn't understand about church here.

"Well, it hasn't done me much good, yet," the driver acknowledged, "but I keep hoping." After a pause, he asked "How'd your visit with the sheriff turn out yesterday?"

Marcus recounted his exchange with Sheriff Caldwell, particularly the lawman's firm instructions not to further trouble Colonel Scobie. When Marcus finished the tale, Bartholomew broke into laughter at once childlike in its spontaneity and cynical in its worldliness.

"What's so funny?"

"'Good, respectable life?' Colonel Scobie is the biggest rumrunner in Gates County," the driver replied.

"How do you know that?"

"Everybody knows that. Might be that I know from more experience than most."

Marcus thought that over for a moment. Bartholomew's strange comings and odd deliveries. His familiarity with Gates Country's obscure, thinly-populated areas. And his widely recognized face. All of those suddenly made a great deal more sense. Bartholomew's revelation also shed light on the reversal of Eden Plantation's declining fortunes. Starting about a decade ago, the turnaround coincided neatly with the onset of Prohibition.

"Might even be," the driver added with a wink "that's how I got to know Gabriel."

"Gabriel moved moonshine for the Colonel?"

Bartholomew nodded. "He wanted to earn extra money for that move to New Orleans or New York he always talked about."

To hear Bartholomew tell it now, Scobie's elegant plantation was not so much a showpiece as a front for modern commerce of the illicit kind. A staging area for bringing hooch down from Memphis or up from New Orleans and the Gulf. And distributing it not just in Gates County, but much of northwest Mississippi.

Gibbs' involvement with Colonel Scobie hadn't started out on the sly as far as Bartholomew knew. Initially, the Colonel was interested only in his music, hiring the trumpeter to play at his frequent parties, balls, and soirees.

But the musician was smart and observant. It didn't take him long to discover the Colonel's other activities. When he figured out how much money could be made in running moonshine, he wanted in. Colonel Scobie must have had a good feeling about the young man. The wily old veteran placed a lot of trust in the musician very quickly.

"Is that what was behind his disappearances? And the sightings of him in strange locations and at odd times?" Marcus wanted to know.

"Some of them, anyway. I can't say for certain about every time," he went silent for a moment. "I will tell you this. Gabriel and I were good friends for a time. We used to talk about our dreams. Me about how I would marry my lady friend and become a respectable fellow. Him about moving on to New York or New Orleans. How he was going to be a big shot musician one day. But he was different after he had that trumpet. Quieter. Didn't want to talk as much. Like he had some big secret."

Bartholomew excused himself and made his way to church. Their exchange gave Marcus much to ponder as he climbed up to the buckboard and set the wagon in motion. At first uncomfortable about a stranger guiding him, Figaro soon grew pliant under Marcus's command. No expert driver, Marcus could still manage a wagon along Gates County's sleepy byways. As Pilate's Point faded into the distance, Marcus followed the directions given to him earlier by Sam Gibbs.

The Ascending Glory Tabernacle, what remained of it, was a long, narrow box. A covered porch protected double doors at one end. An obelisk-like steeple jutted heavenward at the other. Faded whitewash peeled from weathered boards. Weeds, brambles, and sickly sunflowers grew on its grounds. Only the churchyard remained well tended.

There was no particular reason Marcus needed to see the tabernacle. The building itself had no specific bearing on his investigation of Gabriel Gibbs. The *story* of Gabriel Gibbs was another matter entirely. This place, and the now vanished clergyman who had ruled over it, were fundamental to understanding the young musician's life. Perhaps he was becoming a romantic as he aged, but Marcus had needed to see the tabernacle. To make it real to him. Even now, he could almost hear singing coming from inside the ruin. A little too well, in fact. Though the morning had already started to swelter, a chilly tingle traveled down Marcus's spine. Taking reins in hand, he turned the wagon away.

Leaving the tabernacle behind, Marcus guided Figaro along the dusty rural path known as Old Terraplane Highway. He came to where a rutted dirt track intersected the main road, itself not much more than packed earth barely wide enough for two wagons to pass abreast.

Though he had passed several such crossroads already, a massive, twisted oak set this one apart. As Marcus approached, other differences appeared. Opposite the tree were low mounds capped with grayed and weathered wooden crosses. Graves, Marcus realized. In archaic traditions, which it seemed had not fully died out here, those considered unworthy of hallowed ground were often interred at crossroads. If Gabriel Gibbs had died before the creation of a county cemetery, he might well have been buried here. Who had been laid to rest under those mounds? What stories would they tell? Marcus mused that he was indeed becoming a romantic.

A strange assortment of objects adorned the tree, primarily candles and liquor bottles. But a few more puzzling items stood out. A heart-shaped locket dangled from a branch. A knife protruded from the earth at the oak's roots. Nearby, a ragdoll slowly moldered from exposure to the elements.

Cleary, this was *the* crossroad. The one whispered about in relation to Gabriel Gibbs. But what did it all mean? Marcus thought it a pity that Frazer's *Golden Bough* never seriously treated the societies of the New World...and that the curmudgeonly Scottish anthropologist thought of folklore as something inhabiting the increasingly distant country of the past rather than infusing the living world all around him.

Minutes beyond the crossroad, Old Terraplane Highway rejoined the main road. From there, a few more miles took him back to Terraplane, the town where his Gates County adventures had begun.

Driving the wagon into the larger town, a chorus of church bells, both great and humble, flooded his ears. Marcus had intended to do some shopping here, but the ringing bells announced an unanticipated hitch in his plans. Stores in Gates County closed on Sunday. Nevertheless, certain items were essential for his activities. With a little looking around, and light fingers, Marcus "liberated" what he needed: canvas tarp, a crowbar, hooded lantern, pick, and shovel. "All in the name of science," he told himself, hoping no one would suffer too much from his pilfering. Hanging the lantern from the wagon, he loaded the tools in its bed beside Bartholomew's various deliveries for tomorrow. Not wanting awkward questions, Marcus covered his acquisitions with the tarp.

He traveled eastward to the community of Venice, Gabriel's birthplace. Arriving late in the afternoon, he found nothing more than a sad collection of tarpaper shacks and a company store serving nearby Venice Planation. When nobody there seemed to recall much about the Gibbs family, Marcus was only too happy to turn the wagon around. Darkness descending, he lit the lantern.

Homeward bound, Marcus again passed the crossroad. By night, the gnarled oak assumed a sinister shape. Wind teased the tall grass atop unhallowed graves and caused the oak's branches to reach for him. His skin crawled. The Delta had a power, one Marcus also encountered in remote pockets of New England, rendering the mundane damnably suggestive. Little wonder the region was so steeped in folklore. It didn't make his final task, the real reason for his solo excursion, any more appealing.

His pocket watch showed just after midnight as the wagon stopped beneath a faded wooden sign that proclaimed "Gates County Cemetery, Est. 1898." Or it would have, had negligence or ghoulish vandalism not absconded with several letters, leaving behind only the "Gat s Coun y Cemeter."

Marcus hooded his lantern so it cast only a thin, directional beam.

A wire fence marked off the cemetery grounds. To one side stood a small gate. Directly underneath the cemetery sign was another, wider gate. The "corpse gate," as such features had been known until just a few generations ago, served those who only needed to use it once. Except, perhaps, in the case of Gabriel Gibbs.

After cleaning his glasses several times, Marcus removed the tarp, revealing the crowbar, shovel, and pick in the wagon's bed.

To determine if a man documented as dead had returned to the living, Marcus had resigned himself, it was very useful to know what, if anything, his grave contained. Not allowing himself time to think, he set about the repellent task.

As he carried his tools from the wagon, noises behind Marcus brought him to a halt. Horrified, he watched a figure emerge from the bushes. Of all the people he might have expected to encounter here, Aunt Mancie was not on the list. In the lamplight, the Gibbs family matriarch appeared far more vigorous and hearty than on her rocking chair.

"Aunt Mancie, what are you doing here?"

"How come you never asked me about Gabriel?" she challenged him. "You figure the crazy old woman doesn't know anything?"

He hadn't realized it at the time, but her words held much truth. Marcus had the decency to look embarrassed.

"Doesn't matter now," she said. "I reckoned sooner or later you'd turn up here."

"Why?"

"If I wanted to see if someone was alive or dead, I'd look here," she said plainly. "And, if you're opening my grandnephew's grave, it seems only proper that a family member bears witness."

"You didn't tell the others?"

"They might have stopped you."

"You're not going to?"

"Truth is, I'm curious, too."

Digging up a grave was among the hardest, dirtiest things Marcus had done. Taking a break to catch his breath, Marcus looked at his unexpected companion. "Aunt Mancie, do you believe it's possible for people to come back from the dead?"

"Almost anything you can say is possible. Whether it's likely is another thing entirely. And, please, when we're not on the porch you can forget about the 'Aunt' Mancie nonsense."

Hours later, he bent over the exposed coffin of Gabriel Gibbs, holding his crowbar. Standing over the hole, Mancie cradled the pick as if on guard duty. Guarding against what? Marcus didn't ask. He was pretty sure he didn't want to know.

Holding his breath, he wedged the crowbar underneath the coffin lid and pushed down. The lid swung open smoothly, offering no resistance, as if it had been forced before. Discovering it to be empty, Mancie and Marcus exhaled in unison, whether out of surprise, relief, or a mixture of both.

Not only was the coffin unoccupied, its upholstered interior remained unsoiled. As a physician, Marcus was familiar with death and what accompanied it. A body had not lain here, or not lain long enough for decay to leave its mark.

"Mancie, would you pass me the lantern?"

Taking the light from the matriarch, Marcus illuminated the coffin's interior. His careful examination revealed dark hairs and a small fingernail ripped from its owner during some epic endeavor. Breaking out? Breaking in? That was the question. But someone had been here. If not Gibbs himself, then whom? And to what purpose? Marcus pocketed the samples, hoping his companion would not notice.

Chapter Ten

"Can I offer you a ride?" he asked Mancie after covering up the evidence of their deed.

"I hoped you were that much of a gentleman," she replied.

Marcus enjoyed the trip immensely. The old woman, who had stopped seeming so old hours earlier, owned a lively intellect and great curiosity. She questioned Marcus about Boston and his career as a physician. She inquired into his work with the BSPR, appreciating his answers better than most people. In return, she regaled him with local folklore of a distinctly esoteric nature: giant snakes, Hill Folk, Ol' Bloody Bones, Rougaroux, the Singing River, Skunk Apes, Two-Toed Tom, and variations of the ubiquitous ghosts, vampires, and witches.

"Do you believe in any of those things?" he asked.

"It's like I told you back in the burying yard," she replied. "Anything is possible. What's actual is a different matter entirely." She kept her peace for a moment. "But I have a few opinions that might surprise you."

Marcus was uncertain if she teased him. When she refused to be drawn out any further on the matter, he switched topics. "I've never encountered the name Mancie before. What does it mean? Is it short for something?"

"My momma, God rest her soul, went into labor while the Federals swept across Gates County. Right as Union troops were fighting to take Venice Plantation from Nathan Forrest's bushwhackers, in fact. Gunfire going off all around her shack, she held me in her body until the fighting ended and the Blues had taken the place. She swore her baby girl, and somehow she knew I'd be a girl, would be born a free woman. She named me 'Emancipation.' That's quite a mouthful for a child. All I could manage was 'Mancie,' so that's what it's been ever since."

As conversation drifted back toward her grandnephew, Mancie supplied the remaining Gates County parts of the tale. "When Gabriel reached New Orleans, he wrote us that he was playing at someplace called L'Original," she recounted. "He didn't say so, but we knew it was just some Storyville bawdyhouse. Not much came after that. One day, we got the telegram saying he died. Was murdered. Rebekah went to down to bring him home.

"When she got back, an awful fuss occurred. Pastor Heulen had gone and the tabernacle shut, but a lot of people didn't want Gabriel in the churchyard. They still told those stories about him. We had to bury him in that county cemetery back there.

"Poor Rebekah was never right again. Just slipped into her own world. She chatted with Gabriel like he was there beside her. And, like her brother had, she took to wandering. Soon after, she just disappeared. We got a letter from the State Hospital telling us Rebekah had been found, completely senseless, over in Panola County and been committed. Every so often we get a letter from her. Every so often we write. But she's not what you'd call lucid.

"A year gone by, we started hearing rumors. Someone spotted Gabriel in New Orleans. Or Jackson. Then New York. Gabriel, or whoever, was playing that silver trumpet and telling folks he'd 'come back.' We didn't know what to make of it. None of us have seen him. But a lot of folks have their notions and know exactly what they make of it."

Interrupting Mancie's tale, three sets of headlights blinded Figaro and his passengers. Through the glare, Marcus could make out a trio of Model T automobiles and maybe a dozen men. There were words for a group like this: a mob.

"Look a damn Yankee," one shouted, pronouncing the last

two words as one, before offering less savoy comments about Mancie. "Two birds with one stone," another man said as the mob closed in on their wagon.

Mancie looked at Marcus. "How good are you at driving a wagon?" she asked. When he hesitated, Mancie grabbed the reins, swinging the wagon around in a single, fluid motion. With a stern "Get!" she sent Figaro pulling them down the road at backbreaking speed.

Rushing to their automobiles, the men gave chase.

"Climb into the bed and see if anything back there will do us any good," Mancie shouted.

Doing so, he examined Bartholomew's goods. In addition to the tools Marcus had liberated in Terraplane, some of which would make serviceable weapons if the worst happened, he found loose lumber and two barrels. One contained clout nails, likely part of the same load as the lumber. Flour filled the second barrel. Marcus grinned. He could work with these.

Groaning, he tilted the second barrel against the backboard, tipping out 300 pounds of flour. A cloud of flour dust now hanging over the road, Marcus could no longer see his pursuers. Presumably, the reverse was also true. He then dumped the other barrel as well. He noted with satisfaction that about a fourth of the short-shafted, broad-headed nails landed point upward.

The cars roared out from the dust cloud and over the nails. Staccato sequences of hollow pops proclaimed the death of tires. The first automobile came to a hard stop in a ditch. The second spun out of control, rolling over on its side as men scrambled from the wreck. Witnessing the fate of its fellows, the third Model T swerved into the fields, avoiding the hazard, before returning to the road.

Fortunately, Gates County's rutted dirt roads were as hard on cars as horses. Driving Figaro as fiercely as she could, Mancie maintained their lead over the Model T. Unfortunately, animals tired. Automobiles didn't.

As the road passed through woods, Mancie shouted to Marcus "Follow my lead!" Standing on the buckboard, reins in one hand, she hiked up her skirt with the other. With a wild yell, she leapt onto Figaro's back.

Moving to the buckboard, Marcus hesitated. The five-foot jump looked impossibly distant. "Dr. Roads, let me suggest that this is an excellent time to grow a pair," Mancie yelled. Marcus jumped. Landing hard on the animal's back, Marcus concluded no, it was distinctly not a good a time to grow a pair.

Unhitching Figaro from the wagon, Mancie grabbed Marcus's arm and put it around her waist. She guided the horse off into the trees. Behind them, Marcus heard the Model T screech to a halt, its occupants cursing.

Mancie led Figaro through woods and fields on an oblique route to town. Once safely in Underbluff, Marcus checked his pocket watch. Its hands informed him that dawn neared. His body screamed that was a lie, the night had been the longest week of Marcus Roads' life.

As he tied-up Figaro outside of Bartholomew's place, Marcus didn't look forward to the conversation he'd have with the driver tomorrow. He observed Mancie studying him. "Everything fine?" he asked.

He couldn't quite make out her reply, spoken to herself more than Marcus. He thought she said, "Just wondering if you're old enough for me."

After escorting Mancie to Midtown, where she'd spend the night with a family friend, Marcus dragged himself back to the Mississippian Hotel.

Waking at mid-morning, Marcus immediately checked on Mancie. Sore but otherwise unharmed, the pair strolled and discussed the previous evening's events. As they walked, Marcus struggled to find the right words for asking another question about Gabriel. He prefaced it by recalling what Sam Gibbs had said about the difference between church music and worldly music. As he grappled with expressing those still unfamiliar concepts in his own terms, Mancie gave him a look that while, gracious, clearly meant "I know all that. Get to your point."

"When Gabriel made his decision. When he renounced Pastor Huelen to play jazz," Marcus began, "was he really rejecting God and the church as well? Or did he not see it like that?"

"That is a good question," Mancie acknowledged, falling silent as she thought it over. "No person ever really knows another person's soul. And my grand-nephew's soul was harder to know than most. But I don't believe, when Gabriel stood in the tabernacle that final time, he thought he was choosing the world over the church. Old Jericho Heulen would have hated that but at least he could have understood it. What enraged the pastor, maybe even frightened him, was the notion that Gabriel saw music as something 'other.' Something existing outside of sin and salvation. And that maybe music was more important to Gabriel than either of those."

A familiar face derailed their conversation. It was the man's limp that first drew Marcus's attention. A limp acquired, no doubt, when his Model T overturned the night before. In fact, if Marcus was correct, this man had made the "Two birds, one stone" crack.

The man didn't notice him until Marcus put a hand on his shoulder and spun him around. As his injured leg gave out, the man tumbled to the ground. Deducing the leg must be bad indeed, Marcus had an idea. "I don't believe we've been properly introduced." Marcus grinned as he put his full weight on the limb. "We met last night."

Wincing with pain, the man nodded.

"You know I'm a doctor?"

He shook his head.

"The way you're reacting, I suspect that leg is fractured badly. There's a good chance you'll lose it unless you have a doctor set it. Do you have money for a doctor?"

Again, the man shook his head.

"I'll set that bone for you, if you tell me about last night. Do we have an understanding?"

He nodded warily.

Marcus rigged a splint from handy materials and the contents of his black bag. As Marcus worked, the man spilled his guts. He and his companions had been paid five dollars each to scare Marcus, maybe rough him up a bit, but not do any lasting harm. "We didn't expect you to be with anybody else. Or go and pull all those crazy stunts," the man said as if it excused his behavior

77

and he was the aggrieved the party. It didn't and he wasn't.

"Who paid you?" Marcus demanded. His mind ran through the list of possible suspects. The sheriff was unhappy with him. The hotel manager, too. But neither seemed upset enough to try something like this. Or had the supposedly-ill Colonel Scobie feared Marcus might learn too much about his bootlegging operation?

"Some other damn Yankee." Again, the last two words pronounced as one.

"Oh," Marcus replied, his voice venomous. The man had held up his end of the bargain. Marcus turned him loose, saying "You're good to go. Try not to lift anything heavy for two weeks and no running for a month." After pausing, he added, "And I would suggest not making any more trouble for me or for this nice lady. Remember, we both know exactly where to hit your leg to break it again."

"Yes, sir," he groveled resentfully before hobbling away as rapidly as his splint allowed.

"That took ice-cold nerve, threatening a man with losing his leg," Mancie said approvingly.

"It would, if it was true," Marcus answered. "That's not how you treat a fracture. Not even close. He has nothing but a bad sprain. Not that he needed to know that."

Mancie laughed. "Marcus Roads, I believe you may do alright out in the world."

Marcus stormed into the Mississippian Hotel. Time had come for a reckoning with his colleague from New York. Unfortunately, Theodore Fenno had departed.

"Checked out two days ago," the manager announced, taking obvious delight in Marcus's irritation. "But there is a telegram for you. The desk clerk must have overlooked it."

"Must have," Marcus grumbled as he examined the message.

TF in New Orleans. Wrap up Mississippi as soon as feasible and follow. WFP.

Marcus didn't wonder how Walter Franklin Prince knew of Fenno's arrival in New Orleans. Prince had a mole, maybe more than one, at American Society for Psychical Research headquarters. Of course, Marcus assumed the ASPR had a mole in Boston as well.

He reflected on his situation. Marcus didn't understand plenty of things about Gabriel Gibbs' life in Gates County. But nothing suggested the puzzle's crucial pieces would be found here. It was time to follow Prince's telegram, and the trumpeter's footsteps, to New Orleans.

Tomorrow morning, he would again board the Jackson Bell, riding it to its terminus in New Orleans. For now, he needed to have an awkward conversation with a friend down one wagon.

The driver, understandably, was not pleased. Knowing he owed Bartholomew an explanation, Marcus came clean about his activities the previous day, excepting only his visit to the Gates County Cemetery and his unsavory work there. That required being rather circumspect about how Aunt Mancie got involved in the tale, an ambiguity the driver definitely noticed. But the story of the fish-out-of-water investigator and the sexagenarian putting one over on some less than tolerant locals delighted Bartholomew and improved his mood considerably.

Taking Figaro, and borrowing another horse from one of Bartholomew's neighbors, they rode out in search of the wagon. With his limited grasp of Gates County geography, it took Marcus awhile to locate the site of the previous evening's encounter. When he finally did, results were not good. Theodore Fenno's hired goons had not been gracious in defeat, setting fire to the wagon bed. As a silver lining, while the bed had burned out, the flames failed to spread to the rest of the rig. Still, replacing the wagon bed and compensating Bartholomew for lost work while it was repaired, as well as paying for the nails, flour, and lumber which had been in the wagon, would take more than the traveling money Marcus carried on him.

Harnessing the horses to the damaged wagon, Figaro and his companion towed it back to Pilate's Point. Afterward, Marcus and Bartholomew went to the Western Union office. While Marcus would certainly hear from Prince about it later, he telegrammed the BSPR to wire money to cover Bartholomew's damages and lost work.

The driver insisted on one more thing to balance accounts. At his favorite Underbluff speakeasy, he had Marcus treat him to several shots of whisky. Then, finally relaxed and primed to enjoy the story, Bartholomew made the physician tell the tale of his previous evening's adventures one more time.

Chapter Eleven

That left Marcus with his evening free. He would be able to take William Blackmon up on his invitation to explore the historical society's offerings after all. Once again, its president greeted him enthusiastically. As William led him to the reading room, Marcus noticed a painting. No doubt he had seen it on his earlier visit. But, now, he had the context to appreciate it.

A riverboat, in some ways like any other, but notable for its extremely broad hull and shallow draft. Remarkable, most of all, for the unique flag it flew. A white pig on a black background. "That's Pig-Eye Garret's boat?"

Clearly pleased, the historian responded, "Well, look who's learned a thing or two during his time here. Yes. Yes it is. That's the *Duceman.* You noted, of course, its distinct construction. Because of the shallow draft, Pig Eye often avoided capture by fleeing up small brooks and creeks where other vessels couldn't follow."

Being able to connect the dots pleased Marcus. But it was tragic that the social divisions here made it unlikely William Blackmon would ever sit down with Bartholomew Jenkins or Aunt Mancie. They would likely discover that each had different pieces to many of the same puzzles. But, being honest with himself, Marcus acknowledged he could credit his own region only by comparison. Bartholomew and Mancie would be no more welcomed in Beacon Hill than here on the Point.

"You'll have to forgive me, I've got some reports to prepare for the society's quarterly meeting tomorrow. I have to prove to those old bluehairs that I've earned my salary," William said drolly. "But, I'd happy to set you up with anything in the society's collection you'd like to look at."

"Let me see what you have on the Great Gates County Flood." Marcus asked. It might be relaxing to put Gabriel Gibbs out of his mind for an evening and the flood seemed to be the defining event of the county's history.

The society's materials began with a very dry report from the county to Governor Benjamin Humphries discussing the flood, and the loss of Chapel Bar and its residents, with antiseptic generality. It carefully avoided including any unpleasant, or incriminating, humanizing details.

Even duller were local weather records. The establishment of the Weather Bureau of the United States still five years away, it had fallen to amateur meteorologists to record numbers telling the story. While no meteorologist, Marcus possessed a good head for figures. Looking at the data, he felt a touch of sympathy for those who had dithered. The Great Gates County Flood snuck up on people. Beginning with a steady but light rain, like the locals must have witnessed countless times before, it lingered for days before wind and rainfall suddenly and drastically increased in severity. And its elevation meant it would have taken the residents of Pilot's Point longer to recognize the danger than those in lower-lying areas. Like Chapel Bar.

A human face to the tragedy was provided by hand-written copies of articles from the *Pilot's Point Perceptor*, a newspaper which served the community from 1819 to 1866. At the time, the town's name retained its original spelling; not yet having formally acquired its mark of shame.

Even more harrowing were personal accounts of the flood which the society had collected from survivors around the county in a series of oral histories. Their stories overflowed with tragedy. How Thompson Mulligan, despite his valiant efforts, watched the waters carry off his twin brother, Timothy. The destruction of Harrison's Dry Goods and Trading Post, the county's oldest business, never to open its doors again. But there was triumph as well. The survival of all 22 members of the Durst family. The discovery that a venerable statue of the Madonna and Child, brought over from Ireland, remained intact and, indeed, still in place even though the rest of St. James Catholic Church was stripped to its foundation. There was the rescue of Athena, Old Man Hopper's basset hound, found hungry and wet but safe, floating on a plank of wood. Even comedy made an appearance: the terrible night spent by one Eustace McBee, the town drunk, atop the roof of a privy. McBee, apparently, had occupied his time by bargaining with the divine: vowing, if saved, he would devote the rest of his life to doing good works and never touch the demon rum again. While McBee held fast to the first part of his bargain, he quickly forgot the second.

Marcus long ago came to the conclusion that, in any research endeavor, the most crucial information had a way of being buried someplace where no one wanted to look. So it proved with the Great Gates County Flood and demise of Chapel Bar.

Tucked away among rosters and manifests from the various boats moored in Pilot's Point at the time of the flood, Marcus found a report by harbormaster Micah Stillwell which dated from the week after the flood. Amidst the cumbersome document prepared by a man of dubious formal education, Stillwell preserved a picture of the Chapel Bar tragedy differing significantly from that recorded elsewhere.

When it became clear that rising waters put Chapel Bar at risk, Stillwell sought approval from Pilot's Point leadership to release vessels to rescue the imperiled community's residents. Among the authorities mentioned by name were Mayor Adam Gates, Port Commission Chairman Edward Wardwell, Colonel Scobie who was, at that time, commander of the local militia, and Sheriff Odom Caldwell. Had a Caldwell always been sheriff in Gates County? Marcus wouldn't have been surprised.

The harbormaster's report made it clear that a thorough search of the city had located none of those individuals. Reading between the lines, Marcus concluded that, without blessings from one of the people who really ran the city, Stillwell was unwilling to let the risks of allowing boats to leave port fall entirely on his head. And, as a result, the deluge claimed the people of Chapel Bar.

Stillwell never formally submitted his report. Soon after the flood, he received a comfortable position with the Port of Memphis. Coincidence? Maybe. One thing could be said with certainty, though. The city fathers of Pilot's Point couldn't have dithered about dispatching rescue boats.

They had not been in the city at the time.

Chapter Twelve

New Orleans; September 8, 1929

From Terraplane, Marcus caught the Jackson Bell south. He considered stopping overnight at the train's namesake. The Edwards House had a reputation as a fine hotel and, more importantly, the Mississippi State Hospital was in Whitfield, near Jackson. Visiting Rebekah Gibbs might prove insightful. But without knowing anything certain about her faculties or condition, and with the telegram from Prince urging him onward to New Orleans, Marcus remained onboard.

Hours later the train pulled into Union Station, nestled within one of the country's most distinctive cities. While most visitors knew New Orleans for its rich heritage—nowhere else did America's peoples, languages, histories, and even architectures mix so exuberantly, if not always peaceably—as a physician, Marcus also knew the city for grimmer reasons. The Second Horseman felt at home in New Orleans as nowhere else in the United States. Yellow fever, cholera, smallpox, typhus, even bubonic plague, all still paid occasional calls here.

Union Station fronted directly onto Rampart Street. Less than a mile by cab separated the station from the stately Hotel Roosevelt, Marcus's home for the duration of his stay. Even at twilight, the city's heat and humidity made Pilate's Point feel mild by comparison. Despite Prince's exhortations, Marcus was unable to begin investigating that evening. After a prolonged soak in his room's ample bathtub, he slept as he hadn't since leaving Boston.

In the morning, Marcus's investigation began at the office of the Orleans Parish Medical Examiner. As a doctor, Marcus had little trouble obtaining a copy of Gibbs' death certificate. The body of Gabriel Gibbs, male, 21, was discovered in the storied St. Louis Cemetery Number One on the morning of February 4th, 1927. The document indicated a single gunshot wound to the head as Gibbs' cause of death. Estimated time of death occurred sometime the previous day. An individual named Rose Metairie had identified the body.

The death certificate proved helpful, especially if he could locate Ms. Metairie, but hardly decisive. Marcus hoped talking with the coroner might jog the man's memory. Waiting for over an hour before the medical examiner went on break, Marcus discovered him to be a harried man wearing thick spectacles. Underneath a white coat stained with substances Marcus could identify, but preferred not to, he donned a fashionable suit.

Introducing himself, Marcus summarized Gibbs' death certificate and asked if the medical examiner remembered anything else.

Squinting, the coroner scrutinized the document. "If that's what I wrote, that's what it was."

"Anything else you recall about the body?"

"Can't say I do. Otherwise, I would have put it on the certificate."

"Surely…"

"Doctor…Roads, was it?"

Marcus nodded.

"Let me welcome you to the murder capital of America," the coroner proclaimed ruefully. "I've worked hundreds of homicides, and thousands of autopsies, since the one you're asking about. I'm sorry, but I've no further memories of this case."

Marcus couldn't fault the coroner. Still, he wondered, if the victim had been affluent and possessed the right last name, would the man's memory have improved?

"I truly am sorry," the coroner repeated. "Perhaps you'd have better luck with the police," the man's tone suggested he thought

86

that was about as likely as it snowing today.

The police were Marcus's next stop anyway. Their official report added little new information. Cemetery groundskeepers discovered the body. It noted Gibbs' involvement, according to locals, with criminal and/or occult elements in Storyville. Though the case, officially, remained open, the file's most recent notes dated from just days after the murder.

With a little work, Marcus located a lieutenant and sergeant who had worked the case. "If it's the one I'm thinking of," the sergeant replied, "the body was between two tombs."

"Anything else?"

The lieutenant repeated the coroner's words about New Orleans being America's murder capital.

"Lots of folks get dumped in St. Louis Number One. I guess their killers want to save them the trip," as the sergeant chuckled at his own joke the lieutenant at least had the grace to look embarrassed. Perhaps it was only to get Marcus to go away but the sergeant unexpectedly made himself useful. "If it's the murder I'm thinking of, that photographer fellow turned up. Bellocq. I think he took a photo. Talk to him."

"Bellocq?" Marcus inquired.

"E.J. Bellocq," the lieutenant clarified. "Kind of Storyville's unofficial photographer. He's got a studio over on North Robertson."

Commercial photography and traditional portraiture lined the walls of Ernest Joseph Bellocq's studio. After Marcus explained the nature of his inquiry, however, a different set of photos came out. The silver-haired French Creole's private collection contained pictures of Storyville brothels, portraits of its working girls, and even scenes of opium dens from the city's Chinatown. Marcus admired his technique. While treating subjects that polite society refused to acknowledge existed, Bellocq's photos were both candid and humanizing.

The man himself was another matter. Despite his refined French Louisianan accent and foppish attire, Marcus found something off about the photographer. He laughed at the wrong times. He maintained eye contact too long or too briefly. Marcus felt Bellocq looked through him rather than at him. And there was the matter of the private collection within his private collection. Bellocq had photographed more than a few murders and seemed particularly proud of his photos of the infamous New Orleans Axeman's victims. His memory, however, proved to be acute. When Marcus said "Gabriel Gibbs," Bellocq quickly produced the photo.

A body lay in lush grass between two opulent mausoleums, just as the police sergeant had said. Marcus had spent a lot of time looking at the photo acquired from Sam Gibbs back in Mississippi. He had no doubt the body in Bellocq's photo belonged to Gabriel Gibbs. The man had died. One question answered. As to whether he came back...

His physician's eye caught something else. After death, with no beating heart to continue circulation, gravity pulled blood downward. As a result, the parts of a corpse closest to the ground appeared flushed and darkened. But the parts of Gibbs exposed to the camera, the parts turned upward, were the ones that flushed. That could mean only one thing: the musician had been killed elsewhere and his body only deposited in the cemetery after the fact.

"Can I purchase this from you?" Marcus inquired.

"You can have it. If I want pictures of bodies in St. Louis Number One, I won't need to wait long," he tittered. "Now, if you want one of my Axeman photos, we can talk price."

Marcus felt one photo of a dead man was more than enough. He quickly excused himself over Bellocq's chuckling.

Passing the St. James Hotel on his way back to the Roosevelt, a bad penny turned up.

"The fishmonger," Theodore Fenno smirked as he exited the St. James. Of course Fenno had a room at the city's one hotel more prestigious than the Roosevelt.

"You son of a bitch," Marcus hissed. "That stunt in Mississippi could have killed me."

"Quit being melodramatic. I gave strict instructions not to hurt you. This is a serious game, if you can't play dirty, maybe you should go back to Boston."

"Fenno," Marcus said, walking away. "You sure you want to play dirty with a filthy fishmonger?"

For a moment, the New Yorker had the good sense to look worried.

Marcus sighed. He knew he should pity the man. Fenno's son, Edward, was the only thing Theodore ever truly loved. Edward had gone to France as part of the US Army Aviation Section during the Great War. There, his life ended in some nameless farmer's field—whether through enemy action or mechanical failure had never been satisfactorily determined.

Edward's death destroyed Theodore. It also brought him to the ASPR. Spiritualism offered him a link to his departed son. Fenno needed spiritualism to be real. He became a great asset to his society's public and academic profile, if not its integrity. But, in using his brilliant mind to make facts fit theories instead of the other way around, he also challenged one of the few truths to which Marcus still clung.

Yes, the world should pity Theodore Fenno. But his abrasiveness, arrogance, and reflexive belittling of anyone who disagreed with him made that well-nigh impossible.

Chapter Thirteen

That night, Marcus braved America's most notorious neighborhood. Storyville was a sprawling collection of brothels, speakeasies, and music halls serving the high and low alike. Among its 19th century mansions and woeful dives, genteel decadence and lowborn debauchery coexisted unapologetically. Many of Storyville's establishments occupied mansions and townhouses that, like their current occupants, had fallen from respectability.

The neighborhood was also a cradle for jazz, a pilgrimage destination for souls seeking America's modern music. Those hot new sounds blared forth from the doors and windows of Storyville's establishments as well as from the streets themselves. Individually and in groups, buskers performed on guitars, trumpets, accordions, saxophones, and even washboards. One man beat out elaborate rhythms on an overturned washtub and a collection of empty paint cans. A magician performed tricks while singing off-color tunes. And, anomalously, an old man played Corelli on an ancient violin.

For each reveler who paused to hear the buskers, a hundred others packed the streets. Conversations, shouts, and music merged into a Dionysian roar punctuated by the occasional unsettling scream or distant gunshot.

The whole area also smelt faintly of urine.

Originally known as "The District," it later became "Storyville" in dubious tribute to Alderman Sidney Story, the area's political protector and benefactor. In 1917, under pressure from the army, the city made prostitution illegal. But as Mayor Behrman had observed at the time, "You can make it illegal, you can't make it unpopular." Rumors said the brothels here, like the bars three years later, merely went underground.

L'Original, the establishment where Gabriel's letters to his family said he performed, occupied a 19th century townhouse. Not as grand or well-maintained as some but in much better shape than many others. Flanking its crenelated doorframe, two gaslights glowed through panes of red glass. No, the oldest profession hadn't gone far underground at all.

Uncertain what to expect, Marcus halted a moment to steel his nerves, earning him scornful glances and a pointed cough from two Storyville regulars behind him. Marcus pushed open the door.

Leather couches and scarlet drapes filled the establishment's warmly but dimly lit interior. House girls, attired to best display their tangible assets, fraternized with patrons to entice them upstairs, where "business" was transacted. A jazz quartet played on a small stage. Opposite, a formidable bar lined one wall.

Ordering a drink, Marcus sat at a small table near the stage, watching the musicians as he cleaned his glasses and acclimated to his surroundings. As one performer coaxed frenetic notes from a third-hand piano, the saxophone, trombone, and trumpet blared away. Setting aside his instrument, the trombone player sang. His polished baritone vocals contrasted with his bawdy, innuendo-laden paean to Storyville's women and the diversions they offered.

The musical interludes between his verses gave pride of place to the saxophone. Even more than the trumpet, the instrument had become indelibly associated with jazz. And why not? They were a perfect match. Barely half a century old, and familiar in America for less time that, the arbiters of traditional artistic taste held the saxophone in dubious repute. Little wonder the horn found such favor among performers of the equally suspect new genre of music.

As the musicians went on break, and Marcus noticed his empty drink, he set about the task which brought him here. He began his inquiries with the house girls. They were the ones paying him the most attention anyway. The more materially-minded of L'Original's working girls stormed off upon realizing Marcus was not a potential customer. Others seemed to relish the opportunity to hold a normal conversation and proved quite free with information.

One, in particular, delighted in the company of the establishment's most recent arrival. Helene. Shoulder-length curls, dyed a sanguine red almost the color of her lipstick, framed her round face and rosy cheeks. The young woman seemed alternately enchanted and amused by the awkward, urbane New Englander's attempts to navigate the District's cosmopolitan depravity. While she quickly sized up that he wouldn't be clientele, by enduring her teasing, and providing the occasional drink, Marcus paid the price of her conversation. Still, Helene enjoyed baiting him as they talked. Holding his hand, she treated Marcus to lascivious looks and occasionally glanced at the stairs leading to the second floor.

Many would have quickly written off the girl as a gossip. Marcus listened long enough to realize "newsmonger" was a more apt characterization. She had a solid head on her shoulders and served as a good guide into Storyville's complexities. Answering his questions about any criminal or occult associations Gibbs might have had, Helene revealed considerable knowledge about what went on in the city.

In the second half of 1929, both the city's criminal and occult scenes were in transition. As with most large cities, race and neighborhood divided organized crime outfits. Sicilians, Irish, Creoles, Blacks, Spanish, even the East Coast mob now tried its hand in New Orleans. The city played host to all the usual rackets. Theft, extortion, prostitution, blackmail, numbers running, insurance fraud. And, since 1920, bootlegging had been the big one. The illegal liquor trade drove an unprecedented transformation. While organized crime in the city remained fractured, the large-scale operations required for bootlegging, and the even larger profits it offered, gradually consolidated organized crime in the hands a few major outfits, the remainder being assimilated, eliminated, or permanently sidelined into petty larceny.

If organized crime here experienced a slow, steady march toward order, New Orleans' occult scene moved in the opposite direction. Since the death of Marie Comtesse, Helene said, there had been no one to hold the city's various occult elements together. And even the Comtesse, she confided, was no Marie Laveau.

Marcus had heard of Laveau and her intimate connection to Voodoo in New Orleans, but knew no more than that. He asked Helene to fill in the gaps.

The woman, she explained, had been *The* Voodoo Queen of New Orleans. To hear Helene tell it, for decades, Laveau had dominated occult life in New Orleans the way the Medicis dominated Renaissance Florence. No one who had come before or after her possessed the perfect storm of forceful personality, political cunning, theatricality and, making the allowance, supernatural prowess to step into her shoes. The later Marie Comtesse came close and, perhaps, with time could have achieved the feat, had her life not been cut short after mysteriously breaking her neck during one of her bayou revels.

Since then, the occult scene had splintered. Every block had its local practitioner, often resorting to mundane or mystical muscle to expand his or her turf at the expense of rivals. Some groups had become little better than gangs, using fear of their mojo to intimidate merchants and residents into paying protection money. A few, people whispered, had fallen away from traditional practices, following heterodox new rites down dark pathways.

While discussing Marie Laveau, Helene mentioned the Voodoo Queen had been laid to rest in a family mausoleum in…St. Louis Number One. The discovery of Gabriel Gibbs' body in the same cemetery helped fuel Storyville suspicions linking his death with the occult.

Prying for specifics, however, disappointed Marcus. Helene knew the broad strokes but few details regarding occult belief and practice. Absentmindedly fingering a crucifix necklace as she tried to answer his questions, Marcus realized Helene considered herself a good Catholic girl. No doubt knowing too much about voodoo, and its esoteric cousins, crossed a line for her.

Eventually, receiving enough dirty looks from the proprietress, she had to return to plying her "proper" trade. Marcus, in turn, moved on to questioning L'Original's bartenders, bouncers, and regular patrons for what he might glean of Gabriel Gibbs. They recalled a great trumpet player who improved steadily during the time they knew him. Informants remembered him as a polite and kind young man. If he got a little wild sometimes, that was nothing exceptional by Storyville's forgiving benchmarks.

But his focus had always been music. In addition to L'Original, Gibbs played anywhere people would pay him. This included revels in bayous south of the city. Remembering the term "revels" from Helene's description of Marie Comtesse, Marcus prodded for more information. These events seemed to be part bacchanal and part occult ritual, though his informants' vague descriptions left Marcus surmising such events were more widely known of than attended.

That topic led to discussion of two love affairs involving Gibbs. When he started playing the revels, he became very friendly with Queen Lola, a "gris-gris queen" who lived in the swamps and held revels every Friday. His informants intimated that Queen Lola had quite a temper and might already have "disappeared" a beau or two, including a man named Mose who once tended bar at L'Original. Of course, they hinted, she could do worse things than killing a man, even if she allowed him the privilege of staying dead.

That got Marcus's attention but, attempting to learn more, his informants turned cagey. A few suggested something to the contrary. Rather than revenge, Queen Lola could have brought her lover back so he could achieve his musical ambitions.

Nobody seemed to know how to contact Queen Lola. As an outsider, they warned, it was dangerous for him even to try. Nor, they added, should he venture into the bayous on his own. Especially not at night.

Later, Gabriel became involved with a house girl and occasional singer at L'Original. Marcus already knew her name.

Rose Metairie. Her signature appeared on Gibbs' death certificate as the witness identifying the musician's body for the coroner. Marcus's informants also linked Rose romantically with someone named Luc de Amant, apparently a major figure in Storyville's business community or underworld. If a difference existed between the two. At one time, de Amant had owned the property occupied by L'Original.

Rose, the staff told him, had "gone on," becoming a singer at the Moulin. Perhaps she remained a demimondaine or adventuress, but she was no longer just a house girl.

Informants considered Gibbs' death tragic. Beyond that, Marcus found little agreement. Some thought he got too involved with something dark and occult. Perhaps Queen Lola. Perhaps something else entirely. Often, as evidence, they referenced the location of his body as well as his meteorically blossoming musical talent. Others connected it with the endless turf wars and vendettas waged by Storyville's gangs. Some observed "It's just one of those things that happen in the District."

After Gibbs' death, his silver trumpet turned up in a Storyville pawnshop. That surprised Marcus. The instrument was a highly desirable item, especially in such a musical city. Its ultimate fate also came as a surprise. That the instrument disappeared following a burglary involving the murder of the pawnshop's owner seemed a little too convenient. But what did it mean?

A final piece of information came from the staff. Gabriel never played L'Original after his mysterious reappearance. To their recollection, he never even set foot inside the establishment after "coming back." When they heard him play elsewhere, "Resurrection" Gibbs remained aloof from his former associates. But his music had ceased to be merely great. It was the best trumpet playing they ever heard.

Leaving L'Original, the night was young, at least by Storyville's clock. There might be time to catch Rose Metairie at her new place of employment. Threading his way through the crowds and buskers of Villere Street, Marcus became aware of another segment of the District's population, one he had not noticed earlier. Beggars and panhandlers, even more numerous than the buskers, scattered thickly among the pleasure seekers. Missing limbs marked many of them as among those America had let fall between the cracks after their service in the Great War.

For anyone with a smattering of French, including Marcus, there was no mistaking the Moulin. An enormous decorative windmill graced the one-time mansion's roof. The name, and the gratuitous architectural feature, were an obvious reference to, and an attempt to cash in on, the celebrated Paris cabaret. From the staff at L'Original, Marcus had learned that this larger and more elegant venue served as a house of assignation, a place where patrons and prostitutes met to arrange meetings elsewhere. But, in the main, it functioned as a speakeasy and nightclub, not a brothel.

Inquiring after Rose with a bartender, Marcus's eyes followed the man's gesture to the singer currently occupying the Moulin's large, sweeping stage. A striking octoroon woman with perceptive, almond-shaped eyes and curves that reminded him of a Mesopotamian fertility figurine, Marcus understood Gabriel's interest. At her back, the large house band kept their playing subdued, putting the focus on Rose's sultry alto renditions of popular jazz numbers, including "Ain't Misbehavin'," "Honeysuckle Rose," "Sweet Lorraine," and "The Ballad of Mack the Knife."

Looking smart in matching tuxedos, the house band's baby grand piano, standing bass, two trumpets, and trombone put forth a more polished sound than the rough quartet at L'Original, but lacked its raw vitality. Aside from the sex-and-violence undertones of Rose's lyrics, the group was very nearly respectable enough to play an East Coast supper club. Understanding who the real draw was, the instrumentalists' performances remained measured, never overpowering the singer as she crooned and cavorted in an elegant sequined dress.

After her set ended, Marcus bought the singer a drink and inquired about Gibbs.

"We knew each other from L'Original," she began. "He played trumpet in the house band and I was, well, I was a house

97

girl back then. He and I courted a couple times. Starting about the time he cut a record for Ralph Peer. That birddog fellow from Victor Records."

Marcus had no idea what "birddog" meant in this context. But it constituted new information. Even the Gibbs family seemed unaware Gabriel had recorded. If Marcus could get ahold of his records or talk to this man Peer, it might be useful.

"But it was nothing serious," Rose concluded the account of her relationship with Gibbs. "We were never close."

"What about his death? The police don't really know anything, but I get the impression they didn't look too hard, either. Is there anything you can add? Did he have any enemies? Anything he was involved with which might have put him at risk?"

"Like I said, we weren't close. Places like this, you learn to keep your guard up."

"I can appreciate that," Marcus said. He glanced away uncomfortably after Rose treated him to a look that clearly meant "Oh, can you?"

Regaining his composure, he continued. "Even though you two were just casual, are there any names you remember? Any trouble he hinted at?"

It was Rose's turn to look away for a moment. "Let me tell you about myself. I'm the oldest of nine children. Neither of my parents were what you'd call any good. So, I basically raised those kids. I'm still carrying a couple of them along. I want them to have a decent upbringing. And I want to make something of myself. That doesn't leave a lot of time for love. Especially not with a music man. Do you know what I'm saying?"

Marcus might not know what she was saying, but he definitely got the message. And not just from her words. Everyone he'd spoken with at L'Original contradicted what Rose now told him about not being serious with Gabriel. More than that, the singer's guarded demeanor, stiff body language, and reluctance to make eye contact all also suggested deception. But he possessed no real authority or way to compel truthfulness. Hitting a wall, Marcus elected to call it a night.

Chapter Fourteen

Not used to such late hours, Marcus allowed himself to sleep in a little the next day. Hitting the street, he followed up on the lead about Gibbs having recorded.

Marcus had heard that in places like New York and Los Angeles a new breed of commercial establishment appeared: stores selling nothing but phonograph records. He wondered how that would work out for them. In the rest of the country, including New Orleans despite its musical reputation, records were sidelines sold in department stores, radio and phonograph stores, sometimes even furniture stores.

Marcus tried several such establishments both near the Roosevelt and around Storyville. The ones close to his hotel carried little jazz and that "only for a certain type of tourist" as one clerk put it. He had more luck in Storyville, where stores swelled with jazz and blues discs. Many of the clerks knew of "Resurrection" Gibbs but not that the musician had recorded. Marcus's account of a supposed recording session with Gibbs created considerable excitement and more than few clerks asked him to return if he learned more.

Most of them, however, knew Ralph Peer. As Rose had informed him, the man was an employee of Victor Records. With a burst of inspiration, Marcus browsed wire racks full of phonograph records until locating one issued by Victor. The label on the disc identified the company's headquarters as Camden, New Jersey. With that information, Marcus returned to the Roosevelt.

Making use of one of the telephones in the hotel lobby, he attempted to connect with Ralph Peer.

Receiver to his ear, he overheard the hotel operator arranging the call with the long distance operator. Various clicks and pops followed as the call rode the wires between the Pelican State and the Garden State. At last, the phrase "Good afternoon, Victor Talking Machine Company," rewarded his efforts. The receptionist's voice sounded distant against a background of crackles and hisses. After Marcus explained himself she connected him to Ralph Peer.

Even on a long distance call, he couldn't mistake the man's flat, Midwestern tones. Missouri, if Marcus guessed correctly. Maybe Kansas. Talking with Peer, he learned that "birddog" was slang for a job that combined talent scout and recording engineer. Such creatures lived by their wits, traveling across the country looking for promising sounds, recording them, and carrying the discs back to corporate headquarters. There, company executives, "execs" as Peer called them in a tone Marcus might have used to describe a bacterial infection, had the final say on whether to release the recordings for sale. Several genres, notably bluegrass, blues, hillbilly, and jazz, relied heavily upon the initiative of such enterprising birddogs. Peer hinted that musicians and execs alike viewed his profession as shady and on the take. "Not that that would apply to me," he laughed.

Now possessing the necessary background, Marcus came to the point of his call. "I want to ask you about a musician named Gabriel Gibbs. You recorded him a couple years ago in New Orleans."

"I cut an awful lot of discs. And an awful lot of those are in New Orleans. You're going to have to give me more than that."

As it turned out, it only took Marcus mentioning that Gibbs played trumpet.

"Oh, yeah, I remember the session. Beautiful technique. Amazing chops. And he had that gorgeous instrument. I cut four sides with him in the back of a Sixth Ward furniture store. 'Basin Street Blues,' 'Squeeze Me,' and two others. I think at least one of them was original."

"What do you remember about Gibbs himself?"

"Nothing much. He was clean, polite, and sober. That's more than I can say for a lot of musicians. He asked me some questions about music in New York. But that's about all I can recall. There's not usually a lot of personal conversation at these sessions."

"So, what happened with his records? Did they do well?"

"Never got a chance to find out. The record execs wouldn't have anything to do with it," he replied. "They said it's got no bang to it."

"Meaning what exactly?"

"The man didn't sing. And he didn't want any other musicians on the recording. Nobody buys solo trumpet records. Maybe this guy could have changed that, I don't know. But the execs weren't willing to pay to press up a bunch of records just to take a chance on the thing. Damn shame, really. I've still got the master discs somewhere around my office, though."

After New Orleans, Marcus's investigation would likely take him to New York. That meant passing through New Jersey. With that in mind, he secured a promise from Peer to look for the masters and an invitation to drop by the birddog's office for a listen. Though it seemed unlikely, Marcus couldn't rule out the possibility the recordings might contain something useful. More than that, after his experiences in Gates County and meeting the Gibbs family, he no longer saw the musician as an abstract subject of investigation. He wanted a human connection with the man.

Replacing the phone's earpiece in its cradle, Marcus felt a pang of regret. The rest of his day would be spent in investigations more challenging and, possibly, dangerous than talking on the phone. His conversations at L'Original made it clear that untangling the strands of Gibbs' life in New Orleans necessitated a better understanding of Voodoo. He had read a little of Louisiana's syncretic faith. While not a primary concern for either BSPR or ASPR, pertinent articles, scholarly or sensationalistic, circulated occasionally in their journals. He knew better than to trust them. He needed someone local.

The Roosevelt's concierge directed Marcus to a shop on Decatur Street. A woman with thick, lustrous hair, a bright red dress, and galaxies of bangles greeted him enthusiastically. Before Marcus could explain his errand, the proprietress started proffering love potions, brick dust, "authentic" graveyard dirt, fortunes told, and charms and curses for a thousand purposes. Marcus recognized patter when he heard it, doubting he'd find the needed answers here.

After leaving the shop, he heard a thin voice say "You're looking for something."

Scanning the crowd, Marcus beheld a diminutive man whose age might be anywhere from 30 to 70. "You're looking for something and didn't find it in there," the man repeated, puffing on a pipe. It was a statement, not a question. "I will help you," he added, his enigmatic smile revealing crooked teeth.

Although willing, Marcus grew nervous as the man led him through a maze of backstreets, pedestrian walkways, and alleyways. Only his pride's refusal to admit the small man intimidated him, and acknowledgement he had become completely lost, prevented Marcus from backing out. Their wanderings ended in a back alley bodega. Jars of herbs and powders lined rickety shelves. Colored candles piled in wooden crates. A handful of nondescript cloth dolls hung from pegs. An elegant wooden altar that could have come from some venerable Latin American church stood in total contrast.

"Can I ask about the altar?" Marcus began. "I thought Voodoo worshiped…" He fished for the correct term. "Loa."

"Not exactly," his informant answered. "But a common misunderstanding. Loa are not gods, not the way you mean. Voodoo is monotheistic. Our god is benevolent but distant. The loa act as intercessors, like saints. That's why, when my people were forced to the Americas, they easily combined loa and saints. All people tell the same stories, with the same actors, whatever masks they wear."

Marcus had read Jung. Hearing the Swiss scholar so succinctly paraphrased by the little man surprised him.

Setting down his pipe, the informant produced a bottle of rum, two shot glasses, and a pair of cigars.

"I don't smoke, thank you," Marcus declined. Admittedly a quirk, he had the notion smoking was not healthy.

"If we discuss the loa, we honor them with rum and tobacco." When the man insisted, Marcus complied.

In the pages of an ancient book, the man pointed to evocative woodcuts scattered amongst the archaic French typeface as he described major loa for Marcus. Damballah, the all-knowing sky serpent. Maitresse Erzulie, loa of love, beauty, and fertility. Marinette, wise, powerful, and terrible in her wrath. Ogou, the brave warrior. The dread Baron Samedi, loa of death and the dead. And many others besides. He finished with Papa Legba, humanity's great intercessor and the opener of ways.

"Legba likes you." The man laughed, unevenly. "As a solver of puzzles, you, too, are an opener of ways."

The cigar smoke must have made Marcus heady. He could not remember telling the man about himself, what he did, or of his purpose in New Orleans.

"I don't mean to offend, but some people think Voodoo is evil."

"No. Far from it. But it is different from the religion you are familiar with. Loa are not so tight-fisted with the spirit world's power," he explained. "That power can be used. It can also be misused. And some people call anything in Louisiana they don't understand 'Voodoo.' Many things are here beside Voodoo. Most are benign but some are less so."

"Would putting a fingernail or hair in a coffin have any significance in Voodoo?" Marcus asked, switching his inquiries from the general to the specific as he sought to make sense of what he had found in the Gates County Cemetery.

The man frowned. "No. It would not."

Indulging himself, Marcus asked another question bearing upon his investigation. "Can Voodoo bring people back from the dead?"

"Not the way you mean. Yes, a few have that power, after a fashion. But it revives only the body, not the mind. Such a creature could not do what the one you seek does."

Marcus knew he had said nothing about Gabriel Gibbs or his abilities. Had Fenno been here? Could this man be another of his agents? "How do you know so much about me?" Marcus demanded, trying to stand. His legs buckled and head swam. Clearly, the man had slipped him a mickey. Struggling to remain conscious, Marcus dimly noticed crashing to the floor.

SECOND

INTERLUDE

Between New York and Boston; July 1924

"Houdini is a dick," Orson Munn said from one seat over. In the crowded train car, the seat between the two men was conspicuously vacant.

Putting down his reading material, Marcus glanced up at Scientific American's *publisher. "I beg your pardon?"*

"A dick. A detective. Houdini is one. Or like one," Munn explained, raising his voice slightly to be heard over the click-clack of train cars making their way from New York to Boston. "The way he gets into these investigations and cuts to the quick of the matter. That's what we need." Munn paused. "Why? What did you think I meant?"

"I'm sure I don't know," Marcus replied. Briefly, his eyes flickered over the empty seat between them. The 50 year-old celebrity to which it belonged was currently doing pullups in the dining car to entertain admirers and onlookers.

Marcus was not, in fact, sure that Houdini was what the Margery investigation needed. For one thing, general resentment existed among the other judges regarding Houdini's special role in the proceedings. A fear that, after they had done the hard part of the investigation, Houdini would sweep in and claim the credit. More than sour grapes lurked behind those concerns. While a sizable portion of the English-speaking world knew about Scientific American's *contest, most would be hard-pressed to name any of its judges except Houdini. For another thing, rumors surrounded the man...*

The first reason, resentment, explained why the other judges had refused to accompany the famous escape artist and magician from New York to Boston for his first encounter with the medium. Even Malcom Bird, usually so eager to be seen as essential to the investigation, had remained pointedly silent. In their refusal, however, an opportunity lurked.

Walter Franklin Prince had suggested that Marcus, an ASPR member who lived in Boston and had a casual familiarity with the Crandons, was the natural choice to escort Houdini and Munn from New York to the Crandon's residence. Any additional benefits to Prince from that, with Marcus serving as his unofficial agent in the Margery matter, would hopefully remain unsuspected.

When Marcus had arrived at the magazine's headquarters earlier in the day, he was asked to wait while Houdini and Munn concluded a private meeting. Through the solid oak door leading into Munn's office, Marcus picked out some of the conversation occurring on the other side.

"You may rely on me," proclaimed a tinny and rather high-pitched voice. "I'll have the old fraud outed in no time at all."

"Yes, yes. I know. You are going to uncover in mere hours what no one else has managed to bring to light in months," replied a second voice overflowing with sarcasm. Unless Marcus missed his guess, the voice belonged to Malcom Bird, the contest's liaison, with whom Marcus had become acquainted during his periodic visits to the Crandon's house.

"Malcolm, please calm yourself," said a third voice, presumably Orson Munn. "You knew what the deal was when you agreed to participate in the magazine's investigation. Mr. Houdini has commitments and demands on his time that are not like those of the other judges."

"Well, I don't like it!" Malcom protested. "And he won't out her so easily, either. I'm telling you both, she's different than the ones we've looked at before."

The door opened and the displeased Malcom Bird stalked out. Orson Munn followed, arms spread wide in frustration. Last of all came Houdini, instantly recognizable, chuckling and shaking his head. Spotting Marcus and forcing composure on his rather fragile features, Bird took a minute to introduce the pair to the man who would be their escort. "This is Dr. Marcus Roads, a member of the ASPR and a physician."

While Munn simply favored Marcus with a firm handshake, Houdini could not resist additional commentary.

"A physician? Very nice. Did you know doctors can't figure out how I survive some of my performances? There's nothing supernatural about it, of course. But it's nice to know I can still keeping them guessing. Even my friend Sir Arthur Doyle. He's a physician, too, you know. But, in the matter at hand, you may trust me to provide deductions surpassing even those of his greatest creation."

Much of the great escape artist and debunker's conversation continued in that vein all the way from Scientific American headquarters until taking their seats as the train rolled out of Grand Central Station. It came as a considerable relief when Houdini sojourned forth to give an impromptu display of his prowess in the dining car.

And it perversely amused Marcus that, behind the issue of the Journal of the American Medical Association in which he pretended to be so engrossed, he was jotting a note to Prince which summarized the conversation overheard at Munn's office as well as the journey to Boston thus far.

Since accepting what Marcus felt to be an important if less than honorable commission from Prince, his communiqués to the research director had fueled Prince's fears of unprofessional behavior by several of the judges. Bird's deportment, in particular, toward Mina Crandon, the alleged medium known to the world as Margery, could hardly be called impartial. Indeed, it bordered on the salacious. Regarding Prince's other concern, Marcus had ferreted out further rumors that both Crandons led unorthodox intimate lives. Beyond that, despite the exhortations of his patron, Marcus drew a line in the sand and refused to provide specifics. On one matter, however, he could offer happy news. While the man's public pronouncements blew hot and cold, as a judge, William McDougall appeared to be keeping a more objective mind than commonly believed.

Once in Boston, it took Marcus and Munn a while to separate Houdini from the adoring crowds. By the time they departed the station for the Crandons' home, a scowl had etched itself on Marcus's face. The blame for that did not lie with the celebrity, his penchant for self-aggrandizing conversation, or even the publicist and police officer comprising Houdini's permanent entourage. Rather, it resulted from another face Marcus spotted darting from the train only to disappear amidst the crowd. Theodore Fenno had come to Boston. Clearly, people other than Prince had dispatched their agents to keep tabs on this latest development in the investigation.

Marcus presumed that Fenno was here reconnoitering on behalf of the Reverend Fredrick Edwards. The spiritualist clergyman from Detroit currently served as ASPR president. He and his allies resented "the scientists" within the organization passing judgement on their beliefs. So far, the collective weight of figures like Prince, McDougall, and parapsychologist Joseph Rhine had managed to keep Edwards' interference with daily operations of the society in check.

When they arrived at the Crandons' fashionable residence at 10 Lime Street, the maid showed the trio of Houdini, Munn, and Marcus inside. She escorted them to the garden patio where they found the Crandons and several of the contest judges enjoying afternoon tea.

Prince was not there. The ASPR's research director held himself aloof from the Crandons when not actually investigating. And the couple reciprocated his frostiness. Among the judges, only Houdini exceeded Prince for skepticism. Over his lengthy career, Prince had found only a single medium he thought likely to be genuine.

Bird, the liaison, was also absent, not yet having returned from New York. Houdini, of course, had just arrived. The three other judges, however, were in attendance. They had become ensconced, perhaps a little too much, into life at the Crandons'.

It had not been difficult for Marcus to occasionally insert himself at Lime Street, just as Prince had expected. After all, he was an ASPR member nominally part of the same professional circles as Dr. Crandon. In his time at the house, Marcus had

108

developed a feel for the other judges. Hereward Carrington was an eccentric, with his vegetarianism, frequent fasts, and complete teetotaling. He possessed enormous charm and his tales of esoteric adventures in exotic lands, true or not, captivated all but the most timid heart and dullest mind. Daniel Comstock, the engineer and physicist, felt more at home with gizmos and gears than people. Though Marcus never tired of listening to Comstock discuss the strange contraptions he designed to test Margery's abilities. William McDougal displayed an intellectual agility and an inclination to criticize. But he proved not nearly as stuffy as the reputation which preceded him.

Marcus made introductions of the two newcomers. After nodding pleasantly to Marcus, the handsome and affable Dr. Crandon was all big smiles and firm handshakes with his new guests. Conspicuously absent, Marcus noted, were last week's tirades by the good doctor about "that immigrant" Houdini.

But everyone understood that only one introduction really mattered: Houdini to Margery. Heads turned, as they usually did, toward Mina Crandon's twinkling blue eyes and blonde hair worn in a fashionably daring bob. Margery's healthy curves stopped just on the right side of beauty. Just as her gaiety and flirtatiousness stopped precisely on the right side of propriety.

When he chose to do so, the celebrity investigator could pour on the charm as well. "I have come to see the truth of you," he proclaimed to Mina with a bow at once theatrical and Old World. "Thus far, I acknowledge liking what I see."

"Welcome to our house," she replied, blushing. "You won't find any cause for denunciation or expose' here."

Marcus wondered if that was true. He also wondered if it would matter...

Allegations persisted, usually whispered rather than clearly spoken, that in cases where Houdini couldn't find clear indications of trickery, the arch-skeptic had planted evidence or simply pronounced the medium fraudulent. At that point, it became the medium's word against his. In the court of public opinion, the famous Houdini would almost certainly win any such contest. Those rumors had been the other judges' second source of contention regarding Houdini's participation.

Either way, it was to be a showdown between the world's great debunker and its most promising medium. A contest of giants.

Chapter Fifteen

Marcus awoke on his bed at the Roosevelt. Confused images of Houdini and Mina Crandon as wrestling giants who crushed all those around them lingered in his mind. Those thoughts gave way as the previous evening came rushing back to him. While his head throbbed violently, a cursory examination revealed no other injuries.

Then, rolling over to get out of bed, Marcus's side burned. Unbuttoning his shirt, he discovered a tattoo across his left pectoral. Standing, he gazed at it in the mirror. The unfamiliar symbol resembled a Greek cross surrounded by four smaller crosses in circles and bordered with small flourishes.

A visit by a nervous hotel porter interrupted his examination. "The concierge told me to check up on you. You alright, sir?"

"I appear to be fine," Marcus responded tentatively. "You wouldn't happen to know what this is, would you?" he asked, opening his shirt and revealing the tattoo. Making the sign of the cross, the porter departed without another word. That couldn't be good.

After freshening up, Marcus sought out the concierge and inquired how he had returned to the Roosevelt. "The staff found you unconscious behind the hotel. Two porters carried you to your room," the concierge explained in tones clearly indicating that the Roosevelt aspired to a higher caliber of guest than Marcus had proved to be.

"Do you know what this is?" Marcus again inquired,

discreetly revealing the tattoo.

"I'm sure I don't," he replied, his demeanor growing more disdainful.

Suspecting he knew who would, Marcus returned to the first occult shop. It proprietress brightened at his reappearance, resuming her sales pitch. Lifting his shirt to reveal the tattoo, Marcus questioned her about it.

"It is the *veve*, the symbol, of Legba," she responded warily. Instead of viewing Marcus as an easy mark, she now plainly just wanted him out of her shop.

Walking the streets of New Orleans, Marcus tried to make peace with his new addition. As long as he kept the tattoo clean and free from risk of infection while it healed, there was no real harm done. Still, it would be strange to have a sigil from a faith he barely understood, much less subscribed to, displayed on his skin for the remainder of his life. Furthermore, it would be challenging, and that put it mildly, to explain in polite society.

Marcus stopped at the Canal Street offices of the *Times-Picayune*. Talking his way into the morgue, the newspaper's repository of back issues from 1837 onward, Marcus sought additional information on the pawnshop robbery that had claimed Gibbs' silver trumpet. He found it in the March 9th, 1927 issue. A full month after the musician's death, Marcus had expected an earlier date. On the night of March 7th, a person or persons forced entry into Storyville's Trois Boules d'Or pawnshop and killed its owner, Luc de Amant. Marcus recognized, and noted, the name of L'Original's former landlord and Rose's other paramour. An interesting "coincidence."

Police surmised the intruders may have been surprised to find de Amant still at the pawnshop at such a late hour and that the murder may not have been premeditated. "Only a few items were stolen," the story noted, leading police to believe the robbers sought something specific.

Curious, Marcus read ahead several issues until he located de Amant's obituary. The man proved to be no simple pawnshop owner. At one point, his family owned much of what became Storyville, including the properties occupied by both Moulin and L'Original. Over the years, de Amant sold most of that property, retaining only the pawnshop and the family's Basin Street mansion. The obituary noted he was a generous supporter of temperance organizations as well as groups that pushed through the criminalization of prostitution. That struck Marcus. In his experience, individuals did not usually act so contrary to their material interests.

Leaving the *Times-Picayune,* Marcus wandered to the address given for the Trois Boules d'Or pawnshop. He found the establishment still in business, and differing from his expectations. True, it had the predictable display cases full of appliances, jewelry, and musical instruments. But it also offered a considerable number of high-end antiques and objects d'art. It, in fact, compared favorably with many galleries Marcus had visited.

He attempted to engage the clerk in conversation, steering discussion toward the burglary and de Amant's murder. When it became clear the man regarded Marcus as, at best, a kook and, at worst, suspicious, Marcus departed.

Marcus felt that his once thick collection of leads on Gabriel Gibbs in New Orleans had grown perilously thin. Despite the warnings he'd received at L'Original, among the leads that remained, Marcus viewed Queen Lola as the most promising, if highly challenging.

Given the sinister reputation of the Queen and her bayou revels, Marcus thought it couldn't hurt to make inquires back at the police department. After a little effort, he corralled the lieutenant and sergeant he spoke with on his previous visit. The lawmen appeared, at best, ambivalent about his reappearance.

Marcus explained that his inquiries with Gibbs' previous acquaintances in Storyville had left him curious about the swamps and, in particular, Queen Lola and her revels. The sergeant stared at Marcus as if he was out of his mind. So did the lieutenant, for that matter. But he at least attempted to be discreet about it.

"Honestly, we try to have as little to do with the bayous and their people as possible," the lieutenant acknowledged, a note of forced patience in his voice. "Anyway, that's all state law enforcement business these days. But, before that, we did have an inspector who made a study of that sort of thing. John Legrasse is the name. Been retired quite a few years now."

When Marcus continued making a nuisance of himself, the lieutenant dispatched the sergeant to find Legrasse's address and give it to their unwelcome visitor.

Later than afternoon, Marcus knocked on the white door of a townhouse just off Prytania Street in the Lower Garden District. Peach colored, with cream-white trim, a simple colonnaded porch, and Spanish-style iron grills over the windows, the residence spoke of taste if not wealth.

A white-haired man of surprisingly slight frame answered Marcus's knock. Marcus didn't doubt for a moment that he was a former lawman. It was the eyes. Regarding the world from behind rimmed spectacles, they radiated perspicacity. But they were distant, too; the eyes of someone who had seen more than his fair portion of life's unpleasant sights.

John Legrasse invited Marcus inside. The townhome's interior confirmed the impressions offered by its exterior. The furnishings and décor, including a small but handsome collection of antique furniture, reflected good, if highly traditional, taste.

Introducing himself and summarizing his activity in New Orleans, Marcus made a very surprising discovery. Not only was Legrasse familiar with the BSPR, he also knew Walter Franklin Prince. The retired police inspector met Prince at a conference in St. Louis many years earlier. It caught Marcus off guard that Legrasse rather pointedly avoided making further disclosures regarding that encounter.

After his summary of the Gibbs case, Marcus had a distinct impression that the retired inspector had heard stranger things. While Gabriel's murder occurred years after Legrasse left the police, Marcus pumped the inspector for anything he might recall of the matter.

"I can't help you there. Since retiring, I don't pay much attention to the police blotter anymore," Lagrasse confided. "It just gets depressing. On some level, you're a policeman because you want to make a difference. But everything stays the same. Only the names of the perps and their victims change."

"Some of the active duty policemen remember you as taking an interest in the..." Marcus fumbled for the proper term. "The...more esoteric aspects of crimes in the city. And in the swamps."

"That's true," Legrasse nodded guardedly. "It's not something I ever sought out. Might be more accurate to say it sought me out. And I was a little better read than most of the other inspectors. So, it just became my cross to bear." He paused. "We had someone better, once. Inspector Galvez. From a very old New Orleans Spanish family. He's at the Louisiana State Hospital, now. And I doubt very much he's coming back."

The inspector having acknowledged his familiarity with such matters, Marcus began discussing the possible occult dimensions of the Gibbs case. Legrasse was skeptical that the location of Gibbs' body, in St. Louis Number One Cemetery, constituted evidence of occult involvement. With the pragmatic eye of a veteran detective, he pointed out that the cemetery was large, offered plenty of concealment, and near many of New Orleans' most violent neighborhoods, including Storyville. In his opinion, practicality explained the cemetery's popularity as a dumping ground for bodies. Marie Laveau's mausoleum had no more to do with it than the tomb of chess grandmaster Paul Morphy.

"Are you familiar with Queen Lola? She's a...gris-gris queen." The phrase felt alien on Marcus's lips. "Somewhere out in the swamps." With Lola being Marcus's big remaining lead, he hoped Legrasse could shed some light on her.

"Can't say I am, she must be from after my time. But I bet I know her type. Smart. Ambitious. And not a lot of other options to make it in life. They feed on the excitement. The respect. Maybe even the fear they instill in others. Plus, of course, the money."

"Money?"

"Yeah, they can make a pretty penny. 'Donations' from the faithful and the thrill seekers. A lot of those operations have underworld ties, too. Maybe even with a silent partner in New Orleans. They're good cover for bootlegging and other smuggling, the flesh trade, even murder for hire on occasion."

"Do people like Queen Lola really believe they have occult

powers? Or are they just in it for the money?"

"Some are charlatans. Some are true believers. Most, I expect, are a bit of both."

"Would you have any advice for getting in touch with Queen Lola? And how to deal with her if I do?"

Legrasse gave a lengthy sigh. "Dr. Roads, let me tell you how I came to meet Dr. Prince." The inspector hesitated. The look in his eyes was not so much that of a man deciding how to tell a story as of one about to confront the demons of his past.

"It happened in late October of '08. Bayou folk don't like outsiders poking around in their affairs. At least they didn't 20 years ago. I see no reason things would be any different now. Occasionally, something happens that's so big they have to ask for outside help. Or that they can't keep secret. Throughout the first weeks of October, a spate of kidnappings occurred in bayou country...and word got out. Louisiana had no state police force to speak of back then, so the department here in New Orleans put together a detachment of policeman and a couple of investigators, including Galvez and me, to find out what was going on.

"When we got down there, the locals quickly pointed us toward the trouble. That, in itself, tipped us off something was seriously wrong. Some of the braver ones guided us out to the deep bayou, into places even they normally avoid. Our guides showed us an island in the middle of the swamp. Even from a distance, we heard, almost felt, the drum-beats and shouts and cries and carrying-on that sounded less than wholly human.

"Passing through the muck and mire to the island, we found about a hundred people there, most of them naked except for body paint. If it was paint. They were engaged in the worst kind of excesses and goings-on you can imagine. And we saw the missing bayou folks, suspended upside down from crude wooden scaffolds.

"Things were different back then, Doctor. I still maintain we were the good guys more often than not. But, well, there are some things from those days I wouldn't tell someone like you. When we rushed in, it was more like a military operation than a police raid. When all was said and done, maybe half the cultists had gotten away into the swamps, a half dozen lay dead or dying, and we had the rest in custody.

"There's a lot more I could say. Crimes involving the occult don't happen every day here. But they happen often enough. None of us had ever seen anything like this one. Straight Voodoo had nothing to do with it, I can tell you that. And that damned house. Anyway, we came too late to save most of the kidnapped bayou folk. Most of the cultists we arrested turned out to be too feebleminded, crazed, or fanatical to give us answers that made any sense. We had to ship most of them to the state hospital. And most of them are going to die there.

"And they weren't alone. I don't exactly what Inspector Galvez saw, or understood, out there that I didn't. But that raid left him a shell of himself. He stayed at that state hospital, too.

"Among the material evidence gathered at the crime scene was an idol. A little stone thing, not even a foot high. But it's the damnedest thing you've ever seen. I'm not a superstitious man, Dr. Roads, but just looking at that statue, I felt like a goose walked over my grave.

"Nobody at the department knew what to make of it. So I took it to the American Archeological Society conference in St. Louis. I thought identifying the idol could help us learn who those people were and figure out whether we had some larger criminal group or conspiracy on our hands. That's where I met Dr. Prince. He and all those other learned men tried to help. But none of them knew what to make of it either.

"What I'm getting at is that, between bayou folk and cultists, we had about 20 people dead. All over something nobody knows anything about. And we don't know how common things like that are in the swamps. We could guess. But we don't know. There are good people down there, too, Doctor. But even a lot of them are clannish and resentful of outsiders. So, when you ask me what advice I have for visiting this Queen Lola down in the bayous…in a word…don't."

Looking at the floor, Legrasse fell silent for a moment before raising his gaze to meet Marcus's. "But I know what kind of man Dr. Prince is. And, if I take your measure, you're cut from the same cloth. So, when you do go, be polite. Let your people know where you're going to be. And when you're going to be there. Be smart. Bad things happen down there, which means bad things could happen to you. Trust your instincts. If something seems shady, it probably is. And, for God's sake, go armed. Are you carrying a piece?"

Marcus admitted he wasn't.

Walking to a gorgeous Second Empire antique desk, John Legrasse opened the top drawer. Producing a heavy revolver, he carefully handed it to Marcus. "Colt Peacemaker single-action .45 revolver. It's the same piece I carried into the swamps 20 years ago. It got me back. Hopefully, there's some luck left in there to get you back, too."

"I thought you said you weren't superstitious," Marcus gave his host a friendly smile.

"I'm not superstitious," the inspector said. "But I am from Louisiana." He looked at the gun. "You know how to use it?"

Marcus nodded. It had been a few years, but he had done his fair share of shooting with relatives while growing up. And, for a time, fashion dictated that young men of a certain class go armed about Boston.

Thanking the wily old inspector for his wisdom, and his weapon, Marcus departed.

Chapter Sixteen

South Louisiana Bayous; September 12, 1929

Through the Roosevelt, Marcus had hired a car and driver. No doubt Prince would quibble over this expense, too, after the investigation concluded. Easy enough for him, Marcus thought. The BSPR's research director wasn't the one who would otherwise have to throw himself on the mercy of whatever passed for public transportation in rural Louisiana. An hour outside of New Orleans, Marcus questioned that decision. Not only was his driver taciturn and surly, he seemed even more uncomfortable than Marcus with their surroundings.

The previous evening Marcus had returned to L'Original. With Helene's assistance, given under protest, he finally made contact with the right staff and regulars. Spreading a little green-backed goodwill, he acquired instructions to find Queen Lola. Once again, he had the impression the information came second or even third-hand. Hopefully it would suffice.

Given that everyone from the staff at L'Original to the New Orleans police to John Legrasse had warned Marcus against making the journey, maybe his driver was the prudent one after all. As they traveled, the physician's anxieties and doubts warred with his commitment to the investigation.

The road, while not good, was at least worthy of the name. As far as the village of Lafitte, anyway. Beyond that, it was barely wide enough for a single vehicle. Passing required waiting for the road to cross one the good natural islands dotting the bayou. There, enough space could be made for one car or wagon to pull aside and the let the other by.

His directions to Queen Lola's took him only as far as the hamlet of Bayou Rigolettes. From there, the informants at L'Original advised him, he'd need to ask for directions to an even smaller unmarked community known as Fin des Terres.

Making inquiries in Bayou Rigolettes and finding the French he'd polished during his finishing in Europe less than useful, Marcus switched to English. While his conversations started friendly enough, the locals turned frosty whenever Marcus inquired about Fin des Terres. After several failed attempts, a sullen, slack-jawed youth finally provided directions to the community, its name crumpled by the local accent into something like "Fin'ditaer."

The attention of a policeman both alarmed Marcus and delayed his departure. He politely but circumspectly answered the officer's questions about his identity and the purpose of his visit. The lawman let it slip that a child, an infant almost, had vanished from one of the nearby communities and locals suspected foul play. While the officer was scrutinizing unfamiliar faces carefully, he apparently could not envision Marcus connected with kidnapping. Dismissing Marcus with a wave, he enjoined the travelers to "y'all take care, now."

Eastward from Bayou Rigolettes, upkeep of the artificially raised single-lane road became dismal. Marcus's increasingly resentful driver occasionally had to stop and examine a section of nearly submerged roadway before determining it was safe, barely, to continue. While Marcus had no idea what they would do if they encountered a car or wagon coming the other direction, he doubted that happened very often here.

It took the better part of an hour to cover the three miles bringing them to a collection of rough shacks built on tall poles to withstand flooding. A handful of decrepit houseboats, and a lonely general store with a solitary, and dry, gas pump rounded out the community.

"Is this Fin des Terres?" Marcus asked the assortment of old men loitering in front of the store. Encountering a stranger, to say nothing of one who looked and sounded like Marcus, clearly surprised them. The communications difficulties went both ways. Marcus repeated his question several times before realizing the men answered in the affirmative.

"I'm looking for Queen Lola," Marcus continued, forcing his voice to project a confidence he did not feel.

The men now seemed more wary than surprised by Marcus. Without uttering another word, one of them pointed down a lonely trail along the bayou's edge. Returning to the car, Marcus reminded the driver to wait for him. Walking away, he added "If I'm not back in two hours, send help."

The trail cut an eerie path alongside the swamp. Trees draped with thick Spanish moss reached upward and closed in over the trail, casting the world in unnatural twilight. In the water, just a stone's throw away, he heard something move but could not see it. Along the way, like mile markers, tree stump altars stood decorated with burned candles, bottles of liquor, and less wholesome items. Amidst the hanging moss, sticks and bones dangled from the trees on coarse twine, banging against each other in the torpid breeze like macabre wind chimes.

The pathway opened onto a point, jutting like a knife out into the bayou. No trees grew here. The grass had been badly trampled. Broken bottles, empty food tins, and other refuse littered the ground. Marcus noted several stone-lined fire pits dug into the moist earth. A boat dock sat at the point's far end. Next to it, a wooden causeway led to a small island dominated by a raised cabin…

A hut, really. The structure rested atop twisted cedar trunks that looked like muscular, malformed legs. Crossing the causeway, he shuddered at the skulls that capped its wooden supports. Alligator. Bear. Cougar. Some kind of great snake. A simian creature which, to the best of Marcus's knowledge, matched nothing that should exist in the area. And human. Clearly, unmistakably, human.

Reaching the island, he took a deep breath and cleaned his glasses. Close at hand, an iron cauldron bubbled over a large fire. The image of a hut on legs and a boiling cauldron called to his mind tales of Baba Yaga, the terrible witch of Slavic folklore.

While a quick glance revealed that nothing more nefarious than laundry filled the cauldron, Marcus was unnerved. So unnerved that he didn't notice the man until almost walking into him. Tall and gaunt, the man looked as if he might once have been comely. But no more. While his physician's instincts proclaimed the man's relative youth, something was wrong with him. As if he suffered from some kind of wasting disease.

"I'm sorry," Marcus apologized. "I'm looking for Queen Lola." Though the man displayed no obvious symptoms of feeblemindedness, his fixed gaze suggested he hadn't registered, or hadn't heard, that someone spoke to him. Repeating his request, and treated to a similarly blank stare, Marcus tried again, this time with French.

A cackling laugh cut through the air above him. "Don't pay Mose any mind. You're looking for Queen Lola, you've found me." A woman with wild hair, intense eyes, a patchwork dress, and necklaces strung with countless amulets and charms stared down at him from the hut. No one would have called Queen Lola beautiful but she possessed an undeniable magnetism. That did nothing to diminish the Baba Yaga comparison. "But who are you?"

"I'm Dr. Marcus Roads."

The gris-gris queen scrutinized Marcus carefully. "That accent says you've come a long way just to talk to me. And, plainly, you asked the right people to find me. Which means you also asked the right people to be warned away. So, the question is, are you brave, desperate, or stupid?"

Marcus fished for a safe answer. "I guess you will have to decide that."

"That'll do for now," she nodded, kicking over a rope ladder leading up to her hut.

Marcus climbed. As he neared the top, Queen Lola offered a hand. Bracelets of gold, ivory--he hoped it was ivory anyway-- and other materials adorned her muscular arm. While considering reaching for her hand, he also imagined her withdrawing it at the last minute, leaving him to plunge into the boiling cauldron below.

"If I didn't want you here," she said as if reading his

thoughts. "You either wouldn't have found me or wouldn't have made it this far. You mind your manners, doctor. And I promise I'll mind mine."

Taking her hand, Marcus noted the woman's significant strength as she pulled him onto the platform. The gris-gris queen motioned him inside her hut. At its center, a large basalt mortar and pestle occupied a crude cedar table. Burning candles gave off the distinctive aroma of rendered fat. All around were unmarked glass jars of herbs. Heaps of bones, animal parts, dried fish, and a pantheon of frightening idols filled rough-hewn shelves.

Yet, a few parts of the décor stood at odds with the whole. A bottle of expensive French cognac rested on a silver and crystal serving set. A baroque looking-glass hung from one wall. A stack of *Times Picayune* issues rested on a cane chair. Ancient tomes lined a tiny antique bookcase of delicate workmanship. Locked behind hand-carved cabinet doors, the books were visible through a window of delicate brass latticework.

"It's not often I get proper company out here," Queen Lola declared. Removing the stopper from the cognac bottle, she filed two crystal snifters. "*Á votre santé*," she toasted, raising her glass.

"So, Dr. Roads, what do you want?" she asked, setting down her empty snifter. "If you couldn't find it between New England and New Orleans, it's got to be unusual."

"I'm looking for information about Gabriel Gibbs," Marcus began. "I was told you and he used to be…"

"That we were lovers?"

"Well, yes."

"That's true."

"What can you tell me about him?"

"Gabriel? He was fun. But he's wasn't my type," the gris-gris woman said. "I want a man I can own body and soul."

Uncomfortable with the appraising look she now gave him, Marcus tried to return focus to the musician. "And that wasn't Gabriel?"

"Nope. He was too headstrong. Too single-minded."

"Did you two part on good terms?"

"I'm not sure we parted on any terms, really," she said. "He started showing up here less and less. One day, he just stopped coming. Never saw him again." Once more, she studied Marcus. Her expression grew less menacing, perhaps even the slightest bit vulnerable. "You could say he broke it off with me, not the other way around. I wouldn't tell that to most people, it's not good for my reputation. But you've got no stake in that one way or the other.

"Gabriel came to the revels because he could make music and make money. I was just a fringe benefit. I imagine once he was making enough of both in New Orleans, he didn't see a reason to come down here anymore. Gabriel wasn't exactly a skeptic but I don't think he felt like the spirit world had a lot to do with him."

"What do you know about his death?"

"I didn't have anything to do with it, if that's what you mean," she shot him a brazen grin. "Doctor, I'm not someone you ever want to get crosswise with. But Gabriel never did cross me. There was no malice in what he did. Not like…well, you don't need to know about that.

"Hell, I can't look you in the eye and tell you for certain that Gabriel did die. From what I heard, it's got all the right paperwork. But you can never really be sure in New Orleans. And I don't know if he came back. If he did, I had nothing to do with that, either. But I'll tell you this. When somebody's got a passion. A real, true passion. They can do things that seem miraculous, or diabolic, to regular people."

"I don't want to offend. But can I ask you a question about your…religion?"

"Mind your manners. But you've kept them so far. Likely the worst I'd do is not answer."

"People call you a 'gris-gris queen' not a 'Voodoo queen.' Why? Is there a significance to the difference?"

She smiled. "You're no dummy, I can tell that. Most times, a gris-gris woman, or gris-gris man, is someone who works mostly with charms and powders rather than loa. But it's also a respectful way to talk about those who work with spirits other than just loa. That's me. The loa are safe, mostly. At least they play by rules. But they won't do everything. You want real power, you need to broaden your horizons to other powers too."

Marcus remembered the bodega man's words about many things being in Louisiana other than Voodoo. And that, while most were benign, others were less so. While he wasn't sure he wanted the answer, he couldn't resist asking. "Like what?"

"Well, I'll give you one. Empress Lilith. She and I get on really well." Using a key dangling from one of her countless necklaces, Queen Lola unlocked the antique bookshelf. She carefully removed one of the tomes and handed it to Marcus. The ancient leather-bound volume was printed in Hebrew, except for a note on the title page giving the time and place of printing as Prague, 1556. Within the text, sandwiched between the lines of print, he found handwritten French in an archaic, crabbed script. A translation, Marcus presumed, instinctively closing the book and not further perusing those mysterious handwritten lines.

"No idol, though," Queen Lola said. "Her kind doesn't like physical representation. Anyone tells you they've got an idol of Empresses Lilith, watch out. Because they're a danger to themselves and others. But she gives me the best love charms you're going to find. When I say love charms, I really mean lust charms. That's not what people ask for but, deep down, that's what they really mean."

Her talk of other spirits brought John Legrasse's strange tale to his mind. "I heard a story about a big police raid down here about 20 years ago…"

With lightning reflexes, Queen Lola pressed a finger against Marcus's lips. He felt the tip of its blood red nail, long as a small knife, uncomfortably on his skin. "Careful now. Some things have a way of hearing when they're spoken of. And you were about to speak of one of the Outer Ones. See, there's the *Other Ones*, like Empress Lilith. And then there's the *Outer Ones*. Them, I have no truck with."

The gris-gris queen paused. "Except Mam Shub." She nodded toward a statuette on a shelf by itself. Carved from black stone, the figurine looked much like the Venus of Willendorf except for legs terminating in great, bestial cloven hooves. "Mam Shub plays it pretty straight. When everything else has failed, she's always good for a fertility spell. Of course…" Queen Lola shuddered. "Sometimes what her power begets doesn't come out quite right."

Queen Lola made a strange gesture with her left hand. "The one you're talking about with that raid, the Dead-Dreaming Lord of the Deep, that's the safest thing to call him. But there's nothing safe about that one. As long as there have been people in the bayou, there have been those that worship him. Longer, if certain stories are believed. It's said there are *things* in the swamp that serve him, too. As well as some abominable amphibian mélanges that come from the mixing of those things with the meanest of folk.

"I'll tell you something," his hostess continued. "Bayou folk take care of our own problems. I don't know what you heard in New Orleans but the only reason the authorities learned about those kidnappings 20 years ago is that a fellow from down here got arrested for robbery up there and ran his mouth to the police in hope of getting some leniency.

"Those City Men they sent down here botched the job. A lot of the Dead-Dreaming Lord's thralls got away. Yeah, they've been quiet for years, mostly. But occasionally, certain things happen. In fact…well, that's something else you don't need to know about," she eyed him again. "Do you want to know more about the Outer Ones?"

Marcus's mood was dark. Not so much from Queen Lola's tale itself as for the echoes it held. Remarkably similar tales surrounded a certain ill-fortuned and degenerate seaport not far from his hometown of Marblehead. He did not want to know more about the Outer Ones. Actually, having learned as much about Gabriel Gibbs here as seemed likely, he felt quite done with Queen Lola.

More abruptly, perhaps, than good manners dictated, Marcus excused himself.

In the waning light, and with the gris-gris queen's words fresh in his mind, the bayou-side path proved even more alarming than on his way in. Returning to Fin des Terres, Marcus's driver and, more importantly, car were nowhere to be found. The number of men gathered on the porch outside the general store had swelled, and they cast none too friendly eyes on Marcus.

While he wasn't happy about it, Queen Lola was the closest thing to a friend he had out here. At her place, he suspected none of the townsfolk would bother him. Of course, that might prove to be the least of his worries…

Chapter Seventeen

The gris-gris queen cackled at his return.

"Looks like you're stuck with me for a while," Marcus announced, trying to put a brave face on the situation.

"Thought I might be. Look on the bright side. You'll get to see one of my revels," after a moment, she added. "And maybe a bit more."

Marcus noticed that men and women now gathered on the point opposite Queen Lola's island. Fires burned in the pits. As more revelers arrived, instruments appeared. Drummers pounded out deep bass tones that seemed to resonate through the earth itself. Other revelers shook instruments which Marcus knew as maracas, but that Queen Lola referred to as *shak-shaks*, filling the air with the raspy sound of their rattling.

Though the musicians started at a slow, restrained, and almost formal pace, their tempo edged gradually upward. At a point, as if a silent signal had been given, the revelers burst into wild dancing. The speed increased until the drummers pounded forth a furious wall of backbeats. Their cadence was intoxicating, irresistible. Marcus noted that, however unseemly it might be, he swayed along with the primal rhythm. He felt as if his heart beat in time to the revelers' sound.

A solitary trumpeter joined the performance. Pointing his instrument skyward, crescendos of passionate brassy melody soared above the rhythmic bedrock of percussion. With this new addition, the dancers reached new plateaus in their athletic leaps and spins. That Marcus thought himself too well-bred, or too repressively bred, to allow himself to join did not mean he didn't wish to.

Bottles were passed. Without thinking, Marcus took a hearty pull. Rum. But not only Rum. Strange flavors and a tingling sensation in his mouth suggested that certain spices or herbs infused the drink. Marcus knew he should be concerned, especially after what had happened in New Orleans, but couldn't quite manage the effort. Occasionally taking a deep draught from her private bottle, Queen Lola then spewed her mouthful over the gathered revelers. Obviously a ritual act, but with an intent he couldn't deduce.

Eventually, clothes started coming off. Many revelers now danced nearly naked, and some completely so. Marcus had heard the rumors. With a heady mixture of prurience and distaste, he knew what would follow. Or so he assumed. Instead, followed the disrobing, pots of pigment appeared. The revelers painted themselves and each other. Many brushed intricate symbols across their chests. *Veves,* he realized, recalling the word the proprietress of the occult shop had used. But, as nearly as Marcus could tell, none matched the one now indelibly etched into his chest.

A dozen large, muscular men painted themselves in the likeness of skeletons, obscuring their faces with grinning death's heads of white pigment.

Among the most frenzied of the dancers, Marcus noted a young woman with a wild veve painted between her breasts and a large snake draped across her shoulders like a stole. A live snake, Marcus realized, watching it twist and slither over her torso.

Some of the dancers began to...transform. Yes, that word best matched what he witnessed. Their postures, their movements, now totally different from just minutes earlier. It was like watching two different people inhabit the same body in turn.

A physician of curious inclinations, Marcus was familiar with post-hypnotic trances. And the feats possible while under one. Such states frequently underpinned alleged cases of possession, just as the dancers in front of him no doubt imagined themselves possessed by loa. Likewise, trances, and simple charlatanism, explained many supposed mediums. But did they explain all such cases? Both the BSPR and ASPR would dearly like to know.

Pondering that question, Marcus felt a long-nailed hand rest upon his shoulder. He turned to face the gris-gris queen. "This is no regular revel," she shouted over the din. "All the casuals and all the thrill seekers from the city have been turned away. Every man and woman here knows the loa. Or some of the Other Ones. Tonight, a great evil takes place deep in the bayou and we mean to stop it. Are you ready to encounter the Outer Ones?"

To Marcus's surprise, he found he was.

At some point during the revel, a dozen simple boats had put into Queen Lola's dock. Most looked like large canoes, *pirogues* Queen Lola called them. As the gris-gris queen let loose a shriek at once ecstatic and unearthly, the musicians fell instantly quiet and dancers halted mid-pose. With precision than an army would have envied, they began silently filing onto the boats.

A few craft of smaller dimensions but similar proportions moored alongside the pirogues. Queen Lola motioned Marcus to join her aboard one of those. Mose, still and silent as ever, stood at its aft, clutching a large wooden pole.

Without a word, the flotilla shoved off and made its way deeper into the darkened swamp. In contrast to the cacophony which had ruled just moments earlier, the only noise now came from the subtle splash of poles pushing the pirogues through the brackish water.

Even after his eyes adjusted to the darkness, Marcus saw little. It was his ears that announced the danger first. Drums in the distance. Sounding even louder and deeper than ones Queen Lola's revelers used, the unseen instruments must be huge. Not long after, Marcus spotted a great fire in the swamp ahead.

On an island both large and solid by bayou standards, a vast bonfire burned. Tongues of dark red flame licked high into the air. Beyond the fire, bathed in its red-orange glow, the shell of an old plantation house rose at the island's center. Creepers and Spanish moss rested thickly on its walls. While decrepit and abandoned, Marcus marveled at the structure's relative soundness.

Around the blaze, a horde of people circled, cavorted, and shouted. Their movements were animalistic, even bestial. Above the rabble, above the fire, Marcus had the unnerving sensation that dark shapes fluttered in the night sky.

As Queen Lola's boats stealthily approached, he heard the island's occupants chanting. Marcus didn't recognize the language. He was no linguist. But, with its expansive and taxing consonant clusters, it was clearly not Indo-European. Indeed, its strange inflections hardly seemed designed for human speech at all.

As the pirogues split into two groups, the gris-gris queen motioned for Mose to halt. Half of the boats proceeded toward the near shore. The others made a long, slow circle around to the island's far side. From within the folds of her patchwork dress, Queen Lola produced a pair of silver and mother of pearl opera glasses. After surveying the scene for a moment, she passed the glasses to Marcus.

Through the lenses, he watched a single small boat separate itself from the first group and push forward. As a solitary figure leapt from its prow onto the shore, for an instant Marcus thought it was the little man from the New Orleans bodega. Such a thing was, of course, impossible. Blinking, he instead saw a short, lithe youth of perhaps 16, his teeth clenching a corncob pipe. It must have been the pipe that had momentary confused him, Marcus assured himself. After scouting the island, the young man turned back to his allies waiting in the swamp and uttered a shrill birdcall.

As Queen Lola's revelers crossed the last few yards to the bank, the others finally noticed their approach. As men and women poured out of the pirogues onto the island, the earlier arrivals rushed away from their bonfire toward the newcomers. The twelve men painted as skeletons he'd noted earlier served as the reveler's vanguard and shock troops. None under six feet tall, they were bare except for tattered pants, top hats, and the stout, staff-like canes they swung furiously while closing with their opponents.

Fierce war cries arose from both sides as their lines clashed together. As fighting continued, the dark flying shapes Marcus noticed earlier descended from the skies. He beheld a colossal flock of grackles, now perching on the island's cypress trees in their thousands.

The fighting was of a bareknuckle brawling and bartitsu variety. Amidst the chaos, it was easy to miss the finesse and skill displayed by Queen Lola's revelers. The cultists, as Marcus had begun to think of the reveler's opponents—remembering the word John Legrasse had used—favored a brute force approach. Forming a ferocious human wall, they fought to keep the revelers away from a handful of others who hung back; chanting and genuflecting as if desperately trying to complete some arcane rite.

The revelers slowly gained ground, pushing the wall of cultists back toward the bonfire and plantation house.

Among the strange sights unfolding on the island, one in particular drew Marcus's attention. While most people would have found it horrific, it offered Marcus a note of comfortable familiarity amidst his barely believable surroundings. One of the large revelers painted like a skeleton was down, writhing and covered in blood. Even from a distance, and in the darkness, Marcus recognized a life-threatening injury.

Chapter Eighteen

"Take us forward," he commanded.

Not used to being given orders, Queen Lola's eyes flared. Momentarily with resentment, then with respect. She waved Mose to push the boat closer to the island.

Leaping from the boat, Marcus rushed to the man. He had a knife wound to the gut. That wasn't good. Marcus's presence might make the difference between life and death. On the other hand, depending on what damage the blade had done, it might not. Some wounds modern medicine couldn't fix. Even in 1929.

Dropping his black bag beside the man, Marcus swung into action "What's your name?"

"Jean," the man gasped with surprising lucidity.

"Well, Jean, I'm Marcus Roads. You just lay there and relax. We'll get you all fixed up." It might not have been true. But it would do his patient no good to know that.

In a clinical setting, he would have started with a laparotomy, a surgical investigation of the abdomen, to aid in diagnosis and repairing injuries. Marcus was not about to try that in a swamp. Instead, motioning two of Jean's burly fellow revelers to hold the patient down, Marcus explored the wound to evaluate the extent of the injury. And learn whether he could do anything for the man.

Expecting full-body thrashing, gnashing of teeth, and screaming, Marcus was surprised by Jean's gentle moaning and slight writhing. Normally, such a tepid response might support a dire prognosis. But his patient continued to fix Marcus with a focused, coherent gaze.

Through the curious intersection of Marcus's professional and personal lives, he was familiar with the writings of Dr. James Braid. The 19th century Scottish surgeon hypothesized that hypnosis could be used as a substitute for chemical anesthetics. Marcus wondered if the post-hypnotic state of "loa possession" now produced a similar effect upon his patient.

Interesting as Dr. Braid's ideas were, Marcus put his faith in the tried and true: an ether mask. The few drops of ether applied to the wire-mesh mask now placed over Jean's face would make his surgery as painless as possible.

While Marcus worked, he reassigned the two men holding Jean down to boil the water he carried in his physician's bag. No doubt locating a suitable container and scrounging enough burnable wood proved challenging. But, when Marcus next looked up, a fire burned.

With forceps and measured use of his scalpel, Marcus explored Jean's wound. The knife track didn't approach the liver or spleen. That was good, either would have rapidly bled his patient out. He found no evidence of injury to the bowel and did not encounter the telltale odor of such a wound. Marcus would have preferred to also examine the intestines for nicks. But, under field conditions, the risks of such a procedure outweighed the certainty it brought.

As he worked, Marcus ligated the most problematic of the severed blood vessels, the "bleeders" as they were casually called when patients couldn't overhear, using sutures to close the ones he didn't trust to stop on their own. Soaking up the copious quantities of blood, Marcus watched his supply of precious clean towels dwindle.

Having explored to the fullest extent his environment allowed, Marcus cleaned the wound, careful to remove all debris. He then pulled vials of sodium hypochlorate and boric acid from his bag. During his residency at Massachusetts General, Marcus worked under a surgeon who had run a field hospital for the American Expeditionary Force in France. His mentor frequently railed about how a civilian doctor's kit was inadequate for treating traumatic injuries, especially away from a hospital setting. Taking heed, Marcus had adjusted the contents of his bag in accordance with the veteran's suggestions.

The sodium hypochlorate and boric acid were two of those additions. Combined in precise quantities with water, the resulting mixture, known as Dakin's solution, was a weak antiseptic useful for cleaning wounds. Marcus carefully mixed his supplies into the water his assistants had boiled, now cooling beside him.

Movement drew his eye away from the patient. Across the melee, Marcus locked eyes with a cultist rushing madly toward him. Huge, unmoving eyes were but one of the man's disquieting aspects. Clearly, some unfamiliar developmental condition afflicted the cultist. In addition to the eyes, he barely had ears to speak of. Or nose. Prominent nostrils appeared to lead directly into the skull. And there was something distinctly abnormal about the loping gate he displayed while charging.

Carefully setting his instruments down on the comparatively clean surface of his bag, Marcus drew the revolver lent to him by Inspector Legrasse. At another time, Marcus might have panicked. But he tolerated no interference while working on a patient. Calmly holding the weapon and aiming for a moment, Marcus pulled the trigger.

The Peacemaker was not one of those genteel sporting pistols Marcus remembered from his youth. Discharging, the revolver barked like Cerberus. Its powerful recoil stung Marcus's wrist and sent the shot wild. While the peaceable physician had intended a warning shot, the errant bullet caught the cultist in the right shoulder, spinning him around and knocking him into the muck. After a moment, the wounded figure pushed himself onto hands and knees and began crawling the opposite direction. The unnatural speed and agility of the act viscerally repulsed Marcus. The cultist seemed to travel as naturally on four legs as he had on two.

His retreat marked the beginning of a general rout. Their human wall broken, not least of all by alarm over Marcus's gunfire, the cultists fled past the plantation house to the rear of the island. There, finding their boats seized by the other half of

Queen Lola's flotilla, they leapt into the bayou desperately seeking escape. In the darkness, primordial shapes swam slowly but deliberately through the water toward them. Alligators, some ancestral memory informed Marcus. As the reptiles encircled the cultists, the flock of grackles alit from the trees. The frenzied birds cried ecstatically while drawing a living curtain over the inevitable conclusion to the cultists' flight.

Re-sterilizing his instruments with tincture of iodine, Marcus resumed the ligation. Finished at last, he soaked sterile dressing in what remained of the Dakin's solution before packing it in and over the wound. The dressing would absorb any blood that continued seeping, prevent further damage to soft tissue, and, most importantly, reduce the likelihood of infection.

As he worked, Marcus noticed the plantation house being set alight. A new chant, this one rising from the victors, filled the air.

"What's going on?" he wondered aloud.

"Something that should have been done a long time ago, sir," one of the men assisting him answered. Though the boards must have swelled with the water of decades, if not centuries, the plantation went up like kindling.

Marcus completed Jean's dressing with a layer of dry bandages applied over those soaked in Dakin's solution. He then took a small tube of arnica from his bag, generously applying the pungent paste both for its antiseptic properties and for its reputed ability to reducing scarring.

"You're not going to stitch him up?" one of the men holding Jean wondered.

"A good question," Marcus answered patiently, "but no. Usually, you don't want to suture a deep wound like this. It increases the risk of infection because you're basically sealing the germs in." Finally, Marcus applied a medical plaster to hold the dressing in place.

"Are you friends of Jean's?" he asked. Both men nodded. "Okay, listen to me carefully. His life is truly in your hands. He's got a very serious wound." Marcus explained. "If it's taken care of, there's a good chance he'll be fine. If not, there's a very good chance he's still going to die. Either way, he's going to hurt like hell. And there's going to be fever.

"I cannot stress enough the importance of keeping the wound clean. His dressings must be changed, with sterile material, every day. Under no circumstances do you let that swamp water come in contact with the wound. If it gets dirty, you clean it immediately with iodine, carbolic acid, strong alcohol, soap and water. Whatever you can find.

"Do you understand?"

The men acknowledged that they did.

At last, Marcus allowed himself a good look around, taking in the situation on the island. It baffled him to find the large snake he'd spotted earlier at the revel now coiled, protectively, around an infant. The missing child, no doubt, that the lawman advised him of back in Bayou Rigolettes. The woman who had carried the snake picked up the child and handed him to Marcus. Examination revealed the infant to be tired, hungry, and scared but otherwise unharmed.

Jean's proved to be the most serious injury. But hardly the only one. Marcus spent hours dealing with lacerations, fractures, and burns. He helped the last of the wounded onto the pirogues before boarding the gris-gris queen's small boat. A handful of revelers stayed behind to verify the plantation house burned to the ground. And ensure none of the cultists still lurked in hiding on the island.

Without a word, Mose pushed their boat back toward the gris-gris queen's hut. As they traversed the bayou's black waters, Marcus sought to make sense of what had transpired. "What's story behind that old plantation house?" he asked.

On that question, Queen Lola remained as silent as her gondolier.

Returning to the dock where the expedition began, Marcus saw others now joined the victorious revelers. Their deed done, someone had decided to admit the casuals, as Queen Lola had called them, and the thrill seekers after all. He marveled at how many of those who had just fought on the island still possessed the energy to dance and leap as they celebrated their victory.

Sitting on the platform which supported Queen Lola's hut, Marcus dangled his legs over the edge. Watching the revels and taking swigs from a bottle of the curiously tainted rum, he reflected that, strange as it all was, nothing had occurred tonight that definitively could not be explained without recourse to the paranormal. Unlikely? Perhaps. Impossible? No. Still, this was not how things were done in Boston.

With a start, Marcus realized the gris-gris queen sat beside him. When she wished, Queen Lola could be every bit as stealthy as her strange companion. Like Marcus, she dangled her bare feet out over the water. The act possessed a childlike quality which he found at once endearing and horrifying.

"Without medical attention, Jean would have died," Marcus wasn't intending to boast, merely to state a fact and make conversation. "And some of those other injuries would have been crippling rather than inconvenient and painful. It is fortunate I was here."

Queen Lola's laugh sounded like a shriek. "Bless his heart. He thinks its coincidence he came today." The gris-gris queen turned to face him. "Still, you did good out there. Let me give you something that might help you on your way."

"What's that?" he inquired with a mixture of curiosity and trepidation.

"Remember how I told you I want a man I can own body and soul? And how that wasn't Gabriel?"

Marcus nodded warily.

"It was more than just him being a stubborn and headstrong man," she continued. "His soul wasn't mine to take. Nor the devil's, if that's what you're wondering. Gabriel gave his soul to music long before I ever met him." With that, she rose, descended from the hut, and wandered among her revelers.

Later, Marcus watched a craft emerge from the bayou's darkness. Not a pirogue, but an actual boat. Perhaps 30 feet in length, with a wooden deck, even a small cabin, and a single hooded light on its prow. The revelers greeted its arrival with a roar of enthusiasm. While men with long poles maneuvered the boat into Queen Lola's dock, the scent of gasoline fumes mixing with the swamp's natural fecund aroma testified that its actual propulsion came from a more modern source.

Tying up their craft, its muscular crew started unloading

crates. The ubiquitous bootlegging, Marcus realized as eager revelers opened a crate and distributed the brown bottles within. Perhaps a tenth-part of the contraband remained among the revelers to be consumed with abandon. The rest was carried along the trail back to Fin des Terres. Far more than would be needed for local consumption, Marcus suspected that waiting trucks or wagons would carry the hooch to New Orleans.

As the boat's crew lugged the bootleg past Marcus, one cast him a sidelong glance. The rough sailor was not so much a man as a man-shaped mountain. Marcus didn't know why the gold-toothed ogre felt the need to single him out with such an ominous leer.

Chapter Nineteen

New Orleans; September 13, 1929

Simply getting back to New Orleans had consumed much of the day. At first light, Marcus said his goodbyes to the gris-gris queen, walked through Fin des Terres and all the way to the main road at Bayou Rigolettes. There, Marcus hitched a ride from a drayage driver named Claude carrying a load of fresh Gulf shrimp and oysters as far as south New Orleans. The good-natured if rather crude-mannered trucker was glad for the company. And for someone to tell his stories to, though Claude obviously found Marcus's accent as challenging as the physician found the driver's thick Cajun speech. Once in south New Orleans, Marcus hailed a cab back to the Roosevelt.

Upon returning, he immediately complained regarding the driver he hired through the hotel. The concierge, who had clearly already formed his opinion of Marcus, seemed imperfectly sympathetic to his guest's plight.

Departing the concierge's station, he went to the front desk to reclaim materials he'd deposited in the hotel safe before visiting the bayou: extra cash, his correspondence with Prince, and other materials relating to the Gibbs investigation, including the two photographs of Gabriel. As the clerk went to fetch the items, it surprised Marcus when the manager stepped in.

"I am sorry about yesterday," the manager began. "I thought you understood the hotel's policy regarding use of the safe. I regret if it caused you any inconvenience."

"Yesterday?"

"The man you sent to retrieve your materials from the safe. Our policy forbids releasing objects from the safe to third parties. Items can be retrieved only by the guest who deposited them. Or, in contingencies that are fortunately rare at the Roosevelt, their next of kin. That is true even when the third party has written authorization from the guest."

Only one person currently in New Orleans would care enough about what Marcus might deposit in a hotel safe to try that kind of stunt. Suddenly, Marcus grew very concerned. "And you didn't release the materials?"

"Certainly not, sir," the manager patiently continued. "As I explained to you…"

"This man, what did he look like?"

"Towheaded. Hair heavily oiled. A Valentino moustache, and," the manager's lips curled in disdain "he wore spats."

Of course Theodore Fenno wouldn't do his own dirty work, Marcus realized. And, in certain parts of New Orleans, no doubt it would be easy enough to hire a man for such purposes. The "written authorization" left Marcus wondering. Perhaps Fenno's man had handed the clerk any old scrawl, hoping to work a fast con. On the other hand, if Fenno wanted to get fancy and had planned in advance, the ASPR's files probably held enough examples of Marcus's handwriting to try a legitimate forgery. Marcus smiled ruefully at the oxymoron contained within those last two words.

"Thank you," Marcus said with relief. He had intended to reclaim his materials from the safe. In light of this new information, he reversed himself and decided to leave them there. Catching the surprised manager by the collar, Marcus emphasized his point. "I know it's your policy. You've been telling me that all along. But let me make this perfectly clear, even if President Hoover comes in here with Mary Pickford on his arm and they ask for what I've left in that safe, you stick to your policy and give it to nobody but me!" A nasty thought struck Marcus and he sped toward his room.

Kneeling in the hallway outside, Marcus examined the door to his room. Scratches surrounded the keyhole. Over years of

144

use, the same could be said of almost every lock. But misplaced keys made shallow and subtle scratches, noticeable only in multitudes. What concerned Marcus were the handful of deeper, more deliberate marks. With handcuffs and other restraints a commonly used method for detecting bogus physical mediums, a good psychical investigator quickly learned to recognize the telltale signs of a picked lock. Marcus saw them now.

Pushing on the door, it swung open with ease. Inside, the intruder had attempted to cover his tracks. But evidence remained. Any housekeeper who turned down beds so haphazardly would not have kept employment at the fastidious Roosevelt. And one of his bureau's side drawers remained ever so slightly ajar.

Thankful that he had entrusted his most valuable documents to the hotel safe, Marcus assessed his losses. An auxiliary notebook, its pages blank and awaiting content, had been taken. Although he couldn't imagine what good they would do anyone but a physician, so had his back issues of the *Journal of the American Medicine Association*. Most irritatingly, other than the shoes on his feet, his footwear had vanished. That loss included a pricey pair of box-toed Oxfords and a plebian but practical set of workman's boots.

In short, the thief had ignored many items of monetary value. What had been removed was that which could record or contain useful information or that would impede Marcus's investigation through its absence. Everything pointed to Fenno. Or someone in his employ. While it lacked the physical danger of the ASPR man's trickery in Gates County, this most recent violation incensed Marcus more. He had taken the moral high ground and allowed Fenno's nefariousness to go unpunished one time too many. The time had come to consider ways to even the score for the BSPR. And for himself.

Though exhausted by his excursion, he discovered he wanted to be anywhere other than the burgled hotel room. Marcus hit the street. As he walked, thoughts floated through his head. Inspector Legrasse and Queen Lola gave very different accounts of the confrontation which took place in the swamp 20 years ago. While Prince would disapprove of any diversion unlikely to shed light on Gabriel Gibbs, Marcus was curious. He wondered if quick research could yield a better picture of what, really, had occurred.

Strolling back to the *Times-Picayune's* office, Marcus revisited the morgue. He searched back issues for references to that long-ago swamp raid. It took him awhile to find anything. When he did discover something, reported nearly a fortnight after the event, it wasn't an article. It was barely even a blurb.

A handful of lines noted the participation of two dozen of New Orleans' finest in a raid on the bayous south of the city. The action, it stated, related to "criminal gangs" alleged to use the swamps as cover for unspecified illegal activities. Police injuries were described as negligible. It called casualties among the criminals "light" but then, contradictorily, noted a number of fatalities. The piece made no mention of the kidnapped, and murdered, locals. It merely concluded by saying that inspectors John Legrasse and J.D. Galvez jointly commanded the raid.

That final line reminded Marcus about Legrasse's comments regarding the ultimate fate of Inspector Galvez. Back at the Roosevelt, Marcus placed a call to the State Hospital in Jackson, Louisiana. Parsimonious and reluctant informants represented a constant bane for investigators. This time, Marcus got lucky. A file clerk at the hospital proved quite willing to open a window into her institution's workings.

Galvez was indeed a patient at the hospital, she confirmed. Emphasis on *was*. Whatever the detective witnessed in the swamp had shattered his body as well as his mind. The inspector passed away a few years before, at the untimely age of 49. But, Marcus learned, Galvez had not been the only lawman who had seen the state hospital's inside. Nearly a dozen of those participating in the raid had spent some time there, including one John Legrasse.

Marcus heard the clerk's voice quiver as she answered his questions about the swamp cultists who had been taken to the hospital. Like Galvez, most of them died early. Predominantly from a kind of catatonic ennui seizing them shortly after arrival. Those that still lived spent their small hours immersed in nightmares and daytimes in a delusional fugue-state that seemed little better.

Replacing the earpiece, Marcus himself shuddered. He resolved to look no further into that incident 20 years ago. Or, indeed, into Queen Lola. Yes, his visit yielded useful information. And he saw remarkable things. But the deep bayous seemed on a different plane from the BSPR's investigations, even the admittedly unorthodox affair of Gabriel Gibbs. Madness and tragedy seemed to stalk outsiders who had too much contact with those foreboding waters.

Laying on his bed, Marcus reflected on what he had learned about Gibbs in the swamps. That, at least, seemed safe. He wondered if, amidst the spectacle and mystery of his visit, one of the most pertinent bits of information might also have been one of the most mundane. The boat. The bottles. Bootlegging, that emblematic vice of the age. Playing Queen Lola's revels, the musician would have seen it. Clearly, the smugglers made little if any effort to hide their activities. Already familiar with the racket from working for Colonel Scobie in Gates County, he might have viewed rum-running here as a way to make quick cash. If so, could that have been a factor in his death? Unlike his occult connections which, so far, had proved a dead end.

The trumpeter had a possible connection with at least one shady businessman. And Marcus had a hunch. Forcing himself from bed, Marcus dressed and returned to Storyville's round-the-clock carnival. At L'Original, he sought the well-informed Helene's charming company once again. She, in turn, seemed delighted by the reappearance of her strange non-customer.

"Was Luc de Amant involved with bootlegging?" Marcus laughed at himself. A short time in New Orleans had already rendered him much less circumspect in his inquiries.

"Honey, that's no secret," Helene replied, playfully batting her lashes at him. "One of the biggest bootleggers in the District. Also, supposedly, one of the most cutthroat."

"Did Gabriel ever work for him?"

"I don't know that for sure. But Gabriel was a hustler. And between de Amant having once owned this building and both men being interested in Rose, they crossed paths often enough."

That gave Marcus the answer he needed. "Doctor, be

careful," Helene shouted as Marcus departed. "You're taking all the risks of living on the edge but not having any of the fun," somehow, she had managed to combine flirtation with a caution.

Drifting asleep back at the hotel, Marcus turned the new information over in his mind. On the surface, it presented a contradiction. But it wasn't difficult to reconcile de Amant's bootlegging with his support for temperance organizations. Not at all. In fact, it suggested a kind of amoral brilliance. While liquor remained legal, someone like de Amant couldn't hope to compete with the big, established distributers. After Prohibition, however, he could use his muscle to become a major player in the city's bootlegging operations. De Amant, it seemed, had been a plotter.

Chapter Twenty

Marcus spent the following day chasing down leads on a number of Gibbs' former bandmates and residences. The task took Marcus into areas of New Orleans making Storyville feel like Beacon Hill. Individuals who knew Gabriel from before his death remembered the kind, gregarious man recalled at L'Original. But the musician seemed different "after." Those familiar with *that* Gabriel described someone who kept to himself, seldom staying long in one place. He was either barely remembered, aside from his stellar musicianship, or recalled as standoffish. "Resurrection" Gibbs, it seemed, was a very private man.

As Marcus departed one of the many fleabag flophouses on his itinerary, darkness already descending, six large men surrounded him. They showcased the diversity of New Orleans' population, the only admirable thing which could be said of the brutes. Marcus froze as one pressed a gun against his back. As his unwanted, and unwashed, companions swept him into a rusting Nash Ajax, Marcus quietly maligned Theodore Fenno's entire lineage.

The car rattled and belched smoke as it roared through crowded streets. As they traveled, Marcus realized he knew one of his abductors. The giant man's mocking, gold-toothed smile said the recognition was mutual.

The Ajax pulled to a stop between two derelict riverfront warehouses. A white Morris Oxford idled nearby. The fancy

British import contrasted sharply with the decaying industrial neighborhood around it. As the thugs hustled Marcus out of Ajax and toward the Mississippi, a man resembling an elegantly-dressed bulldog stepped from the Morris. Recalling the photo in the *Times-Picayune* obituary, the man reminded Marcus of a younger version of the late Luc de Amant.

"You've been asking questions about Uncle Luc," the bulldog said accusingly. "Poking around things that are none of your business. I've got to put a stop to it. Permanently."

Fenno wasn't to blame. Marcus cursed his own recklessness. He hoped Helene hadn't tipped off the man. His instincts said no. More likely, his visit to the pawnshop and asking questions about de Amant's murder had proved a fool's errand. Hoping to play for time, Marcus played a hunch. "Gabriel discovered what you and Luc de Amant were up to, didn't he? And you killed him for it."

"If that bitch has been running her mouth…" He cursed. "Not the first time Uncle Luc's soft spot for skirts has made trouble. No matter, she'll get hers later." Walking back to the Morris, he turned to his hired muscle. "Take care of this for me."

"Put him in St. Louis Number One when we're done, boss?" asked gold-tooth. The ogre's soft brogue mixed with thick Louisiana patois argued that his parents had seen Eire.

"No. Unlike Gibbs, people might ask questions about this one. Strip him and dump him in the river," with that simple, antiseptic prescription for murder the nephew departed. Before driving away, he called out once more. "And, this time, make sure you do your job before you dump him. I don't want any more monkey business like we had with Gibbs."

As gold-tooth held his gun on Marcus, the others roughly removed his clothes. One halted, eyes widening as he regarded Marcus's chest. The tattoo, Marcus realized. "Oh no. Oh no!" the man repeated. The others followed his gaze.

"I'm not messing with no gris-gris shit!" another said.

"Damn it. After seeing him in the swamp, I should have been wise," gold-tooth announced. "Come on, boys. We're not getting paid enough for this," he concluded. Piling back into the Ajax, the men rattled off into the night leaving Marcus alone on the riverbank.

Considering her previous romantic entanglement with Luc de Amant, Marcus strongly suspected that Rose Metairie, Gibbs' love interest turned songbird, was the "bitch" the nephew had mentioned. Unless he moved quickly, the singer faced mortal danger.

Bursting into the Moulin, Marcus made such a scene that even the house band ceased playing and stared at him. All except the standing bass player, so engrossed in his plucking that he remained oblivious to events around him. The singer herself appeared surprised, and then irritated, by Marcus's reappearance. Before Rose could react further, he took her wrist. "De Amant's nephew is on his way. He thinks you've talked about what happened to Gabriel. You're in serious trouble. We've got to get you someplace safe!"

Her expression now grimly earnest, Rose nodded.

Able to think of only one place in the city he considered absolutely safe, Marcus hailed a cab to the Garden District. Leaving Storyville behind, he turned to Rose. "Now will you tell me what really happened with Gabriel?"

"From his playing in the swamp, Gabriel learned about Luc's bootlegging and got himself involved." Her words confirmed Marcus's suspicions. "I lied to you. I loved Gabriel, even if I knew he'd never really love anything but his music. I tried to warn him off. Luc was bad news. Bad things happened to people that got too close to him.

"Luc had some scheme to get rich off land speculating in the District, something he'd been nursing for years," Rose continued, trying to remain composed. "Getting rid of Alderman Story was part of it. Gabriel overheard Luc and his boys planning the hit. Gabriel was no angel. He had no problem with bootlegging. But he wanted no truck with murder. There's a regular at L'Original who's a city hall man. Marcus got him to warn the alderman. Must have worked, 'cause Story's still walking on God's green earth."

Face in hands, Rose started crying. "When Gabriel left that night, I went to Luc and told him someone warned Story. I thought doing him a good turn, he might do me one. And he did.

He got me out of that working house and turned me into a proper singer at the Moulin. I never mentioned Gabriel. But he must have worked it out just the same. And Gabriel died."

She sobbed. "I killed him. I killed Gabriel. Sure as if I pulled the trigger myself. That's why, when he came back, I couldn't face him. I thought he'd have it in for me. And why I didn't want to tell you about any of it the first night you came to the club."

"You did not kill Gabriel." Marcus awkwardly put his arm around the woman, not wanting to give the wrong impression. "De Amant chose to try to kill Story. And he chose to kill Gabriel. You're not guilty of anything other than wanting a better life for you and your siblings," Marcus said. That wasn't entirely true, she had been dangerously naïve. Especially for someone with so much time in Storyville under her belt. Saying so wouldn't have helped either of them.

John Legrasse again displayed his mettle, reacting with aplomb when Marcus showed up on his doorstep, this time not only after dark but with a Storyville jazz singer in tow. Marcus poured out his tale. "That'd be 'Big Jim' Kessler," Legrasse interjected after Marcus described the man who'd casually ordered his death just hours ago. "Yeah, he's de Amant's nephew. He's well-known to police, but too rich and too well-bred to take down easily."

As he and Rose sat in Lagrasse's comfortable parlor, their host dug into his stash of sly whiskey, pouring his guests drinks to calm their rattled nerves. Afterward, he and Marcus put their heads together. Luc de Amant sold his family's Storyville properties when prices were sky high. He must have had a pile of cash. New Orleans' guardians of public morality, not content with outlawing prostitution and alcohol, wanted Storyville razed to the ground. If that happened, land values would plummet and de Amant could snap up most of the District with his cash. When the area was redeveloped, he'd make his money back ten times over.

One thing would have stood in his way. Sidney Story embodied that uniquely Louisiana breed of politician: a smooth operator, probably even a crooked one, genuinely beloved by his constituents. As long as Alderman Story lived, Storyville remained safe. De Amant and Big Jim, they surmised, aimed to remove him from the equation.

After piecing the men's machinations together, they turned to immediate matters. Tomorrow, the inspector would take Rose to the police to tell her story.

"She'll be safe," Legrasse concluded. "If anything happened to her afterward, it would be too high profile even for Big Jim, too easy to tie to him." Beyond that, he gave no cause for optimism. "This is New Orleans. I'm not going to lie to you. I'd bet everything I have on Big Jim walking or getting slapped on the wrist. If years in law enforcement taught me anything, it's to take your wins where you find them."

Marcus wanted one more win before leaving town. The investigation would soon shift to New York, where Theodore Fenno and the ASPR had the home field advantage. Marcus needed to neutralize that. Besides, he owed the man payback.

In the morning, before heading to Union Station and departing back east, Marcus entered the offices of the Orleans Parish Commission for Public Health and Hygiene. "I'm Dr. Marcus Roads," he introduced himself to a clerk. "I am a physician licensed to practice by the Commonwealth of Massachusetts. Yesterday, at the St. James hotel, I encountered a man displaying symptoms of yellow fever. I recommend immediate quarantine until his condition can be determined. His name is Theodore Fenno."

Chapter Twenty - One

New York City, September 18, 1929

Reversing his route over the rails which had carried him to New Orleans, Marcus arrived in New York. After rural Mississippi and far-flung but low-lying New Orleans, New York's manmade canyons of iron, concrete, and glass required readjustment.

Settling into his room at the Martinique Hotel, Marcus squared away his belongings. Taking no chances after New Orleans, he entrusted his essential items to the Martinique's hotel safe. To these had been added two thick discs of shellac resin with handwritten labels.

Realizing that, compared with the distance between the Big Easy and the Big Apple, a visit to Camden, New Jersey represented only a slight detour, Marcus stopped there on his way. Exiting the train, the smell of smoke inundated him as it rolled up from factories along the Delaware River. Through the haze, Philadelphia's skyline was a dim outline on the far shore. Wandering through streets flush with new manufacturing money, Marcus found a smaller industrial area centered upon Front Street and Big Timber Creek. There, a multi-story factory of redbrick housed one of the world's centers for manufacturing phonograph records.

Walking through the doors of the Victor Talking Machine Company, Marcus was escorted to Ralph Peer's office. The birddog sat behind a large wooden desk covered with ledgers and paperwork. Well-groomed and donning a nice suit, the round-faced Peer more closely resembled the "execs" he had railed against during their phone conversation than the shady, ill-kempt birddog archetype Marcus had imagined. All around the man and his desk were metal shelves lined with hundreds, maybe thousands, of discs. A surprisingly venerable and ragged gramophone hummed in one corner.

"Dr. Roads," Peer announced. "It's good to have a face to put with the voice." If anything, the thousand miles of telephone wire strung between them during their first exchange had muted the man's pronounced Midwestern accent.

After small talk, Peer filled Marcus in on what had transpired following their phone call. "As soon as we hung up, I hunted up those master discs from the session with Gibbs," he said, indicating two records in plain blown sleeves resting on the gramophone's edge. "I've listened to them several times since then. The man is good, no doubt about it. It really is a shame the execs wouldn't have anything to do with it. You want to have a listen?" the birddog cracked a smile.

Eagerly, Marcus said yes.

Peer took one record in hand. "Both the songs on this disc are covers of popular tunes, 'Squeeze Me' and 'Basin Street Blues.' There's nothing uncommon about that. What's unusual is what Gabriel Gibbs did with them. Before we listen to his versions, I want you to hear Fats Waller play 'Squeeze Me' and Louis Armstrong on 'Basin Street Blues.'"

The Fats Waller original of "Squeeze Me" had a sensual, earthy jazz sound with strong blues undertones. As they listened to Gibbs' version, Peer commented on what Marcus had already picked out: its unmistakably mournful edge. At times, it was very nearly a jazz dirge. To Marcus, knowing what he did about the artist, that made sense. For Gabriel, "Squeeze Me" wasn't just another song. It was the tune he was playing when Pastor Heulen caught him making worldly music at the tabernacle. And the song he later played there to declare his defiance, leading to the young man's traumatic break with his mentor, estrangement from his family, and becoming a pariah in Gates County. A pivotal moment in his life. Perhaps *the* pivotal moment.

Whatever the song meant for Fats Waller, when Gibbs played "Squeeze Me," he sounded a requiem for his former life.

Armstrong's "Basin Street Blues" was edgy and carnal, a sly musical tribute to Storyville and its temptations. But Gabriel Gibbs' take on the same song rung with hope and inspiration. Again, Marcus wondered if biography made the difference. Arriving in Storyville, which clustered around Basin Street, represented a hopeful moment for the young musician from Gates County. The passing of an important milestone toward the life of fame and glory Gabriel hoped would be his.

The songs on the second disc were both original compositions by Gibbs. It intrigued Marcus to see Peer's handwritten title on the first side. "Gabriel's Trumpet."

"This one is the kicker," Peer announced as he put it on the gramophone's platter. "First time I heard it, I hated it. It's growing on me. It's jazz, but I've never heard anything quite like it. The kid could arrange a song, no doubt about it. I don't think this would sell well but the critics would love it."

The song began with several bars of fast, syncopated playing. By the time Marcus recognized it as an odd arrangement of the old folk tune "Dixie," Gibbs had moved on to waves of staccato trumpet runs reminiscent of falling rain that became faster and faster. In the following section, the musician stuck to his instrument's lower register, lending the muted, sonorous notes an almost aquatic feel. Slowly, the fourth and final section emerged from the third, interweaving bits from old spirituals and hot new jazz numbers.

The other side of the disc, labeled simply "Noodling #1," consisted of the trumpeter showing off by playing a variety of long notes. As Peer noted, while impressive on a technical level, it was a stretch to call it music. "It's kind of interesting. But to really make it something, you'd need to be able to fit more than three minutes of music on a side."

Marcus thought he might finally be developing an ear for jazz. He recognized the proficiency of the recordings, appreciated the quality of the music, and could pick out the salient differences between Gabriel's versions and those of the artists he covered. "So, would you call him a good player or a great player?"

Peer considered the question carefully. "On the precipice between the one and the other."

"Can you put that in some kind of context for me?"

"Well, I wouldn't trade Armstrong or Waller for him. But I can't imagine kicking him out of the studio, either."

"I can hear that," Marcus acknowledged. "Is there any way I could get copies of Gabriel's records?" Through Peer's recordings, Marcus experienced his first direct, personal connection with the musician whose life sometimes felt as if it might subsume his own. Certainly, the man increasingly became "Gabriel" to him not "Gibbs."

Peer shook his head at Marcus's request, then halted. "But, tell you what, you can have these. If you never mention it to anyone. It would be my head if the execs found out. But I think the odds of them ever asking about these discs again are pretty much zero."

Stepping out of the Martinique the day after arriving in New York, Marcus discovered the Southern weather had followed him. The city sweltered unseasonably and the copy of the *Times* he scanned while catching a cab to Harlem was filled with the heat deaths of the very old and very young.

Eventually, Marcus turned its pages to less morbid fare. Ecstatically, he read of progress on the city's Museum of Modern Art, scheduled to open in November. It amused him to read that Mayor Jimmy Walker was receiving criticism for the "unseemly" act of discussing his policies in a series of short "talkies" being shown in cinemas throughout the city. And, as the home of Wall Street, the paper bulged with analysis, opinion, and counter-opinion about the nation's jittery stock market. While some saw trouble ahead, others predicted 1929 would finish as a banner year for America's investors.

Dangers other than the heat, his cabbie informed him, stalked Harlem. A fiend dubbed "The Broadway Butcher" had killed a dozen young men in the neighborhood. His depredations were not confined to the areas of Harlem near Broadway. If anything, the killer seemed shy of that well-known thoroughfare. But reporters, always fond of sensationalist alliteration, found the moniker irresistible.

Requesting the cabbie let him off at the corner of Lennox Avenue and 110th Street, Marcus stepped onto the streets of Harlem.

He had never witnessed a place quite like it.

The neighborhood pulsed with purposeful energy. Streets buzzed with commerce of every type. Vendors proffered hot peanuts, boiled crab, and roasted sausage out of carts and stalls. From truck beds, burly men purveyed coal, ice, and wood. And everywhere were young boys selling "the numbers," the private, and illegal, lotteries ubiquitous in Harlem and throughout the city.

As remarkable as the neighborhood's energy was the couture of the men and women on its streets. Their attire, while overlapping broader fashions of the day, found its own unique expression. Men wore form-fitting single-breasted tailored suits. Some younger men preferred distinctive suits with wide lapels, wider shoulders, and a high waist. Fedoras, porkpies, and trilbies were the order of the day for headwear. Women favored skirts with hemlines balancing daring with tasteful. Or dresses which dropped rather than bunched at the waist, giving their wearers a svelte, natural appearance. Brightly colored cloche hats, with their distinctive bell shape, accented the ensembles. For both men and women, fashions proclaimed confidence; looks not merely asking but demanding to be seen.

Marcus's quest involved a very specific kind of commerce. He didn't have to work hard to find it. An estimated 500 speakeasies packed the neighborhood, most of them also offering music. Even Storyville would be hard-pressed to match such a density.

He moved through Harlem with a drive and determination he had not felt in Mississippi or New Orleans. The neighborhood, after all, offered an incentive absent from his earlier travels. Somewhere, perhaps in one of these buildings, perhaps on these very streets, was Gabriel Gibbs. A face-to-face encounter with the man now presented itself not only as a possibility, but as Marcus's ultimate goal. He would meet the man. Then he would know what to make of him.

Using the article about Gabriel from the *New York Sentinel* that he'd first consulted back on the train to Gates County, Marcus tracked down the names of a few places Gabriel had stayed and several clubs where he played. Talking with people there, Marcus got more names. Which lead him to still more names. Like post-resurrection Gabriel in New Orleans, the musician always took single rooms and seldom stayed anywhere more than a week. Gabriel even turned down rent-free living arrangements with other musicians. Whatever his secret, he clearly valued privacy.

Marcus, however, found praise for the man's musicianship to be uniformly superlative.

Everyone in Harlem knew the story of Gabriel's return from the dead. They either didn't believe it, didn't care, or treated him as a celebrity for it. Perhaps not knowing him before he came back made a difference but, in contrast with New Orleans, people here seemed content to take Gabriel's money or perform with him, whether he was alive or dead.

Perhaps Gabriel's itchy feet had more to do with avoiding someone than wanting secrecy. From the informants he spoke with, Marcus learned of other parties actively inquiring about Gabriel. As least two others also trailed the trumpeter, one black, one white. Cursing to himself, Marcus concluded Theodore Fenno had secured an early release from his New Orleans quarantine. That was disappointing but also unsurprising given the resources and social standing at the man's disposal. But of the black man, Marcus had no notion. Especially as descriptions of the individual differed wildly.

Chapter Twenty - Two

Resolving to visit one more club before calling it day, Marcus stood outside an establishment in the basement of a 133rd Street brownstone. While its sign proclaimed it "The Catagonia Club" everyone referred to it as "Pod's and Jerry's." Walking down the steps and through a red door, Marcus entered a dimly lit space crowded with about two dozen tables. A well-stocked bar occupied one entire wall.

Though already early evening, the establishment had not yet opened for business. Its only occupants were a group of musicians talking and laughing on a ramshackle stage at the club's far end.

"You looking for something, man?" one of them called out.

As his eyes adjusted to the dim light, Marcus approached the players. "Yes. My name is Marcus Roads. I'd like to ask some questions about a man who used to play here if that's alright. A trumpeter. Named Gabriel Gibbs."

The men hesitated, looking at each other as if hoping someone else would make decision.

"Well, he's not a cop," one of them said about Marcus at last. The man sat on a bench in front of a beat-up piano, the front top of its case missing. "A cop wouldn't have bothered introducing himself," he added.

"Wouldn't have asked for permission to question us either," said another, a lithe young man holding a clarinet between his legs.

"Okay, stranger," the piano player said. Not only raw presence but the arrangement of the chairs on the stage marked him as the ensemble's leader. "We were going to have a little smoke before practicing. If you want to join us, we can talk about Resurrection Gibbs."

The pianist introduced himself as Willie "The Lion" Smith. He spoke in a distinctive fashion, referring to himself in the third person. "The Lion runs the music here. And these are his cubs." Bernard Addison played guitar and, when the band did a traditional number, pulled out his banjo. Buck Clayton trumpeted. Dick Fullbright played standing bass. Johnny Mullins blew sax. Artie Shaw was the clarinetist who'd spoken earlier. Arthur Trappier banged drums from the group.

Introductions concluded, Smith reached for his single-breasted, silk-lined jacket. Seeing the tiny, needlelike cigarette the Lion produced from the jacket's pocket, Marcus felt relief. This would be nothing compared to the thick cigar he'd forced himself through in New Orleans. At least that's what he thought until the dank, pungent smell of its smoke hit his nose.

Cannabis Sativa, colloquially known as marijuana or, in faster circles, reefer, was not illegal...although it came under increasing regulation. It was, however, scorned for its association with poor minorities and its alleged incapacitating and addictive properties. At least it was in the social circles where Marcus normally traveled. As a physician, he thought its incapacitating and addictive qualities were more widely spoken of than supported by clinical evidence. Nevertheless, smoking it had never occurred to him. After his experiences in Louisiana, however, marijuana seemed like a minor indiscretion.

Taking the cigarette from the Lion, Marcus inhaled. Never before had he imagined "hot" and "sharp" as flavors. But, as his throat and lungs felt burned and cut, he realized they were. He exhaled with a spasmodic cough. The musicians smiled and laughed. Addison, the guitar player, slapped Marcus on the back, attempting to halt his coughing fit.

The next time the cigarette came around, Dick Fullbright advised him "Don't fight the smoke this time. Relax, take it in. Hold it."

While the sensation remained unpleasant, Marcus found he could follow those instructions. After a few moments, he exhaled a cloud that appeared blue-gray in speakeasy's gloom. Each time the cigarette made its way around the circle it got easier.

"So," the Lion looked at their guest. "You an alligator?"

"Alligator?"

The musicians snickered at Marcus's response.

"An alligator. A jazz cat," the Lion continued, presumably believing that would clarify the matter.

With Marcus still uncertain as to the proper response, Arthur Trappier stepped in "I don't think our new friend knows the lingo."

"Well, we've got to fix that!" the Lion smiled.

The musicians initiated Marcus into the curious cant that, from its origins in Harlem, radiated out across the country to anywhere one could find the syncopated sounds of jazz or the sour taste of illicit hooch.

A man was a *gate* or a *cat*. Particularly one in the know, or *hep,* as the musicians said, or who liked or played jazz. The opposite of *hep cats* were *Jeffs* or *squares*. They called swaggering, ostentatiously dressed young men *sports* or *sheiks*. Conversely, a woman was a *Jane*, a *mop*, or *sister*. A *bearcat*, if she possessed a feisty streak. If attractive, she could be a *doll,* a *smarty,* or a *roll*.

"But never a *jelly roll*," Johnny Mullins commented to raucous laughter. Marcus didn't understand the joke.

"A jelly roll," the Lion explained, "is a very particular part of a woman's body. You can also use it for a really mean lady. But I wouldn't advise it unless you've got quick feet!"

Marcus giggled. Taking another turn on the cigarette, he imagined himself writing the term "jelly roll" in his patients' files. For some reason, the utterly inappropriate thought struck him as deliciously entertaining.

It amazed Marcus to learn the plethora of terms musicians used for cannabis. In addition to reefer and marijuana, it could be *gage*, *Indian hop*, *pot*, *tea*, and a dozen other things Marcus lost track of. He had once heard an artic explorer speak at the

Boston Athenaeum. In his presentation, the polar adventurer mentioned that the Esquimaux had more than a dozen words for snow, testimony to the critical role it played in the lives of those northern people. If that rule held true across cultures, then this pungent weed was surely the glue which held jazz together. Funny that people made such a fuss over a little plant that wasn't affecting him at all.

The musicians continued teaching him terms related to the drug's use. A *viper* was someone who smoked it habitually. *Teapads* were establishments where jazz and marijuana comingled. "You're in one right now, Clambake, with a bunch of vipers," Mullins said.

"Clambake?"

"It means a musician from New England, usually. But you can use it for anyone from there." Shaw clarified.

Marcus tried to work out if he had been insulted.

"Relax, Johnny's just razzing you," the Lion said in a conciliatory tone. "We wouldn't take the trouble of calling you Clambake if we hadn't decided you're not a Jeff."

"Wait!" Marcus exclaimed, his mind suddenly returning to a previous part of the conversation. "What about Jelly Roll Morton?" A name Marcus knew from jazz, it now left him confused in light of what he'd learned earlier.

"That's his way of bragging about his success with the ladies," the Lion explained. "Don't get me wrong, as pianist, Jelly Roll will do. But if one-tenth of what the man said about himself was true, he could walk on water. And play piano while doing it."

At that, the others chuckled, Clayton and Fullbright exclaiming "And how!" in unison.

His education concluded with *ofay*, *bull*, and *the man*. Terms for the police. "Not words to call them to their faces," Artie Shaw emphasized. "Unless you can get away with it," he added with a smile.

"So, tell me about Gabriel?" Marcus asked once the flood of new terminology had slowed to a trickle and then stopped.

"We'd already been hearing the handle 'Resurrection Gibbs' up and down Seventh Avenue for a bit before he showed up here," Addison began.

"The hotshot new horn blower in town," Clayton chimed in with, perhaps, a trace of envy. "And with that heebie-jeebies backstory, too."

The Lion picked up the tale. "Anyway, he looked up Pod and Jerry, that's the cats that own this place. And impressed them enough they told us to give him a run through. So, the Lion had him play a couple of tunes. First thing we noticed was that fine silver piece he plays. Solid chops, too. And no doubt he was finger zinger, moving those digits so fast you could barely see 'em. But the most impressive thing were those balloon lungs of his. I never saw Resurrection run out of wind!

"So, the Lion thought, let's bring him in, he'll do well. With him on board we'd swing to beat all hell!" the pianist paused. "Turned out we had musical differences. More than that, the Lion didn't expect Resurrection to turn out so high hat! You know, a real upstage type."

"High hat?" Marcus repeated. "Upstage?"

"Uh-huh," he nodded, leaning against his piano. "Never wanting to mix with us outside of gigs. Keeping to himself. Never talking. He'd play his gigs, grab his sawbucks, and go. Like he thought he was better than us.

"So, that's the Lion's hand," Smith concluded. "But why's a cat like you interested in him?"

"Truthfully," Marcus admitted, "I'm interested in the resurrection aspect. I want to know if it's true. If it is, how? If not, what's the real story? I've been tracking him all the way from Gates County, Mississippi, through New Orleans, and now here." Finding his tongue looser than he expected, Marcus shared much of what he'd learned about Gabriel's musical career while investigating in Gates County and New Orleans. As he recounted the story Sam Gibbs had told about his brother besting King Oliver in the trumpet contest, Marcus noted the musicians smirking at him. "What's so funny?"

"Everybody in jazz knows Oliver's got the gum disease something fierce," the Lion explained.

"That's right," Buck Clayton, the trumpeter, added. "It's an open secret that those trumpet solos on his new albums are actually Red Allen, his number two."

"Why would gum disease makes a difference?" Marcus asked.

"Part of being a great horn player is having a tight embouchure," Clayton explained.

"That's the way you use your lips and teeth to blow into the mouthpiece," Addison clarified before Clayton continued.

"With bad gum disease, you can't hold your embouchure. You can't control your playing so well and you lose power from your sound," the trumpeter said. "Don't mistake me, even now, besting the King is no mean feat, but it's not what you'd call a miracle."

"So, Clambake," the Lion said, turning the tables on Marcus. "What's your opinion? You think he came back from the dead?"

"I'm a physician. In that world, resurrection isn't something we think happens," Marcus had witnessed some strange things, but his statement held true enough. "But can I look you in the eye and tell you absolutely that he didn't come back? No. This is an odd case, that's for certain. What do all of you think?"

Opinions were divided. Finally, Smith chimed in, proclaiming "The Lion has seen a lot of *bullshwa* in his life. Never seen a cat come back from the dead, though." After a moment, he added furtively, "Still, there's something powerfully strange about 'Resurrection' Gibbs." When the musicians' debate wound down, he pronounced "Well, we need to warm up before Pod and Jerry open for business. You play anything, Clambake?"

Marcus admitted he didn't.

"How about sing?" someone asked.

Marcus suspected that a few years of enforced participation in the children's choir of Marblehead's Congregationalist Church wouldn't count for much with his current companions. It seemed easier just to say no.

"Well then, how about you find some wood to slap and help Arthur out with the beats."

After the Lion counted down from three, the band exploded into bombastic jazz, the sound driven by their leader's furious piano. Clearly, the Lion was a finger zinger, too. Smith's fingers produced pulses of strident notes as his hands leapt up and down the keyboard. With its missing front, Marcus could watch the piano's guts move.

Standing, Marcus started slapping out a rhythm on the piano's side.

Instantly, all sound stopped and the other musicians stared open-mouthed at their guest. The pianist's eyes bored into Marcus's own with icy sternness. "Nobody," he hissed "touches the Lion's elephant box but the Lion."

"I'm sorry," Marcus stammered, wondering if he'd have to make a quick break for it.

"'S okay. You didn't know. Now you do." As if the incident had never occurred, the Lion and his band resumed their music making.

Returning to his seat, Marcus began banging on the wooden tabletop in time to the music. The Lion looked over at him and nodded approvingly.

Melodies danced back and forth between the Lion's keys and Artie Shaw's clarinet. On guitar, Bernard Addison took occasional turns in the lead. Arthur Trappier's drums and Dick Fullbright's bass anchored the band. Buck Clayton's trumpet and Johnny Mullins' sax came on like waves, sometimes gently lapping at the rest of the band's sound. Other times, sweeping it all up with a furious crash.

As the music continued, Marcus reflected on the difference between the jazz played in New York and its cousin in New Orleans. Each city's music could almost be viewed as an extension of its speech. Storyville's sound was honeyed, sonorous, and drawling. Harlem delivered its music in rapid, precise clips.

Pushing back his chair, Marcus stood and did a kind of dance as he continuing beating on the table. It was nice to put Gabriel Gibbs out of his mind for a moment and relax. He was having a very good time, in spite of marijuana's much vaunted properties coming to nothing.

As the night's first customers wandered through the basement door, Marcus realized the time had come to excuse himself. While he hoped the band enjoyed this as much as he had, his participation would not help the musicians earn their keep in front of paying crowd.

Marcus thanked them for their time and for making him welcome. "No need to thank us," the Lion said. "I wouldn't hang up that black bag if I were you, but you held your own. You're a cat now. Come back anytime."

Making his way back up the steps to 133rd Street, Marcus experienced a curious falling sensation, as if constantly being pulled backward and to his right. He felt giddy and light headed. It had, after all, been a long day. Perhaps he had not allowed himself proper time to recover from his travels. He took a moment to steady himself on the iron railing. Finally feeling ready to continue, Marcus discovered that Artie Shaw and Buck Clayton had joined him.

"We just wanted to make sure you were alright," Clayton said, lending Marcus a steadying hand.

"And maybe give you a bit of perspective," the young clarinetist added.

"See, the Lion, he talks like everyone but him is a crumb," the trumpet player explained. "Take that into account. When he says Jelly Roll Morton 'will do,' what he means is 'the man is incredible.' And when he says Resurrection Gibbs 'will do well,' he's really saying 'I've never heard anything like it.'"

"And that was the problem," Shaw continued. "The 'musical differences.' I think the world of the Lion. But he only wants one king of the jungle, if you take my meaning."

"But, whether he admits or not, the Lion saw it, too." Clayton looked at his own instrument. "I could blow this thing my whole life and never sound like that."

Back at the Martinique, Marcus sat in the hotel dining room, immersed in a dreamy daze. He ordered a bowl of tomato bisque and a steak sandwich with a side of hot chips. And, when he finished, to his great surprise, he ordered another.

168

THIRD

INTERLUDE

New York City; February, 1925

In the end, Marcus had played his part. And a bit more.

For his trouble, he'd received a summons to the ASPR research director's office. Though he knew to expect it, it shocked Marcus to see the frail looking Malcom Bird behind that sturdy desk instead of the robust Prince. To Bird's right sat a smirking Theodore Fenno. Other faces, new men Marcus didn't recognize, occupied the remaining seats. All were arrayed to face him.

Whether Walter Franklin Prince had resigned in protest or been told his services would no longer be required depended on who you believed. On what you wanted to believe...

The investigation which had so commanded the world's attention was over. Houdini had been the first nay-sayer. Hardly a surprise. But, in the end, Hereward Carrington alone endorsed Mina Crandon, better known as Margery, as a genuine physical medium. Neither she nor, as time would show, anyone else would ever claim the Scientific American *prize. But the matter hadn't ended there.*

For once, the papers ignored Houdini, and the other judges, and continued publishing glowing accounts of Margery's powers. The role played by ASPR members in the investigation infuriated the society's president, Rev. Edwards, and many of its big donors: elderly East Coast aristocrats who wanted the comforting promise of a life beyond as they navigated their winter years. McDougall, Prince, and other leaders of the society's skeptical faction had been marginalized in a bureaucratic coup. To preserve their dignity, most had departed.

Even so, many people were taken aback when Edwards replaced Prince with Bird, whose only research qualification came from a brief stint teaching mathematics at Columbia. "I would like to offer you this opportunity to withdraw your recent report regarding Mina Crandon," Bird treated Marcus to a forced smile. "It has not yet formally been received by the society. So it can be withdrawn with no complications."

Paradoxically, it had been William McDougall and not Walter Franklin Prince who drew Marcus directly into the investigation. Through it, the two had become acquainted well enough for McDougall to intuit that Marcus had no special loyalty to the Crandons. One morning, the former President of the ASPR had shown up at Marcus's practice, bearing with him a glass specimen jar.

The jar, McDougall explained, contained ectoplasm. Or, rather, possible ectoplasm, that Margery appeared to produce during her séance the previous evening. Ectoplasm, that material supposedly resulting when living beings interacted with the etheric plane, represented a holy grail of spiritualism and paranormal investigation. Unfortunately, no agreement existed regarding its creation, properties, or even appearance; save that it was generally considered to be soft, viscous, and malleable.

McDougall, pressing the glass jar into Marcus's hands, explained he wanted a physician's opinion on the substance within.

Marcus had examined "ectoplasm" many times before. Frequently, it bore a most uncanny similarity to commercial cheesecloth. He'd seen other specimens that had striking parallels with wax, India rubber, or even paraffin. A quick examination told him, at least, that the substance in the jar was none of those things.

McDougall's sample was pinkish-gray with a thin, greasy sheen. Putting on gloves, he removed the substance and examined it tactilely. Superficially lumpy, it possessed a soft, elastic quality. His autonomic reaction to the sample surprised

170

Marcus. No sense of wonder or mystery accompanied beholding, and holding, the strange material. Indeed, it possessed an organic familiarity.

Carving off a sliver of the substance so thin as to be translucent, Marcus affixed it to a glass slide which he placed underneath his laboratory's new Leitz microscope. There, he discovered capillaries and fingerlike cells. The regular, repeating patterns of organic, terrestrial life.

Marcus had a suspicion, but need confirmation.

Unfortunately, proof wouldn't be as easy to come by as it would have been even ten years ago. The proliferation of refrigerated trucks and train cars had transformed most of Boston's butchers into mere retailers. Killing, dressing, and packing had shifted westward to places like Chicago, Kansas City, and Fort Worth. There, the vast plants of Upton Sinclair's The Jungle, *a novel that still gave Marcus nightmares, processed America's meat with factory-like efficiency.*

Fortunately, there was one group that, following millennia-old proscriptions, still slaughtered locally. Taking a long stroll, Marcus ambled toward the areas of Brookline, Dorchester, and Roxbury, at the heart of Boston's Jewish community.

Marcus entered the first Kosher butcher shop he encountered, his specimen jar of ectoplasm cradled under one arm. There, a very tolerant butcher graciously allowed Marcus run of the shop in attempting to match the jar's contents with the various bits of offal on premises.

It was among the small intestines of the Bos Taurus, *the common cow, where he found the closest match. Marcus carried a small segment procured from the butcher back to his lab. True, the homogenous blob in his jar differed greatly from intestines in their natural state. But it would have required no great skill to open the intestines up and pulp them a little. The microscope, however, would not lie. Placing the sample from the butcher's under the Leitz, Marcus failed to distinguish it from the one presented by McDougall.*

Informing him of that conclusion, the ASPR man had asked Marcus for a written report.

Now, following McDougall's departure from the society, that

171

report was being rejected.

"Why are you worried about me?" Marcus protested. "Joseph Rhine claims he observed Margery using her hands and feet to move objects. Compared to Rhine's opinions, mine are nothing." Truth be told, Rhine represented only one of many reports questioning Margery's authenticity that had been submitted to, and rejected by, the society since Edwards' coup. Rhine's simply ranked as the most prestigious name among them.

"Rhine's report has not been accepted, and will not be accepted, by this society," Bird proclaimed. "Furthermore, it has been suggested that he look to apply his talents, whatever those might be, elsewhere."

There it was. The threat was made by analogy. But made nonetheless. Recant. Or get out.

"No, I can't tell you with 100% certainty that the specimen is cow intestine and not ectoplasm. But, if it looks like it came from a cow, the responsible thing to do is to treat it as if it came from a cow. Not from some astral borderland between this world and the next. The burden is on the advocate to prove. Not on the skeptic to disprove. That's how science works."

"President Edwards believes the old guard like McDougall and Prince relied too heavily on that axiom. Spiritualism is different and necessitates different methodology," Bird explained.

"Think of all the knowledge and advancements we've forfeited by insisting on proof of those first steps just in hope of convincing those who will always doubt us," Fenno gushed. "It's time we start pushing forward for those who have the vision to come with us."

Putting his fingers together, as if trying to appear clever, Bird spoke more calmly than his colleague. "Think of it this way. If, every time an aeroplane had taken flight since 1903, it had to be proven it was not suspended by wires or resting on a mountain of cheesecloth, how far would aviation had come?"

Marcus noticed Fenno jump as if goosed. He wondered if the ASPR's new research director knew of Theodore's family tragedy. If so, the flight metaphor had been poorly chosen.

Either way, Bird continued "President Edwards knows how much good work you've done for the society. He, personally, told me he hopes you'll embrace the new way of doing things. Can I tell him you're willing?"

"You're saying that, from the ASPR's current viewpoint, the only people qualified to rule on the validity of paranormal phenomena are those who already believe in them?"

"That is precisely what we are telling you," Fenno replied emphatically. Bird looked irritated by the man's bluntness but did not contradict him.

Standing, Marcus exited, turning his back on Bird's dyspeptic frown and Fenno's angry shouts of "You're a fishmonger and all you'll ever be is a fishmonger!" Marcus hoped rumors he'd heard about Walter Franklin Prince organizing a scientifically-grounded society to rival this new incarnation of the ASPR would prove true.

A Harvard education and a medical career both encouraged a proficiency with Latin. Walking out the door, Marcus turned and made his parting remark "You may tell President Edwards 'Quis custodiet ipsos custodes?'"

Chapter Twenty-Three

The next day, Marcus carried on with his investigation. Despite unsettling dreams, which he suspected had again involved Fenno, he felt relaxed and well rested.

Outside a boardinghouse known for catering to musicians, he spied a man waving his arms enthusiastically while talking with its lodgers. The man was not subtle. Even at a distance, Marcus overheard his booming voice utter words like "Gibbs" and "Trumpet." Thanking the lodgers for their time, the man departed, ambling in Marcus's direction. Resembling a thinner William Howard Taft, whom Marcus had once heard speak in Boston, this man was clearly not Fenno. Passing Marcus, the man nodded affably.

"Do we know each other?" Marcus asked.

"I don't believe so," he replied. "I presume you're the other white inquiring about Gibbs? Charles Fort," the man introduced himself.

"So, you're Fort. I'm Marcus Roads." The men shook hands. Marcus knew of Fort. In the intellectual war over the paranormal, Charles Fort occupied a strange middle ground. The man spent his life scrutinizing centuries of newspapers and journals from across the globe, identifying and collating reports of anomalous phenomena. Strange weather. Unexplained falls of schools of fish or swarms of frogs from the clear blue sky. Anomalous artifacts. Spontaneous human combustion. The transit of objects and people from one point to another without crossing the intervening space, a phenomena Fort dubbed "tele-portation." Those, and a hundred other strange things, found their way into Fort's books. Rarely did the man take a position on any of his findings. For him, a report's existence was what mattered.

For his trouble, Fort earned scorn from believers and skeptics alike. The former maligned him for having these accounts at his disposal but not pushing an interpretation. Specifically, their interpretation. For skeptics, by publicizing the stories he discovered, Fort implicitly encouraged belief in the supernatural. That was more than enough to merit their derision.

The pair talked about their respective investigations. Discussing Gabriel with Fort proved cathartic. While Fort grasped the case's significance, Marcus could trust him not to blab to the ASPR. Or BSPR for that matter. And if, a few years down the road, some of the things Marcus shared with the man happened to find their way into one of Fort's books, by then it wouldn't matter.

Though Fort lived in New York, the Bronx if memory served, encountering him out and about in Harlem surprised Marcus. From what Marcus understood, the man was more Mycroft than Sherlock. His proclivities ran toward armchair research not active investigation. Politely, he put that point to Fort.

The man's sheepish grin acknowledged the remark's truth. "Disappearance and reappearance cases are special favorites of mine. Many of the best ones come from 19th century Britain. Sadly, you don't get them often anymore. So, with one happening in my city, I couldn't just stay at home. Of course," Fort added, "you have the advantage over me."

When Marcus didn't understand what he meant, Fort clarified. "Reading as many accounts as I have, you see patterns. Everything which disappears reappears somewhere else. Everything that appears, presumably, came from somewhere. Most people are content seeing only their side of that equation, not the whole picture. You've been where Gibbs is from. You're where he is now. You're seeing both sides. Figure out what adds up, and what doesn't, and you'll crack the riddle." Fort paused.

"But I think you've missed one thing already."

"What?"

"Inside the coffin, did you find marks from clawing?" When Marcus's eyes widened, Fort saw Marcus took his meaning. "That's right. Victorian England saw many cases of premature burial. Well, not that many, but enough to make the entire society positively paranoid about it. And New England's had a few instances recently. I don't know how they'll react. But, as a Bostonian, you might do well to invest in two-way coffins. The real point is, England or New England, in every case of premature burial, the interred person clawed the blazes out of the coffin's inside trying to get out."

He had found no such marks in the Gates County Cemetery. "I'm dealing with someone getting in," Marcus realized.

Fort smiled approvingly at the deduction. Producing a white cotton handkerchief, he wiped away beads of perspiration which the unseasonable heat coaxed from his brow. "Dr. Roads, I dislike restaurants. But, traveling here, I noted one with a sign boasting of its refrigerated air. If we are going to continue this, perhaps we should adjourn there?"

Marcus agreed, allowing Fort to lead him down Pleasant Avenue into a part of Harlem where Italian immigrants predominated. Fort indicated a snug little place with an exterior of vibrant red trim occupying a corner storefront. "Rao's," the marquee over its door proclaimed. In addition to its refrigerated air, it also advertised fine dining.

Discovering Rao's to be a Sicilian restaurant, upon taking their seats, Fort launched into a scattershot discussion of strange events which had befallen Italy's south over the past century. A red rain that fell in Sicily in 1849. Red dust a generation later in 1872. A sea monster, not of the typical serpentine variety, sighted off the coast in May of the same year. And then there was the curious coincidence of timing linking Messina's 1908 earthquake and a prodigious rain of meteors in Spain.

Italian cooking, slowly edging toward the mainstream, still represented something of a daring taste. In the eyes of those like the Beacon Hill establishment, it remained the food of working class and politically unreliable immigrants. Not quite so suspect as, say, Chinese cuisine but not entirely respectable. For those, like Marcus, whose tastes ran toward the avant-garde, that reputation only added to its appeal. Fort, however, appeared out of his element. Upon the arrival of an immaculately tailored waiter at their table, Marcus's gregarious tablemate grew bashful. "You order for us," Fort nudged.

The waiter's rich accent instantly called to mind images of the sun-drenched Mezzogiorno. Marcus deferred to his recommendations, clear only on the fact that they'd ordered some kind of pasta. With their order placed, conversation turned to the two men's backgrounds.

Fort discussed his childhood in Albany. Initially, he wanted to be a naturalist and developed his passion for collecting very early in life, starting with birds, minerals, and seashells. After graduation, Fort traveled much of the US, the British Isles, Europe, and South Africa. Returning home, he worked as a journalist with a shaky sideline dabbling in fiction. The former inspired a new focus for the man's collecting: the accounts of strange phenomena that had become his life's work.

It intrigued Marcus that no single "Eureka" moment had birthed the man's obsession. Rather, it appeared to be the natural result of combining his endless exposure to news with his childhood interests and the natural bent of his personality.

Later, Fort had received an inheritance yielding just enough income to devote himself fully to research and collating. He now split his time between the US and UK, perusing centuries of obscure journals to find stories of the phenomena which interested him.

Marcus, in turn, told his own tale. Fort's enthusiastic response to Marcus's formative years in Marblehead surprised him. "Did you know that, in 1858, a strange object fell from the sky just outside Marblehead?" Fort asked excitably. Marcus admitted he did not.

"Local experts proclaimed it a 'furnace product,'" Fort continued. "Like the kind that results from smelting iron or copper ore. More likely it was meteorite. But, in that case, why not simply describe it as such?" It disappointed Fort that Marcus knew nothing of the object. "A pity. Perhaps your ancestors could have told us things not in those reports."

In the course of investigating for the BSPR and, before the schism, the ASPR, Marcus had met some very strange people. But none of them exceeded Fort for eccentricity. If the man always comported himself like this, Marcus doubted his gatherings and discussion groups were the most coveted invitation of the social season.

To Fort's great interest, Marcus recounted some the strange experiences as a physician which led to his interest in the psychical and supernatural. During his residency at Massachusetts General, Marcus witnessed a patient awaken after surgery and immediately provide an uncannily accurate description of the hospital's third floor storage room. She even mentioned a shelf lined with dolls and stuffed animals the staff kept on hand for young patients.

He had examined a head trauma patient who periodically spouted bouts of gibberish that another doctor, a second-generation immigrant whose parents were Jews from Hamburg, swore to be fluent Yiddish. That would have been less remarkable had the patient in question not been a rustic Yankee from western Massachusetts who had never left his native county before moving to Boston three months earlier.

"Xenoglossia," Fort commented, giving the phenomenon a name which Marcus had not known before.

Then there was the patient who awoke from a coma with a surprisingly current knowledge of Red Sox scores and the, accurate as it turned out, certainty that his favorite uncle had passed.

Several witnesses placed another patient, an elevator man at the Dreyfus Hotel, at the hotel when it collapsed in 1925. In fact, at the moment of the disaster the man had been recovering from a severe fever at the hospital.

All of those were atop a pile of more "mundane" impossible recoveries and bright lights at the ends of tunnels.

The waiter's return interrupted Marcus's accounts. Placing two platters in front of them, heaped with ropy pasta drenched in red sauce and capped with a meatball as big as a man's fist, the waiter smiled. "*Caluri*," he announced, pausing a moment.

"Hot," he corrected himself, warning his diners.

The pasta was hearty and filling, the sauce spicy, and the meatballs succulent. Both men fell quiet, tucking into their meal with obvious gusto. Fort broke the silence first. Changing topics, he inveighed against the "twin tyrannies" he believed sought to "monopolize and corrupt our understanding of the world." The first, Fort claimed, were the spiritualists, who were "desperate to link every anomalous phenomenon to the souls of our departed. And shout down any alternate explanation." Marcus could be sympathetic. He had witnessed that process at work. In the ASPR. And, despite the best efforts of himself, Prince, and others, even within the BSPR.

Fort unleashed equal venom against conventional science. "It invariably pronounces against everything not already in harmony with its systemizations," the man thundered with an energy that very nearly sent his meatball escaping off its plate.

As a physician, even one involved with investigating strange phenomena, Marcus felt stung by that pronouncement. Though the signs had always been there, the revelation was quiet and sudden: he felt greater kinship with the scientists than the spiritualists. Marcus's compulsive if casual reading habits also gave him a passing familiarity with the seismic revolutions currently underway in the world of physics, encouraging him to question Fort's assertion. "But, surely, Einstein? Or Heisenberg?" Marcus protested.

"A palace coup. A succession crisis within the royal house," Fort replied. "Watch. The moment Einstein and Heisenberg dethrone Newton and their other predecessors, they will be set up as the new gods. Until someone else comes along to dethrone them."

That argument, Marcus thought, was more emotionally felt than logically sound, actually undercutting Fort's point rather than reinforcing it. Still, when Fort further opined that "Those with a psychological need to *believe* in marvels are no more prejudiced and gullible than those with a psychological need *not* to believe in marvels," Marcus could not disagree. Indeed, he thought instantly of both Fenno and Houdini, each man embodying one category of those targeted by Fort's jeremiad.

Having the distinct impression that Fort could easily talk in circles on the matter all night, Marcus tried to steer conversation back toward the matter of Gabriel Gibbs.

Chapter Twenty - Four

"There are many well-known cases of strange disappearances," Fort responded. "The entire population of Jamestown for one. Though mundane explanations admittedly present themselves. The writer Ambrose Bierce, for another. But, with Bierce last conclusively seen at a hotel in the Texas desert and allegedly headed south to join the Mexican revolution, supernatural causes are hardly needed. And the British diplomat Bathurst, of course.

"Then there are some lesser known but more intriguing examples. A young man named Sherman Church worked for the Augusta Mills in Battle Creek, Michigan. One day in 1900, he reported to work and promptly disappeared. He was never observed leaving the mill. An exhaustive search for him occurred on premises and beyond. Yet no trace of him was ever found.

"Gibbs is part of a rarer set of data. A strange reappearance. Off the top of my head, I can think of a few cases resembling his. One is that of the authoress Agatha Christie."

Marcus, like nearly everyone in America, Canada, and UK with access to a newspaper or radio, knew the case. It had dominated the news for over a week in 1926. The famous writer disappeared. After a nationwide search, she was located ten days later in a hotel. She had registered there under an alias which happened to include the surname of her husband's alleged lover. According to some accounts, at the time of her discovery, Christie suffered under a confused or amnesiac state.

"Again, there is a range of plausible explanations," Fort said, "mostly defaulting to publicity or scandal. It helps, needless to say, that Christie is very much in the public eye. The disappearance and reappearance of such a person would, naturally, excite great curiosity and generate a huge volume of data. An impoverished musician from American South, on the other hand. You really had no choice but to go and dig."

Marcus winced. Sharing his activities in the Gates County Cemetery had been an enormous act of trust on his part. Presumably, Fort had not considered how accurate, and macabre, his turn of phrase was in connection with that aspect of Marcus's investigation into Gabriel Gibbs.

"You said a few cases?" Marcus inquired. "What about the others?"

"Well, there is the matter of Princess Caraboo," Fort responded. "Or, perhaps, Mary Wilcox."

"I've never heard of her."

"In 1817, in the village of Almondsbury in England, there appeared a strangely dressed young woman making sounds which villagers presumed to be a foreign language. They brought her to the local magistrate, a Mr. Worral, who, rather than imprisoning her for vagrancy, remanded the young lady to his own care. I have found no record of what Mrs. Worral thought of that," Fort laughed before continuing.

"During her time with the Worrals, the lady continued making sounds that witnesses presumed to be speech. She also began drawing comb-shaped symbols that were believed to be writing. Some of her scribblings are still held at Oxford. A variety of historians, linguists, and self-appointed experts visited her to try to make heads or tails of the young lady's communication.

"Eventually, one of them, a Portuguese sailor named Enes or Enos, who had spent time in the East Indies, declared he understood her. He offered his translation of what he claimed the woman said. Her name was Princess Caraboo, royalty from the Island of Javasu, presumed to be Java in the Indian Ocean. After being kidnapped by pirates and enduring a lengthy captivity, she had jumped ship near Bristol and wandered aimlessly until being

184

taken to the Worrals.

"The account provided by Enes, or Enos, contained exotic, wondrous, and lurid details of life in Java and among her pirate captors. Both the princess and her translator became minor celebrities. Then a distinctly non-Javanese woman called Mrs. Wilcox, of Devonshire, appeared. She identified Princess Caraboo as her daughter, Mary, who had simply taken off one day without explanation.

"At that point, Princess Caraboo, or Mary, had a breakdown which many people interpreted as a confession. Mr. Worral, it should be noted, remained unconvinced of Mrs. Wilcox's claim. Certainly the magistrate saw no need to charge the young lady with imposture or, indeed, even remove her from his home. Eventually, presumably out of the goodness of her heart, Mrs. Worral paid for the young lady's passage to America to begin a new life.

"The Princess Caraboo affair also produced a score of sensationalistic pamphlets and broadsheets from Bristol all the way to London, advocating for or against the Princess's story. Or, rather, what the Portuguese sailor claimed was her story, as she spoke no words anyone else claimed to understand. Without going into detail, it deserves mentioning that many of these publications, both pro and con, reflected only a tenuous awareness of the facts of the case.

"I grant all of that is exceedingly convoluted. Here, to my mind, are the salient points. One, Princess Caraboo tells what is presumed to be a story in what is presumed to be an unknown language. Two, many pamphlet publishers, who were themselves liars and possessed motives of financial gain or publicity, claim Princess Caraboo lied. Three, aside from what other likely liars claimed, we have no idea what Princess Caraboo actually said. Including whether or not she ever used the name Princess Caraboo for herself."

"But there is a fundamental difference between those two and the Gabriel Gibbs case," Marcus interjected. "Neither Agatha Christie nor the princess were alleged to have come back from the dead. What do you know about cases of resurrection? Alleged resurrection?" the physician in Marcus corrected.

185

Fort laughed. "I could present you with an overflowing file of resurrections. Somewhere around 3,100 of them memory serves."

Marcus balked, dubious of such a large number. Sensing his companion's skepticism, Fort elaborated. "Allow me to explain. The vast majority of those are people who were pronounced dead, either in the absence of a body or because an existing body had been misidentified, and later turned up...often creating great inconvenience.

"These cases are interesting not for what they tell us about the resurrected dead, but for what they tell us about the living. Human perception is notoriously fickle and people have a way of seeing what they want to see. In most of the accounts in my files, people were declared dead because, on some level, someone wished them so. So a spouse could remarry. To collect insurance money. And so forth.

"That is the fulcrum on which the Gibbs investigation turns," Fort concluded. "Did he truly die and came back? Or was he merely...elsewhere...for the interval?"

"He is dead," Marcus pronounced. "I acquired a photo of his body in New Orleans. Earlier, in Mississippi, I acquired a photo of Gibbs in life. Both show the same man."

Fort frowned. "If you say so. You know, I am sure, how easily such images can be staged. As well as all the optical and psychological factors which may complicate such a seemingly simple matter," he countered. "Still, I'm inclined to believe you. Not because you're a physician. If anything, that should predispose me to the contrary. But because you appear to be a sincere seeker of truth who tries to shed pre-perceptions. The question then becomes what do we know of resurrections? Outside of those 'resurrections by paper' I mentioned earlier."

"I have a few examples from my work. Many physicians do," Marcus said, expanding upon his most remarkable experience. Antonio Silvano was a Genoese immigrant carried into the hospital after being struck by a streetcar. Despite Marcus's best efforts, Silvano died. Marcus remained as sure of that as he could be. Nevertheless, several minutes later, the man gasped, sat up on the table, and called out the name of his deceased mother…terrifying a pair of hospital orderlies. Silvano and his wife were profoundly grateful to Marcus, despite the physician's honest protestations that he had played no part in the man's inexplicable return. To this day, he received an effusive card from the couple each year on the anniversary of the event.

Again, Fort frowned. "But you're talking about people who died. I'm talking about people who were dead. If you take my meaning." Though Marcus did, Fort felt the need to continue elaborating. "Someone who laid inert in a surgical theatre for a handful of minutes is not the same as someone eulogized and buried who then turned up weeks, months, or years later. Well after bodily corruption should have done its work.

"But my files do have a few examples of that sort of thing," Fort acknowledged, summarizing several instances.

In 1846, a whaler named Ebenezer Allen drowned when his pilot boat capsized off of Mystic, Connecticut. He was dragged to shore and declared dead. The next day, however, Allen rose as if nothing had happened. But he swore off the sea as unlucky and took work in the shipbuilding trade. Ironically, he drowned again less than a year later while fishing in the Mystic River. That time, being dead took.

In 1909, in the village of Rycote in Oxfordshire, a young woman named Emma Osgood died after a short illness. Neighbors considered the death especially tragic as Osgood was two days away from marrying her childhood sweetheart. A death certificate had been filled out, the body was at the undertakers, and plans were being made for a funeral rather than a wedding when Osgood showed up again. The constabulary swore that her body could now not be located. Several locals gave testimony before the magistrate supporting the woman's claims to be Osgood. While her marriage took place, the revivified Osgood vanished months later.

For his third anecdote, Fort turned to a more recent case. In 1925 Montana, a man named Smith was shot six times in a dispute with his neighbor. Documentation supported his death and burial. A month later, a man appeared and claimed to be Smith. Authorities found Smith's grave empty. The living man had scars matching the locations of Smith's bullet wounds.

Evidence suggests the majority of locals accepted the man as Smith. Stories also circulated that, after his return, Smith displayed preternatural resistance to normal injury. He even signed with a traveling show, giving performances as the "Unkillable Man." A train crash in Wyoming later debunked that moniker.

"Many such cases are no doubt deliberate imposture. Or accidental deception, as in the case of someone who returns in the kind of amnesiac state claimed for Agatha Christie. The question is are any of them genuine?"

"It seems an unlikely prospect, doesn't it?" Marcus concluded. "Though a tantalizing one. My rival from the ASPR, the man I mentioned earlier, is nuts over the prospect of bodily resurrection."

"I don't know why. Even should that be true, what would that get him?"

Marcus's face must have betrayed confusion.

"It's important to read between the lines in these accounts," his companion explained. "The most important data is often in what is not said. Resurrected people never seem to last too long after they come back. Even the man from Nazareth is said to have returned for only 40 days.

"In the case of imposture, I expect maintaining the ruse eventually becomes untenable and imposters vanish as mysteriously as they appeared. But let's take the contrary position. Around 30 million people die every year. Even if every alleged report of resurrection were genuine, clearly it is not a normal thing. And I think nature itself agrees. Consider the examples I mentioned. It's as if some mechanism exists by which the universe rights the balance and returns such people to their proper side of that greatest of walls.

"To put it plainly," Fort concluded, "authentic or not, I suspect our man Gibbs is living on borrowed time."

On that sobering note, Marcus noted that both their plates were empty. At some point during their conversation, the waiter had discretely placed the check on the table. When Fort glanced away awkwardly, Marcus took the hint. While Fort's inheritance allowed him freedom to pursue his unorthodox interests, the man hardly seemed wealthy. And, of the two of them, Marcus had gained more from the exchange. He reached for his pocketbook, realizing it was one more expense he and Prince would likely have words over later.

Out on Pleasant Avenue, Fort smiled, thanked Marcus for the meal, and departed with a nod.

Chapter Twenty - Five

Marcus spent his cab ride back to the Martinique lost in thought. Not so much about the information acquired from Fort as about the man himself and his unorthodox perspective. Marcus was no longer a believer. If, indeed, he had ever been. But he had no love for dogmatic skepticism. Perhaps his position had come to match Fort's more closely than he had realized.

The specifics of their conversation returned over the night as Marcus struggled with sleep. Most notably, Fort's suggestion that if Gabriel's resurrection was fraudulent, he would likely soon vanish. And his more ominous pronouncement that, were the resurrection somehow genuine, a supernatural Sword of Damocles hung over the musician's head.

Days passed. Marcus continued interviewing Gabriel's universally distant acquaintances. On another matter, his thoughts had evolved. Because of his medical knowledge, Marcus had served as an expert witness in several trials. He knew eyewitness testimony could be unreliable. But either eyewitnesses had grown even worse or two different black men trailed Gabriel. One was polite, well-spoken, and a bit of dandy. The other was intimidating and nearly incoherent. To use the local terminology, he seemed "bugsy."

The investigation detoured as a sinister possibility struck Marcus. He feared that one of the city's top news stories somehow intertwined with his personal investigation. Two informants, referring to separate Broadway Butcher victims, had told him the same thing: I thought it was Gabriel until I saw him at a gig later. Hoping to test a theory, Marcus visited the police.

Of the NYPD's 32nd Precinct, it could be politely said that most of its policemen did not appear to come from the neighborhood they policed. They, too, displayed surprise at finding Marcus in their station. Surprise, and if he could judge by the ruddy-faced desk sergeant, more than a little suspicion.

"Would it be possible to examine photos of the Broadway Butcher's victims?" Marcus asked.

"You some kind of sicko? Clear off, I've got work to do," the sergeant replied curtly.

"Please, I want to check something. If I'm right, it would benefit the police."

"For all I know, you are the Butcher. Move along, pal."

"I'm not the Butcher. I'm a physician."

The sergeant eyed him uncharitably. "Don't they say Jack the Ripper was a doctor?"

Marcus determined it was time to leave. "*Ofay*, thank you for your time."

"What did you say?" the sergeant's expression combined anger with disbelief of his senses.

"I said, 'Okay, thank you for your time.'"

"Yeah, that's what I thought you said."

There was a spring in Marcus's step as he departed the station. On impulse, probably a foolish one, he'd used the derogatory slang learned from the Lion and his musicians. But it delighted him that he'd done so…and gotten away with it.

Back on the street, euphoria evaporated as he pondered how to proceed following his setback. The only other group with a finger on the city's pulse to rival policemen were journalists. Actually, if the 32nd Precinct offered any indication, journalists might know more. Marcus tracked down the offices of the *New York Sentinel*, the publication whose piece on Gabriel he'd read on the train to Mississippi.

Like any good paper, the *Sentinel's* newsroom was a study in controlled chaos. Marcus's presence elicited no special note or concern. He located the reporter responsible for the Gibbs piece. Abbot Stevens was a young woman with a newly-minted journalism degree from Howard University.

Introducing himself, Marcus praised her story about Gabriel. Like every reporter Marcus had met, she basked in the knowledge that someone valued her work. Despite that appreciation, she remained sharp-minded and inquisitive. "What can I do for you?" she asked. "I doubt you came all the way from Boston just to compliment my writing."

No flies on this reporter, Marcus thought. "I hope you'll help me check something out. If I'm correct, it's a scoop for you," he explained to her.

"I'm game," Stevens replied. "What do you need?"

"Do you have photos of the Broadway Butcher's victims?"

She gathered the relevant stories from the *Sentinel's* morgue, spreading them on her desk. Looking at the photos, Stevens whistled. "They could all be cousins." It was true. Some were an inch taller or shorter. A little fleshier or thinner, though none very fleshy. A shade darker or lighter. But none more different than that.

"Thank you. This was worth my time," she smiled.

Marcus thanked her and left. What he hadn't mentioned was that Gabriel Gibbs would fit seamlessly into that gallery of victims. Perhaps Stevens had worked that out for herself but, if so, the journalist held her tongue. Either a murderer with coincidently specific tastes stalked Harlem or someone was trying to kill, or re-kill, Gabriel Gibbs and doing a very poor job of it. And a lot of people had been caught in the crossfire.

That revelation did not in itself suggest a course of action. His investigation's mandate didn't include trying to catch a killer. It was also way out of his league. As he had told Prince at the investigation's beginning, he was no Pinkerton. It would be good to warn Gabriel, but that required finding the man…something Marcus had been trying to do anyway. So he resumed tracking down the web of names and address of clubs and lodgings connected with the trumpeter. At one, he learned of another close call for the musician. A boardinghouse where he was staying had burned to the ground, killing most of its lodgers. Gabriel, serendipitously, had been performing when the fire occurred.

Morbid curiosity drew Marcus to the site. A hole in the ground filled with charred timber and detritus marked all that remained of the St. Ignatius Street Boardinghouse. At its rim, a makeshift memorial had sprung up: flowers, candles, and handwritten signs proclaiming "We Miss You" or "Now at Peace."

Nearby, a figure skulked in the shadows. The imposing man wore the remnants of a once fine suit. His face was drawn, almost skeletal. He resembled the woodcut of Baron Samedi, loa of death and the dead, Marcus had seen in New Orleans. A shrill birdcall disturbed his circumspect observation of the man. Perched on an electrical wire, a grackle stared down at him. While not unheard of, grackles were uncommon this far north. Aunt Mancie's comments about the birds, and their singular behavior during the melee in the bayou, flashed through his mind. Though Marcus would have denied it, in his mind the bird's presence took on an ominous aspect. It also called his attention to the gathering gloom of Harlem's late twilight and that, as he contemplated the stranger, few other people could be seen.

Even without the associations of Gates County and New Orleans, the lurking man triggered something primordial. Marcus fled.

The following day, departing Club Hot-Cha, where someone named Clarence said he'd never heard a better trumpeter than Gabriel but didn't know anything else about him, Marcus spied a fashionably-dressed young man leaning against a wall while writing in his notebook. Priding himself on modern taste in the arts, Marcus could not fail to recognize one of America's greatest poets.

"Mr. Hughes?" he said. "I'm Marcus Roads. I'm a huge admirer."

Langston Hughes turned toward him. The poet wore a warm expression that still stopped Marcus in his tracks. Though it held no malice, Hughes' intelligent, perceptive gaze pierced Marcus like a knife. Nervous and starstruck, Marcus cleaned his glasses and could think of nothing cleverer to say than "What are you working on?"

"A sketch." Marcus saw that nothing but words filled the man's pad. "A prose sketch," Hughes corrected. "Perhaps it will become a poem. Perhaps it will just be one of those contrivances cluttering our desks forever."

Sudden inspiration struck Marcus. The poet was known, and indeed celebrated, for his curiosity about the world around him. "You're looking into Gabriel Gibbs, too, aren't you?"

"I am." He nodded. "you're the other one, then?"

"You've run into Fort?"

"Indeed," Hughes chuckled. "Quite the character."

"I guess we're all looking for the same thing."

"We are all looking for the same man," Hughes said pointedly. "But not, I think, the same thing."

"What do you mean?"

"You look at Gabriel Gibbs as a puzzle. Something to be solved, labeled, and cataloged. I will give you credit for being ahead of Fort. For all his enthusiasm, I think the man sees only one more datum for his collection. I see something different. If you'll accept the observation, my perspective is greater. Resurrected or not, his story is about renewal. For a society. For a people. For a community. One might say he's the living embodiment of the Harlem Renaissance." Hughes grinned modestly. "Or, perhaps I'm grandstanding and wanting to justify a poem about him."

Marcus felt dressed down by the poet. Again, Hughes looked him over. "Despondency is a suit few men wear well, Marcus. I implied that your view is limited. Not that it would always be limited. Walk with me. Regard the world through my eyes for a while."

And, for just awhile, Marcus Roads, admirer of the avant-garde and devotee of the new art, forgot all about Gabriel Gibbs.

The pair strolled Harlem's streets. As they wandered, Marcus's companion pointed out landmarks and offered commentary upon life in the neighborhood. Their progress was frequently interrupted as Hughes stopped, or was stopped, to talk with residents. Marcus envied the poet's gift for conversation, engaging everyone from street vendors to other artists with an easy eloquence. The man's speech possessed an inherently lyrical quality transforming even casual conversation into prose and poetry.

Hughes had opined Gabriel might be a living symbol of the Harlem Renaissance. But in the mind of Marcus, and millions of others beyond Harlem's borders, Hughes himself held that title. False modesty or not, Hughes brushed the label away.

"I am just one more person who has found himself here," the poet's eyes twinkled as he sought signs that Marcus recognized the sentence's dual meanings. "I came to New York to study at Columbia. Alas, even there, they saw color too strongly. But, while here, I fell in love with Harlem. First she became my mistress. And then my true love. Oh, I might have strayed a little: England, Paris, Washington, Lincoln College in Pennsylvania. But Harlem always called to me. And, in my heart, I always remained faithful. As soon as I had degree in hand, I came." Though that love of place, Hughes opened a unique window for Marcus into Harlem's Renaissance.

The poet began by referencing the changing lives of black Americans over the past half century. "Our past is always with us," Hughes told Marcus, "but cannot exclusively define us." The Harlem Renaissance, he believed, resulted from contemporary blacks seeking a new definition and new identity for a new age. It was a movement driven in large part by artists who, rejecting stereotypes and straightjacketed convention, grasped for new approaches to literature, drama, and art in which nuanced portrayals of individuals could serve as a lens for American blacks and the human condition as a whole. Many of their innovations, such as Harlem's jazz, already influenced broader American culture. Not only finding favor but fueling mainstream trends.

Two other events had catalyzed a renaissance already in motion. Returning home after risking their lives in the Great War, hundreds of thousands of black veterans felt confident demanding a greater voice in their homeland. At the same time, the Great Migration started from the South, Midwest, and even Latin America and the Caribbean northward, especially to New York. These arrivals further energized Harlem by bringing new sounds, new traditions, and new arts.

Hughes and his fellow luminaries were bohemians in the old-school sense. Dismissive of the neighborhood's bourgeois, and finding them as devoid of passion as their bourgeois counterparts elsewhere, Harlem's poets, writers, and artists strove for the common touch as they celebrated the life of the street.

As Hughes concluded by putting it to Marcus that "Life's struggles and triumphs, joys and sorrows, are all here," the pair arrived outside an elegant three-story townhouse. Hughes led Marcus up the steps and through a doorway flanked by an elegant corniche.

Chapter Twenty - Six

With great delight, Marcus realized Hughes had brought him to one of Harlem's, and America's, most celebrated intellectual salons. The poet presented Marcus to its hosts. The activist and suffragette Ruth Logan Roberts enthusiastically opened her home for regular gatherings of Harlem intelligentsia. Her husband, Eugene, Hughes carefully noted to Marcus, was a prominent local physician.

Having exchanged pleasantries with the hosts, Hughes introduced Marcus to the others in attendance. Saturated by names and faces, while Marcus could not keep track of everyone he met, many of those present stood out.

Countee Cullen, his first name pronounced *Coun-tay*, was another of Harlem's celebrated poets and writers. As Marcus discovered, he was also a fellow Harvard alumnus. Harold Jackman, the poet's companion, hovered around Cullen. While a teacher, the true reason for Jackman's fame could be found in his epithet "The Handsomest Man in Harlem." Jackman's face, Marcus acknowledged, embodied the Classical aesthetic, fit for a bust of Grecian marble.

Older than the rest, Jessie Fauset had a lengthy career as a woman of letters, editor, novelist, and poet who had studied at the Sorbonne. The poet Virginia Houston was celebrated by some and condemned by others for the uncompromising explicitness of her verse. Zora Neale Hurston, a writer as well as an anthropologist and folklorist, had studied under Frank Boas and alongside Margaret Mead. Her husband, Herbert Sheen, played jazz as both vocation and avocation. Eugene Gordon embodied much of what Hughes had said about the Harlem Renaissance on their walk to the salon. A veteran of the Great War, Gordon returned home to become a journalist and activist, founding and editing the *Saturday Evening Quill* literary magazine and later adding fiction to his oeuvre.

The youngest of the salon's attendees, Elmer Simms Campbell, appeared, at most, 23. Hughes effusively praised the introverted young man's work as a cartoonist, already finding favor in Harlem Renaissance publications and mainstream magazines alike.

Carl Van Vechten, the only other white in attendance, was an artist and photographer. He was an admirer and advocate for many artists of the Harlem Renaissance as well as, famously, a friend of Gertrude Stein. And, Marcus discovered, if you were unaware of his association with Stein, it didn't matter. Just talk to the man for five minutes and he'd let you know.

The guests mingled and made small talk while enjoying cocktails. Hughes seemed to be everywhere at once, leaving Marcus to make his way on his own. Fortunately, he discovered points of commonality with several attendees.

Though their time at Harvard did not overlap, it had been close enough that he and Cullen could reminisce about experiences there. With Fauset he could discuss Paris. Sheen, a pianist, was delighted by the story of Marcus's encounter with Willie "The Lion" Smith. "And you're still in one piece?" Sheen joked. "You know, the Lion is the best pianist in Harlem. If you don't believe it, just ask him." Though he had not met Resurrection Gibbs, Sheen knew of the musician and the excitement he generated.

Efforts to uncover information which might advance Marcus's investigation, however, yielded mostly disappointment. Van Vechten, the photographer, was unfamiliar with his New Orleans counterpart, Bellocq. Marcus had hoped the New Yorker might shed some additional light on the strange man whose assistance, it had to be acknowledged, had proved invaluable. Raised in New Orleans, Eugene Gordon had tales of a Storyville even wilder than the one experienced by Marcus. But the journalist departed the Crescent City long before Gabriel's arrival.

Only with Zora Neale Hurston did conversation ultimately shed light on the man who had brought Marcus to Harlem. Neale enjoyed sharing accounts of her anthropological work in the south and the Caribbean. Relaying them clearly and entertainingly, Marcus immediately sensed in Hurston the same kind of natural storyteller as Bartholomew Jenkins and William Blackmon.

When Marcus referenced his recent travels to the Delta and New Orleans, Hurston's eyes briefly flickered to Hughes, with whom Marcus had arrived. Though the poet was engaged in animated conversation with Jessie Fauset, Hurston quickly put two and two together. "Gabriel Gibbs?" she asked.

"In both Mississippi and New Orleans," he explained, answering her question. "I tried to get as much of the local folklore as I could, hoping it might help me make sense of things."

"You were thinking a zombi?"

Marcus blushed.

"There's no shame in it," she responded. "So many wild tales circulate about Gabriel Gibbs that the mind naturally wanders to wild answers." She paused, as if gauging what she could trust Marcus with. "I will tell you this. During my travels in Haiti, I met a zombi. Or someone the local villagers believed to be a zombi. No one would ever mistake him for normal. In fact, even now, I instinctively want to say 'it' not 'he.' And not in a million years could he have played an instrument, painted a picture, written a poem, or done any of those things which are the human spirit's zenith. Whatever Gabriel Gibbs is, he's no zombi."

"That's what I heard from the locals I asked," Marcus added. He was tempted to talk about his strangest experiences in Louisiana. But the encounter in the New Orleans bodega felt too intimate, too personal. As for the night in the swamp, in hindsight Marcus had trouble believing it himself. Instead, holding his tongue on those incidents, he posed Hurston a question.

"Do you believe it's possible to come back from the dead, Ms. Hurston?"

"Categorically, no. But an anthropologist sees some very strange things."

"Funny," Marcus observed. "A physician might give the same answer."

"Everyplace I've been and every culture I've studied," Hurston continued, "I've found that human beings have a powerful need regarding death. I'm not talking about needing to believe it's not the end. Though there is that, too. I'm talking about a need to make death mean something."

While they were unfailingly polite, Marcus perceived a certain reticence from some of the guests. Eventually, he found himself in the corner next to Dr. Roberts. "I enjoy these gatherings," the other physician told Marcus, "but they're really Ruth's affairs. Mostly, I just sit back, watch, and listen."

Inevitably, the two talked shop. Despite the segregation of American medicine, a topic the men danced around uneasily, much of practicing medicine was universal. The connection created by sharing a profession that was more than a profession also allowed Marcus to broach the delicate question of his reception at the salon. The cool reception he received from some. Had he done or said something wrong-footed?

"Don't take it personally," Roberts replied. "There are some whites that come to Harlem just for the thrill. To see something they think is exotic. Like they're paying to see a spectacle at the nickelodeon. So we learn to hold our distance until someone proves their bona fides.

"But if Langston brought you here, that's good enough for me. The man delights in surrounding himself with every type of strange character. Except phonies. He can smell a poseur a mile away."

One guest who did not keep his distance was Hubert Delany, an assistant district attorney for New York. Flashing a winning smile as he wrapped Marcus's wrist in his enthusiastic hand, Delany explained he was running for New York's 21st Congressional District. Even Marcus's protestations that he lived in Boston did not deter Delany from expounding on his plans for the district. Before the evening ended, Marcus found himself making a modest contribution the campaign. From his own pocket, of course. He could never get that past Prince as legitimate expense.

With the tardy arrival of the poets Arna Bontemps and Richard Bruce Nugent, the salon got underway in earnest.

It opened with Cullen giving a reading of his recently published poem "The Black Christ," a work written in evocative rhyming triplets, made further majestic by the poet's velvety tenor voice. Approval and applause at the end of his reading gave way to discussing the age-old discussion of how, and if, the idea of a just, loving god could be reconciled with a world full of pain and hardship.

Another reading followed as Virginia Houston performed one of her work in progress. Reactions to the piece divided more sharply than for Cullen's poem. While some adored it, others were off-put. Marcus was both at once. Its meter and powerful use of language entranced him. At the same time, he had no doubt he blushed a brilliant crimson at its frank portrayal of sexuality.

With no one else interested in giving a reading, as Delany updated the others on his campaign, the salon's focus turned to politics. Many of the participants traded barbs, albeit generally good-natured ones, with Zora Neale Hurston who appeared more conservative than the others.

There was ghoulish speculation as to the nature and origin of the Broadway Butcher. Hughes took macabre relish in observing that New York had seen such creatures before. And would again. Adding to that, Hurston noted every culture in the world produced such individuals on occasion. Supporting that, she shared several grisly tales from her anthropological travels throughout America and around the globe. While Marcus's discovery at the *Sentinel's* office hung on the tip of his tongue, whether out of reticence at being a newcomer and outsider or hesitation at passing on something which might be no more than extraordinary coincidence, he remained silent.

The poet Nugent then opined widely on Harlem's upcoming

social calendar, a scene to which he seemed even better plugged in than Hughes. Falling silent, he rolled a thick cigarette. As the fragrant tobacco drifted through the room, the gathering returned to mingling and small talk.

Marcus had the impression that Nugent's social update, followed by his cigarette, had become a kind of ritual formally marking the end of the salon. By the time he and Hughes left, Marcus had exchanged cards, and promises to keep in contact, with Countee Cullen and Dr. Roberts.

From Elmer Campbell, who had said little during the salon, Marcus received something else. The young cartoonist had spent most of the evening drawing with a charcoal pencil in a large tablet. At the end, he gifted the physician a sketch of Marcus and Hughes standing together in the Roberts' foyer. Rendered in rough but evocative charcoal strokes, the dapper, dignified, and rather diminutive poet stood next to the tall, gangling physician.

Back on 130th Street, in the unseasonable and stifling air, the pair resumed their walk. Ruminating on the works read by Countee Cullen and Virginia Houston, Marcus asked Hughes about his current projects.

The poet confided he was considering branching out, making the leap to a novel. Already, he gathered notes for such a work. A portrayal of the life of American blacks through the lens of the triumphs and tragedies of a single, typical family. He still wrestled with the basic question of where to set his story, but leaned toward Kansas. "I grew up in Lawrence, that city between the banks of the Kansas and the Wakarusa," Hughes said before acknowledging the work would be semi-autobiographical…but could only be so much so. "You know what Tolstoy wrote of families?"

Marcus nodded.

"My family was many things, Dr. Roads. Typical was not one of them."

References to the problems within his family transmuted into comments on the problems the poet saw in his country. Hughes revealed a sympathy for communism, expressing a desire to travel to the Soviet Union someday. While Marcus grasped that the matter might look different as part of a community America treated so poorly, as much as he admired the man, Marcus could not condone communism. Sensing mutual awkwardness, they removed politics from the table as a topic of discussion.

The conversational impasse was broken as the pair passed a corner where two young men painted a large mural onto a brick wall. Their work presented a brightly-colored microcosm of Harlem life. Streets and buildings were rendered with lines meeting at strange, crazy-quilt angles that captured the neighborhood's energy and unpredictability. It was peopled with figures that, in contrast, they captured in motion with curves. Slender, graceful, almost liquid.

Unsurprisingly, Hughes knew the artists…and stopped to chat with them. The eldest, perhaps 21. His younger counterpart, no more than 19. Throughout their conversation, the men glanced curiously at Marcus. Eventually, Hughes recognized the faux pas. "Forgive me. Allow me to introduce Charles Alston," he said, indicating the eldest "and Mike Bannarn. Two of our most talented up-and-coming visual artists." Hughes paused. "Gentlemen, this is Dr. Marcus Roads. He, like me, is a student of the Gabriel Gibbs mystery."

Adjusting the cadence of his speech and infinitesimally tweaking the long "e" at the end of he, me, and mystery, Hughes transformed his simple sentence into verse. Again, Marcus envied the poet his mastery of the English language.

"Resurrection Gibbs, couldn't leave him out." Bannarn smiled, pointing out one of the figures on the mural in progress. The musician stood next to an open grave, which looked out of place rendered in the middle of Lennox Avenue, one of the trumpeter's feet still inside. Marcus had no doubt the artists had seen the musician, the Gibbs family's distinctive delicate features were there in paint. With his silver trumpet pointed heavenward, a stream of notes issued forth. Adjusting his glasses, on closer examination Marcus saw the notes were, in fact, tiny silhouetted dancers, rendered with the same artful fluidity as the mural's other figures.

As Marcus and the painters contemplated the rendering of Gabriel Gibbs, Hughes carefully scrutinized his own likeness in the mural with, perhaps, the faintest trace of vanity.

"Such a great musician," Alston effused. "And one hell of a tale. If there wasn't a Resurrection Gibbs, I think someone would just invent him. He's like the whole Harlem Renaissance all rolled up into one. Resurrection. That's what it's all about.

"Of course," the painter added, "Nobody really comes back."

Though Bannarn didn't actually say anything, his uneasy shift in posture made Marcus suspect the younger artist wasn't quite so certain.

Collective respects paid to Gabriel Gibbs and his meaning, the men returned to their topic of conversation prior to Hughes' introductions: a boycott of the Harmon Foundation by Harlem artists, which Alston and Bannarn sought to organize and of which Hughes was broadly supportive. Though soft spoken, Alston did most of the talking. Nodding and occasionally providing short affirmations of his friend's statements, Bannarn projected a quiet intensity.

Seeing their new acquaintance lost, Alston provided context. The Harmon Foundation organized traveling art shows of works by all black artists for all white audiences. Ostensibly a philanthropic service to both communities, the young artists found its underlying assumptions demeaning.

"Nobody needs to box me up, Dr. Roads," Alston said as part of his explanation. "I'll put my work beside any artist in the world, even Picasso, and let the viewer be the judge."

Bannarn chimed in, declaring "It's about the colors on the canvas, not the color of the artist."

Marcus signaled agreement with those sentiments. Hughes and Alston resumed talking, Bannarn paying keen interest. While the conversation fascinated him, Marcus was not a part of it, giving him freedom to peruse the mural in progress. In addition to spotting Hughes and Gabriel, it pleased him that he recognized several other figures. He found the image of Cullen the poet accompanied, in art as in life, by Jackman the Adonis. Hubert Delany, the district attorney and would-be congressman, strode confidently down the street in a tasteful suit, pressing the flesh with the people of Harlem.

"Who is that?" Marcus exclaimed, startling the others out of their conversation. He indicated a tall, broad-shouldered figure in a tattered suit looming in shadows. Even rendered in pigment, his image projected menace.

"Young people call him the Gray Torpedo," Alston said, adding "'Torpedo' is slang for a rough, dangerous customer. Older folks, especially ones who came here from the South, call him the Haint. Young or old, they want nothing to do with him."

"I've seen him," Marcus announced. "He was outside the ruins of the St. Ignatius Street Boardinghouse."

"We've all seen him," Bannarn said. "I just wish I could un-see him."

Eventually leaving Alston and Bannarn to their mural, Hughes and Marcus continued their wandering. As they walked, Marcus observed to the poet that Charles Alston's comment that Gabriel Gibbs was "like the whole Harlem Renaissance all rolled up into one" mirrored, albeit more colloquially, the sentiment Hughes had expressed when he and Marcus began talking.

The poet smiled. "And so you begin to see. Gibbs isn't just a curious puzzle like you thought. Or a news story like Fort believes. He's part of a context. It is impossible to understand him without it."

Marcus nodded. "I just wish I could figure out where the man is going to be next."

"In that, we are correspondent," Hughes laughed. He stopped suddenly, gazing upward. Marcus followed his eyes. A playbill hung from the lamppost:

Gabriel "Resurrection" Gibbs
Saturday, September 27
The Savoy Ballroom

Chapter Twenty - Seven

As screams filled the Savoy, Marcus found himself unable to move. Not because the shooting of Gabriel Gibbs surprised him. If anything, the contrary. Increasingly fixated on Charles Fort's musings that, genuine resurrection or not, doom nipped at the musician's heels, as well as Gabriel's connection with the Broadway Butcher, a sense of impending tragedy had possessed Marcus. Now that things had unfolded precisely as he feared, a kind of paralysis possessed Marcus.

Even so, his height allowed him to get the lay of the land. Over a sea of panicked patrons fleeing the gunfire, he spotted the shooter and fit another puzzle piece into place. Marcus recognized the man: the menacing presence outside the ruins of the St. Ignatius Street Boarding House, the Gray Torpedo of Alston and Bannarn's mural.

Already, a trio of the Savoy's star dancers grappled with the Torpedo, attempting to restrain him. The dancers, Frankie Manning, Shepherd Nesterman, and "Snake Hips" Tucker, were lovers not fighters. But they possessed an Olympian athleticism that would have allowed them to go toe-to-toe with any prizefighter in the country. Screaming "Abomination! Abomination!" and wielding his empty revolver like a club, the Torpedo struggled vainly to escape the dancers and reach the fallen trumpeter.

The spell broke as suddenly as it had appeared, Marcus snatched up his black bag and forced his way through the chaos toward the stage. He noted Jack La Rue, the ballroom's fearsome chief of security, and his men roughly shouldering their way through the crowd toward the fray. Grateful for their quick response, Marcus wished it could have been faster.

Their nerves frayed by suspicions and fears, upon arriving at the club he and Hughes warned La Rue to be on the lookout for trouble. Hughes did most of the talking. Marcus figured a warning would carry more weight coming from the poet, no less of a Harlem institution than the Savoy itself, than from some Beantown square.

La Rue would be none too gentle with the Torpedo. Even at the best of times, Hughes had informed Marcus after their conversation with man, the Savoy's chief bouncer relished "discussing" breaches of the club's policies with his fists. That was not Marcus's concern.

He and Hughes continued toward Gabriel. Or tried to. Threading his way through fleeing patrons, Marcus felt like a salmon swimming upstream. Reaching the wounded musician, Marcus dropped his black bag and stepped forward.

Taking a knee beside the man whose life Marcus had come to know as well as his own, the moment overwhelmed him. He gazed with wonder at the delicately-featured figure around whom so many mysteries swirled. As time seemed to slow almost to a stop, Marcus was acutely aware of completing the circle that had begun in Walter Franklin Prince's library.

White tuxedo shirt soaked with crimson, the trumpeter sprawled across the overturned drum kit. The sight of Gabriel, looking impossibly small and frail, roused Marcus from his reverie and reminded him of his physician's calling. Seeing the musician's chest rise and fall, even if only weakly, Marcus sighed with relief. Gabriel wasn't already beyond his help. As Marcus glanced over his shoulder, a knot formed in his stomach. "Where's my bag?"

He cursed himself. For a few moments, he'd allowed Marcus Roads the supernatural investigator to overpower Marcus Roads the physician. Now, the black satchel holding the essential tools of his proper trade was nowhere to be seen."

"Where's my bag?" he repeated loudly, his voice carrying

even over the surrounding commotion. "We have to find it." Hughes, La Rue, and the others fanned out across the ballroom. Even Fenno, Marcus noted out of the corner of his eye, searched. Marcus had been surprised and disappointed by the ASPR investigator's abrupt reappearance, grumpily dragging himself into the Savoy minutes before the show. Ensuring his rival could not mistake his displeasure, Fenno sat, brooding, at the same table as Marcus and Hughes.

Despite their best efforts, the bag was not found. Perhaps an accidental kick knocked it into the darkest of the Savoy's dark corners or under a remote table. Perhaps an opportunistic patron had nicked it. The method didn't matter, only its absence.

"Does the Savoy have medical supplies?" Marcus asked La Rue.

"First aid kit," the security chief answered.

"Bring it."

Like Queen Lola in the swamp, La Rue's expression indicated someone used to giving orders not taking them. Marcus didn't care. And, whatever thoughts traveled behind La Rue's handsome tough-guy features, the man did as told.

Marcus began removing Gabriel's bloody tuxedo shirt to examine the injury. Halting suddenly, his eyes went wide. He greeted La Rue's return with gratitude. Not for the tiny first aid kit he carried but because it gave Marcus time to work out a new, and unexpected, complication.

Opening the tin box confirmed Marcus's skepticism. Vials of iodine and merbromin antiseptics as well as aromatic spirits of ammonia. Bottles of aspirin and laxatives. Blunt-nose scissors, absorbent cotton, band-aid strips and dental floss. Dental floss? It seemed inadequate for the day-to-day needs of a large nightclub. To say nothing of treating a life-threatening injury.

Hughes read Marcus's gaze without need for commentary. "What do we do?" It was strange to see the poet, for once, uncomfortable and without answers.

Marcus thought a moment. "Dr. Roberts." Hughes nodded in response. Ruth Logan Roberts' house, home to Harlem's most famous cultural salon, was also the residence of her husband, the physician Eugene Roberts. Surely he would have a bag Marcus could borrow. But how to get it? Time was not merely of the essence. It was matter of life and death.

Marcus kept himself in good condition. Good but not great. And, anyway, he needed to remain here doing what he could to prevent the musician's condition from deteriorating. Fenno? Not even an option. The diminutive Hughes seemed in solid health but hardly an athlete. "Who is the quickest person here?" he asked anyone who happened to be listening. "One of the dancers, maybe?"

La Rue disappeared into the crowd. Instead of a dancer, he returned with a young boy. Clifford Stryker was the fastest numbers runner in Harlem which, Marcus presumed, explained why the twelve year-old had been hanging around the Savoy at such an hour.

Borrowing pen and paper from Hughes, Marcus dashed off a quick note to Dr. Roberts explaining his need. Handing it to the boy, Marcus gave clear instructions. "Clifford, my patient's survival depends on you," he said, indicating the trumpeter. "Take this message to 130 West 130th street, run as fast as you can. Don't give this message to anyone other than Dr. Eugene Roberts or his wife, Ruth Logan Roberts. They're going to give you something, a black bag, probably. Bring it back as quickly as possible. Do you understand?" Marcus knew his manner probably patronized the young man. But the situation allowed no margin for error.

"Yes, sir. One-hundred thirty West 130th. Dr. Eugene Roberts. Or his wife, Ruth," Clifford repeated with perfect precision before adding, "And get back here like the Devil."

"Very good," Marcus acknowledged. "Now, go!" By the time he finished speaking Stryker had already vanished. Marcus returned attention to his patient. On the one hand, moving someone with a bullet wound was risky. On the other, the Savoy's main room, loud, crowded, and dirty was no place to treat a serious injury. Normally, Marcus would have wrestled with the unlovely options. Bur the "unexpected complication" he'd discovered swung the balance in favor of moving the trumpeter.

Carrying his wounded patient, Marcus led a procession into

the greenroom. Carefully, he laid the musician on a table. As he continued removing the blood-soaked shirt to treat the injury, the physician looked at the others in the room. "This man requires immediate treatment. Everybody out."

Everyone complied. Almost. Langston Hughes leaned against one wall. Theodore Fenno, still fuming over his recently escaped quarantine, sat stubbornly at a table. Having experienced Hughes' gaze, Marcus had no illusions about winning the necessary battle of wills to make him leave. Fenno, he could probably overawe. To Marcus's surprise, he didn't want to. The man was a rival. But he, too, had made the journey. It felt wrong to deprive him of its conclusion.

Returning attention to his patient, Marcus stared at the musician's small breasts, carefully wrapped to further minimize them. This was the key. Sex was a difficult secret to keep, explaining Resurrection Gibbs' obsession with privacy and frequent relocation. It also shed light upon the revelation Marcus had while listening to the trumpeter perform minutes earlier. With his growing ear for jazz, Marcus realized the musician on the Savoy's stage sounded very similar to the one on Ralph Peer's records. Very similar, but not identical. Of all the women who might have impersonated Gabriel Gibbs, only one could not be well accounted for in the time since the musician's reappearance. "You're Rebekah, aren't you?"

Wincing, his patient, Gabriel's younger sister, nodded.

"You're not in danger. I made your injury sound severe to get everyone to leave and give you some privacy." He hoped that was true. Instinct told him it was. She was in pain and had difficulty breathing deeply. But she remained conscious and her vitals appeared good.

"Proper medical supplies are on the way," Marcus continued. Something else he hoped was true. He gave his patient a warm smile. With no evidence the bullet had punctured a lung, while her talking wouldn't help matters, it wouldn't really hurt either. And it might get Rebekah's mind off her injury. "It seems like you've had quite an adventure…" Marcus said leadingly.

"You don't owe us anything you don't want to share," Hughes assured her before admitting, "but we'd really like to hear."

"It's okay, I'd like to tell," she said, fighting through the pain. "And, in case I don't make it, someone should know."

"Hold on," Marcus cautioned her. If a dozen or so words were hard to get through, there was no way she would be able to tell her story. Though he lacked his black bag, he suspected the Savoy had its own options for treating Rebekah's pain.

He looked at Hughes. "Please fetch La Rue for me." As the poet moved, Marcus draped his jacket over Rebekah's bare torso.

Hughes returned with the ballroom's chief of security as his side. "You need something, Roads?"

"Cocaine." Marcus called back to La Rue.

"What?" he asked as if not believing what he'd heard.

"Cocaine. Bring me some."

"Cocaine is a controlled substance," La Rue protested as if reading off a script "It is dispensable only by prescription."

"In case you've forgotten, I *am* a doctor. And I'm proscribing it for this patient," Marcus answered in calm, professional tones. "You can save the dog and pony show for the bulls. I know there's cocaine around here. Find it."

Returning after a short absence, he handed Marcus a fancy sachet of dusty white powder. "This better be worth it," La Rue grumbled. "It cost me a ten-spot to snag from a bartender. He wanted twenty. After I countered with twenty and black eye, we came to terms."

Marcus barely heard the man's bravado. Hoping to dismiss La Rue with a glance, when the bouncer bristled Marcus feared there'd be trouble. But after La Rue's gaze faltered first, the Savoy's chief of security slunk from the greenroom like a chastened child. Alone again, or as close to alone as he'd get, Marcus uncovered Rebekah and draped his jacket across a nearby chair.

Restricted for good reason, and easily abused, cocaine did have legitimate medical uses. One of them was as a potent and fast-acting topical anesthetic. The perfectionist in Marcus cringed at having to eyeball the dosage but, after making his best professional judgement, he banished hesitation from his mind.

Dropping several pinches into his hand, he delicately applied the powder around Rebekah's wound.

Chapter Twenty - Eight

As the numbing agent took hold, Marcus watched her breathing deepen and the rictus of pain around the corners of her mouth subside to a mere grimace. "Feeling better?"

Leaning up and resting on one elbow, Rebekah nodded. "Some water, though?"

Making himself useful, Fenno poured her a glass of water from a pitcher on his table.

"I almost don't know where to start," she began. "As long as I've been aware, I've known Gabriel was different." At first, Rebekah's voice was weak, her speech halting. She gained vigor as she continued. Whether that supported a positive prognosis or simply meant that adrenaline, willpower, and cocaine were doing their work, Marcus had no way to know until proper instruments arrived.

"Most folks are built from a little good, a little bad, and a lot of normal," she explained. "My brother wasn't like that. He was larger than life. But like a child, too. Not much strung the two together. Gabriel awed me. And I pitied him. Sometimes I felt like his big sister, not his little one. That's a strange thing. But it made me love him even more. Probably even more than I thought I could love anyone.

"And he loved me. Sometimes he could be thoughtless, but I never met anybody more loving than my brother. One time, I must have been about eight, my best friend had her birthday party. Pa bought me a new party dress and ma did my hair up nice. My friend lived a couple miles up the road and I wasn't big enough to go on my own. Ma and Aunt Mancie had their housework and all the other men were busy on the farm. So, Gabriel walked me to the party.

"A big cloudburst happened while we were there. Rain came down in sheets for hours. Lightning and thunder, everything. After it stopped, I was afraid to walk home because I'd get my new dress all muddy. Gabriel carried me on his back the whole way. He was little for his age and I'm only two years younger. I don't think he was really any bigger than I was. He cried from the weight of me the whole second half of the way. But he did it anyway because he loved his little sister.

"I loved his passion for life. And his basic decency. He was honest about himself and his life. And too focused on his passions to bother with deceiving anybody. I especially loved his passion for music and never got tired of hearing him play. When he blew trumpet, he seemed more real, more alive, than anyone I've ever known. One day, Gabriel vowed he'd headline a big Harlem show. I believed him, too. And I knew I'd do whatever I could to get him there. As it turned out, that took a lot more than I expected.

"I'll tell you all something I've never admitted to anyone, not even Gabriel. I was never big on Pastor. I tried to love him because Gabe did and because he helped Gabe with his music. But he always left me cold. After what he did to my brother, I prayed that God would smite him with some terrible affliction, like he did to Job. I know you're not supposed to wish that on anyone. Especially a man of God. But he'd hurt Gabriel…and I wasn't going to let that go."

She paused, as if considering whether to add something. "It might even be that, after Pastor made himself a hypocrite by showing up for King Oliver's big to-do, I whispered louder against him than anyone else.

"But I'm getting ahead of the tale. After their showdown in the tabernacle, Gabriel didn't have anything left but music. I encouraged his practicing and playing all those parties and dances. When he took strange and started wandering and disappearing, the family worried about him. Ma and Pa kept talking about putting their feet down and forbidding him to play anymore. I knew that wouldn't go well, so I talked them out of it.

"But I worried, too. To find out what was really going on, I began following him when he left the house. It didn't take long to figure out what the deal was. He'd started moving liquor for Colonel Scobie. I confronted Gabriel about it.

"The way he explained it, along with what he made from playing, the money from rum running let him devote himself fulltime to music. There was never any talking my brother out of anything related to his music. His confrontation with Pastor proved that. And there are more dangerous things than rum running. Especially when the sheriff likes your family and is already taking his cut. I promised Gabriel it would stay our secret, if he promised not to do anything dumb.

"So, things continued apiece. There came a stretch when Gabriel stayed away for several days. I figured the Colonel had just been moving even more moonshine than usual. Then, one night, my brother turned up at the house, exhausted, and with that silver trumpet in hand for the first time.

"He sat me down and told me how he got it. I didn't even have to ask. He wanted to talk about it.

"He had been at Eden Plantation one night playing one of the Colonel's parties. After his guests had gone, the Colonel called Gabriel into his study, just the two of them alone, and told my brother a story.

"It was about the last days of the war. Everybody saw the writing on the wall. Union forces were pushing their way through the county and a bunch of its rich families got worried about what would happen to their possessions when they fell into Yankee hands. So, they made a deal with some river pirate called Pig-Eye. He'd sail their valuables to safety, plus what remained of the Confederate gold in the county treasury, in exchange for a cut. I guess they figured they'd be able to recover their treasure later.

"This Pig Eye put his boat into Able's Creek. It's up north in the county, well away from the prying eyes of regular folks who might be upset that the society people were getting their valuables safely away when everyone else wasn't. They met the pirates there and loaded up their treasures. But the weather must have been on the Yankee's side. Can't say I'm surprised. Big rains came that nobody expected and rising water made the creek dangerous. After it was all loaded up, the boat swamped. It sunk right there with Pig Eye and his crew aboard. And all those society folks lost their riches.

"Sixty years later, Colonel Scobie and Sheriff Caldwell got to talking. Turns out those two were already thick as thieves over the moonshine. They figured with all the innovation that had taken place since the war, and with the hot summer lowering water levels, it might be possible to dive the boat's wreck and recover all those valuables. Old Colonel Scobie was one of the ones there that day back in '65. He'd stood on the shore in the rain and watched the boat go down. So he knew right where the wreck was. Sheriff Caldwell's grandfather had been there, too. I'm sure there were others.

"So the colonel and sheriff bought hoses, a compressor, a second-hand diving suit with one of those big metal helmets. I don't know what all else. But, because the diving stuff wasn't failsafe, they wanted something else. Someone who could hold his breath a mighty long time. From my brother's trumpet playing, the colonel knew he already had someone like that working for him. Gabriel.

"The Colonel must have genuinely liked my brother at least a little bit to level with him like that. He told Gabriel exactly what he wanted and promised him a share of whatever was recovered.

"My brother agreed and, soon after, they started. Colonel Scobie, the sheriff, and a few of their most trusted men were there, with Gabriel doing the actual diving. It didn't take long to find the wreck, but things got hard from there. The boat had settled on its side. Over the years, it got pretty far buried in the mud. And that's not a clear creek. The water's dirty and gets lots of leaves and other things in it. So, when he dived, my brother couldn't see more than a few feet in front of his face.

"He found those strongboxes full of Confederate gold. They were too heavy to go anywhere. A lot of the other stuff got ruined. Gabriel told me about all these fancy picture frames he brought up. Fancy, but empty. Their paintings had all rotted away. And some of the stuff that should have been there was just gone, washed downstream to the Mississippi.

"But Gabriel found things. Candlesticks. Jewelry boxes. Even a chest of China porcelain that, somehow, hadn't broken or even chipped. And the trumpet. Colonel Scobie must have seen how Gabriel looked at it, because he offered my brother a deal. It was a priceless family heirloom, the colonel said, but he'd let Gabriel keep it if he forfeited the rest of his share. It wasn't a fair deal. Not one soul in a million would have taken it. But, far as my brother was concerned, he'd swindled Colonel Scobie. I guess any deal where both parties feel they've cheated the other is a fair one."

So Gabriel's silver trumpet turned out to be the same one tied to the Scobie family after all. More than that, Rebekah's account of treasure from the sunken riverboat and how the trumpet had come into her brother's hands offered Marcus the key to two other puzzles. First, he now knew where the leaders of Pilot's Point had been on the day that the Great Gates County Flood claimed Chapel Bar. The day Pilot's Point became Pilate's Point. Second, more than just moonshine had funded the revival of Colonel Scobie's flagging family fortunes. According to Bartholomew the driver, the colonel's efforts to restore Eden Plantation reached their glorious crescendo about two or three years ago. A date coinciding nicely with the appearance of the silver trumpet.

"It took Gabriel a while to clean that trumpet up and get it playing again," Rebekah continued. "The bell was banged-up pretty badly, too. So he had to fix that. And I helped him, of course. My brother didn't commit to a lot of things. But if he got an idea in his head, he'd see it through no matter what. That trumpet became his calling card. And it was a remarkable piece. Again, I'm getting ahead of the tale but, in the time since I've become Gabriel, I've tried other trumpets a few times. I've never found another that sounds as sweet or loves its owner as much as that one."

"That day King Oliver came to town, I went down to the fairground with my brother Sam to hear Gabriel play. I felt so torn that I thought I'd be pulled in two. I wanted him to win, I really did. It's what he wanted. But I also knew what winning would mean. He'd be out of Gates County and never look back. And that's exactly what happened. But I felt so proud of him for beating the King. Afterward, he gave me a hug and said 'thank you.' I'm not sure he ever loved me more than at that moment. But my heart broke the whole time.

When Gabriel got on that train for New Orleans, part of my soul went with him. We didn't hear much from my brother, but I hung on every word. Every night I tried to imagine his life down there. I told myself I'd go visit him when I got old enough."

Rebekah paused, drawing a long breath. "Pa got the telegram about Gabriel's murder while buying supplies in Pilate's Point." Marcus watched a spasm flicker across her face. More than just her wound, it testified to a memory still intensely painful. "He came home with a look on his face like he was the one who died. And he just told us. No lead in. No cushion. Nothing," Her voice faltered as she relived that horrid moment. "Time stopped. I thought the world would end. Turned out, that wasn't even the worst of it.

"After all we'd been through with Pastor Heulen and Gabriel's reputation, Ma thought it would be easier to bury him in New Orleans. I love her. But I don't think I'll ever forgive her for that. Pa wouldn't say anything against her. Sam wanted to, I think, but didn't. Aunt Mancie was the only one who had my back."

Marcus could not suppress a smile at that.

"I told them they could try and stop me," she went on, "but I was going to New Orleans and get my brother come hell or high water. He would get buried in Gates County if I had to dig the hole with my hands.

"On the train back home, my forehead pressed against that cheap pine box they'd given him down there, I kept thinking about that vow he made. It broke my heart he'd never see that Harlem spotlight. Then I made a vow of my own. I'd make Gabriel's dream come true. I don't know if you've ever grieved, really grieved, for someone. There comes a time when you've cried every tear a body can make. Then you've got to figure out what to do. How to go on."

As Rebekah took a sip of water, Marcus thought Fenno stirred uncomfortably in his seat.

"I decided my brother would headline that Harlem club after all," she continued. "He'd get a standing ovation for it, too. How? I'd become Gabriel. Maybe folks would think reports of his death were greatly exaggerated. If not, Gabriel already had that supernatural reputation. It would make my job easier. I almost wanted to thank Pastor Heulen for it.

"Having that goal dulled my grief. I threw myself into planning how to take my wild notion and make it real."

"When I got back home with his body, my folks told me we couldn't bury Gabriel at the tabernacle churchyard. At first, I saw red. Even though Pastor was gone and disgraced, his former flock wouldn't let us bury my brother where he'd gone to church. I couldn't believe it. After apiece I realized, for what needed doing, it was a blessing. The tabernacle was too close to farms and homesteads. The county cemetery wasn't near anything.

"The new moon happened just a few days after the funeral. That night, I went back and dug up my brother. It's the worst thing I've ever done. I'm not just talking about digging up my flesh and blood. It's terrible work all on its own. But it needed doing. To convince folks Gabriel had come back, that pine box had to be empty. Someone might be crazy enough to check.

Marcus meet Rebekah's gaze with difficulty. "You ripped off a fingernail in the process, didn't you?"

Rebekah nodded, eyeing him carefully. "Uh-huh. My crowbar slipped when I opened the coffin.

"I pulled Gabriel out. After catching my breath, I dragged his body to the nearest creek and dumped it. That turned out to be Able's Creek. So, all the while, I'm thinking about how it's the same creek his trumpet had come out of and wondering what that meant. Afterward, he must have floated downstream and into the Mississippi. The week next, a body washed up in Issaquena County just south of Gates County. It was in bad shape. But even if it wasn't, it wouldn't have mattered. When identifying a body, nobody looks for a man who's already buried.

"I knew I'd have to disappear to make my plan work. After Gabriel's funeral, to lay the groundwork, I started acting out of sorts. That wasn't hard. I was still in a bad place.

"When I vanished, I went back to New Orleans. I needed Gabriel's silver trumpet to pull this off. Folks wouldn't believe it was really Gabriel without it. More than that, the trumpet was like the ruse in a two-bit medicine show charlatan's trick. You've seen that trumpet. You can't take your eyes off it. If folks were looking at the trumpet, they weren't looking at my face and maybe thinking, 'Does Gabriel look a little different?'

"In New Orleans, I never did tell anyone about being Gabriel's sister. But I retraced the steps of his life down there. I went to that club he played at. And to another to listen to some singer he'd apparently been gaga over. She looked pretty, but didn't seem like much to me. I even went to the cemetery where they found his body. Spent the whole night there wandering around in a daze. But, mostly, I asked after the trumpet. I found it in some Storyville pawnshop. Fancier place than I expected to find in the District. When I tried to buy the trumpet, the clerk told me to go away, it wasn't for sale. Seemed like something about me made him awfully nervous.

"As I said, I didn't have any choice but to get that trumpet. That night, I went back and broke in. There was a man inside doing the books. Not the one from earlier, an older fellow. He surprised me. I surprised him. We scuffled. In the course of things, he fell and hit his head on a shelf. He didn't get up again.

"I feel bad. But I don't feel as bad as I likely should."

"Remove any guilt from your conscience," Marcus interjected. "That man was responsible for your brother's death. He didn't pull the trigger but he was responsible all the same."

She nodded thoughtfully. "Can't say I'm surprised. Something in his eyes. More like a mad dog's than a person's." Rebekah halted a moment, refocusing on her tale. "Anyway, I grabbed that trumpet and went.

"From New Orleans, I went back to Mississippi, to Whitfield. I began working a laundry job at the State Hospital. It's not a happy place and the work was brutal, but it gave me a little money to live off. I had another reason for picking that job, though. It was the perfect way to explain my disappearance. The hospital didn't mind if employees used the mailroom. I sent a letter to my family saying I'd got committed. It was postmarked from the hospital. Why wouldn't they believe it?

"A fellow working in the mailroom got sweet on me. If anything came for me, he'd set it aside. James is a good man, he'll make someone a fine husband someday. I felt guilty about stringing him along like that, but I didn't have a choice.

"And, of course, if anyone telephoned, there was a Rebekah Gibbs 'at the hospital.' Just not as a patient. As long as their questions weren't too specific, my secret would be safe.

"I worked every day. Each night, I went home to the little shotgun shack I'd rented on the edge of town and woodshedded with the trumpet until dawn. I'd get a few hours' sleep and do it all over the next day.

"Flourishes, licks, runs, riffs, I learned them all. I'd listened to Gabriel so many times, I might as well have had a phonograph in my head. The hardest part were those long, steady notes of his. But they were his signature, so I had to be able to do them. Finally, I got the trick of it. And I got pretty good with that trumpet. Not to be prideful, but maybe better than Gabriel."

From informants Marcus had spoken with, as well as from his own ear contrasting Ralph Peer's records with the trumpeter who had just performed at the Savoy, there was no "maybe" about it. Post-resurrection Gabriel, which was to say Rebekah, was the superior musician.

"After a year," she continued, "I started going into Jackson on weekends and playing on Farish Street, building my chops and gathering up nickels, dimes, maybe a quarter if I got lucky. I wasn't claiming to be Gabriel. Not yet. But I was learning to pass as a man. Dress like one. Walk like one. Talk like one. I didn't get it right all at once. There are some funny stories…well, that's for another time. Before long, I started playing in the clubs for cash instead of on the street for coins. The good clubs smelled like beer and stale smoke. The bad ones? Well, add vomit to that list. But when folks cheered for me, I understood a bit about why my brother loved playing.

"Like I said, I didn't plan to be Gabriel yet. But one night I played a gig at the Brown Circle. Turned out someone in the crowd used to gig with my brother in Storyville. Never caught his name but after the show he came up and called me 'Gabriel.' I bolted through the backdoor fast as I could. But he'd seen me, heard me play, and still took me for Gabriel. I'd passed the test. He told folks about seeing 'Gabriel' alive and playing. That's when Resurrection Gibbs was born.

"With the cat now out of the bag, I figured I might as well be in New Orleans. 'The Big Time,' Gabriel always called it. Even after leaving Mississippi, I kept up the ruse of being in the State Hospital through my friend in the mailroom.

"New Orleans meant the end of being Rebekah by day and somebody else by night. I was Gabriel all the time. Asleep or awake. Eventually, I mostly forgot I wasn't him. I made a real name for myself, for Gabriel, in Storyville. But I had problems. Too many people knew Gabriel there. I was always dodging somebody who'd known my brother or faking my way through conversations I knew nothing about. Having coming back from the dead, Gabriel got plenty of attention from the occult folks. Plus, some lug named Jim Kessler had it in for me. One night, leaving a gig at Mahogany Hall, somebody took a shot at me. That was the last straw. I had put by some money and figured it was time to make Gabriel's dream come true. I caught the next train to New York."

Chapter Twenty - Nine

As suddenly as he had vanished, Clifford Stryker appeared in the greenroom, coated in a sweaty sheen and clutching a black bag as if it was the most important object in the world. Protecting the musician's secret, Hughes intercepted the boy before he could get a good look at Marcus's patient. Taking the black bag from Stryker, the poet carefully passed it to Marcus.

As Marcus eagerly popped open the satchel's brass clasps and examined its contents he was dimly aware of the boy apologizing that a run-in with the police had delayed him. It seemed the 32nd precinct's finest had been skeptical that a young Harlem boy had legitimate reason to be in possession of expensive equipment like the contents of a doctor's bag. Even with Marcus's note as proof, it taken some fast talking and pleading by the boy to convince the bulls to turn him loose.

No two physicians' kits were the same. Some of Dr. Roberts' choices were ones Marcus would not have made and, he was sure, vice-versa. Still, there was no doubt he could work with what he found inside.

Instead of an ether mask, Eugene Roberts favored the direct approach. Injecting Rebekah with a syringe full of morphine, Marcus would know the truth of her condition soon enough. "In a moment," he told her, "you're not going to feel anything. Just lay there and relax. Take a nap if you want to. We'll talk more afterward."

After irrigating the wound, Marcus began his examination.

Rebekah had been lucky. The Gray Torpedo's bullet entered through her left torso, likely headed for the heart or other vitals. But, striking a rib, it had deflected upward. Marcus's normally ever-present modesty never troubled him while working. Palpating his patient's chest, his sensitive fingertips quickly located the bullet lodged along the left pectoral muscle. Very lucky indeed.

He had less concern about the bullet's current location than the damage it had done going in. He treated and dressed the wound, little different from what he'd done in the swamp just a week ago.

Then, scalpel in hand, Marcus made a small incision over the bullet and the irrigated the cut. By surgical standards, the bullet's removal was both easy and simple. Marcus sutured the small incision, as usual taking satisfaction in his excellent stitch work. Rebekah Gibbs might not even have a scar to remind her of the evening. Not that she'd need one.

The whole procedure took less than an hour. Still, morphine was potent stuff. It would be another hour, maybe two, before Rebekah Gibbs regained sufficient presence of mind to talk.

Waiting for Rebekah to regain lucidity, commotion outside the green room disturbed Marcus. Walking to the door, Hughes cracked it slightly. His expression announced that, whatever he saw, it excited the poet's interest. Slipping outside, Hughes carefully closed the door behind him.

Marcus again checked Rebekah's vitals. Still positive. He then took a moment to clean and sterilize Dr. Roberts' instruments before returning everything to its proper place within the bag. Only then did he allow himself a moment to rest. Sitting, he and Fenno exchanged awkward glances in uncomfortable silence.

"Will she be okay, fishmonger?" when the ASPR man's question broke the quiet, his tone was civil.

"I won't swear to it until she gets up off that table and walks away but, I think, yes."

Minutes later Hughes reappeared. Drawing close to Marcus and Fenno, in tones at once somber and animated, the poet recounted what he'd seen and heard. The police had arrived to collect the shooter from La Rue and his bruisers. They hadn't departed before beginning their interrogation, either.

Marcus had already connected the gunman with the second black man trailing Gabriel Gibbs. And recognized him as the menacing figure skulking in shadows near the remains of the St. Ignatius Street boardinghouse. The Gray Torpedo who featured in Alston and Bannarn's mural. But Marcus had never suspected he was also looking at the monstrous remains of a human being who had once been Pastor Jericho Heulen.

Marcus turned that over in his mind. It seemed, having lost everything else, the man couldn't let go of his pride, jealousy, and rage. They drove the pastor to seek revenge on Gabriel while burning everything human out of himself. The remaining shell wasn't much different from the walking dead Marcus learned about in New Orleans, but animated by hate rather than sorcery.

Marcus wondered what Charles Fort would make of that. And what strange analogs might lurk in the man's files. Though probably a blessing for keeping Rebekah's secret, it disappointed Marcus that Fort hadn't joined them. After Hughes spotted the playbill heralding Gabriel's performance at the Savoy, Marcus phoned Fort to invite him. But, even with the game afoot, the idea of a nighttime visit to the popular Savoy proved too much for the Bronx recluse.

"The police expressed their interest in speaking with Gabriel Gibbs," Hughes concluded with a droll smirk. "Taking the liberty of putting words into your mouth, I told them you pronounced it would be hours before 'he' recovered enough to talk."

As if on cue, Rebekah Gibbs coughed and began stirring. "How are you feeling?" Marcus asked while moving toward his patient

"I guess about as well as I could expect," after a moment she recalled she had been in the middle of telling her story. "Where was I?"

"Arriving in New York," he prompted after concluding Rebekah had sufficiently recovered her faculties.

"That's right," she nodded groggily. "Harlem had so much

going on. Music. Theatre. Society. All this energy everywhere. New ideas floating around. I'd never seen anything like it. But I stayed focused and threw myself into the music. I got big fast. No one cared if I was resurrected. Some of them, I think, got a kick from the idea. After all the trouble I'd had in New Orleans, though, always staying on the move seemed the safest thing."

"Did you know so many people were looking for you?" Marcus asked.

Rebekah shook her head. "I just didn't want people seeing too much or asking too many questions. It's hard keeping some secrets in close quarters."

"That probably saved your life," Marcus commented, describing the near misses she'd had with the Broadway Butcher who, he realized, was almost certainly Pastor Heulen. "It's very likely he also set the St. Ignatius Street Boardinghouse fire, you were fortunate to have a concert that night."

"But that's not how it happened," Rebekah protested. "I didn't have that gig, not originally. Heading back to St. Ignatius that night, an old woman got in my face. She warned me away, telling me to find someplace, anyplace, else to be. I didn't exactly believe her but she gave me the nerves so badly that I went out and found that gig just to calm down. When I got back, the boardinghouse had burned up."

"You've no idea who she was?" Marcus inquired.

"No. Just a toothless old lady in a black shawl," Rebekah replied. "After that, I carried on with my music. I know it's nothing compared to the folks who died at the boardinghouse, but I lost everything in that fire except the trumpet and the clothes on my back. So, I had to start from scratch. But I've led a charmed life here, getting bigger and better gigs: Tillie's, Pod and Jerry's, Connie's Inn, the Log Cabin, Small's Paradise, the Radium Club, Lafayette Theatre. When Moe Gale told me I'd got the Savoy spot, it was the happiest moment of my life. That gig would fulfill my brother's wish.

"Has fulfilled his wish," she corrected herself. "Unless you gentlemen, and I hope you are gentlemen, tell anyone differently, history's going to say Gabriel Gibbs headlined the Savoy Ballroom and brought the damn roof down. I've made my brother's dream come true. Now, I have the choice to get my old life back.

"I never imagined Pastor Heulen would show up here, too. Even with that spotlight shining in my face, once the shooting started, I could tell it was him. He's not the kind of man you'd mistake for anybody else. In the end, I think he and I might be a little alike. Neither of us could let Gabriel go, even after he died. Except, maybe, I'm ready to now."

"You want to go back to being Rebekah?" Marcus asked.

"I love my brother and always will," Rebekah's smile was bittersweet. "but I swapped two years of my life for two years of his. I don't want to miss out on any more of mine."

"Then perhaps Gabriel Gibbs dies tonight of his wound?" Marcus suggested.

"With no body? How are you going to pull that off?" she asked.

"I am a physician," he replied. "Mister Hughes and Mister Fenno are well-regarded locals. With their collusion, I suspect we can manage something."

At that, Rebekah Gibbs' bittersweet smile lost its bitter.

Chapter Thirty

The three men helped Rebekah out the Savoy's rear door. "You'll be okay. Keep the wound clean, change the dressing every day, and don't exert yourself for a bit," Marcus advised, her before adding, "There's a family in Gates County that would be very glad to see you. You can't bring back Gabriel this time, but you can bring back yourself."

They watched her, silver trumpet tucked under her right arm, walk down the alley and out of sight.

"I believe it is past time for me to depart as well," Fenno announced. Ambling the opposite direction, he tipped his hat. "Mr. Hughes. Fishmonger." It was Fenno's customary slight but, Marcus thought, absent its usual malice.

Returning to the greenroom, Marcus opened up about the case in a way he hadn't previously, not even with Fort. Hughes, in turn, offered his thoughts and insights. They talked long into the night about the case and what it meant.

When the pair finally exited through the main doors onto Lennox Avenue, dawn's rays greeted them. "I don't believe I shall compose anything about Gibbs, either of them," Hughes concluded. "I cannot tell the real story and anything else would be but a pale shadow of the truth." Shaking hands, the two men parted. As Marcus walked, it seemed the city's heat wave had broken. The morning was crisp, almost cool. The first whiff of autumn traveled on the breeze.

Over his shoulder, Hughes called after him. "I won't tell you what to put in your report, Marcus. But, whatever it is, be truthful with yourself about who it really serves."

Returning to Boston, Marcus wired the Gibbs family in Gates County. Addressing the telegram to Ma and Pa Gibbs, he regretted to inform them that their son was dead, but at peace. And, in the time following his departure from Mississippi, there was no dishonor to be found either in his life or his death. On the matter of Rebekah, he offered better news. While he could make no promises that she would come home, their wayward daughter was free and happy.

Delayed by a final errand in in New York, it was dusk before Marcus reached the newly constructed art deco apartment building on Commonwealth Avenue he called home. Departing the Savoy and returning to the Martinique to collect his belongings, he realized someone in the city deserved the real story behind last night's events. At least in part.

Not Fort. Marcus liked the man but did not fully trust any confidences made to him to remain private in perpetuity. Instead, he returned to Harlem, eventually locating the boy Clifford Stryker.

"I understand you're the top numbers runner in Harlem?" Marcus began.

Uncertain how to respond to a barely-known upper class white inquiring about his questionable livelihood, Clifford eventually opted for the bold approach. "That's a fact."

"Am I right in thinking that, beyond just having quick feet, part of your job is knowing when to hold your tongue?"

The boy nodded.

"Good. There's something you deserve to know. But you've got to keep it to yourself. Do we have an understanding?"

Again, a guarded nod.

"You either have heard or will hear that my patient last night died. That is not true. I cannot tell you the reasons why the public story is different from the real story. I promise you the reasons are good ones. But it wouldn't be right to make you spend the rest of your life wondering if you had been a little faster, if you hadn't had that run in with the bulls, would that man would have lived. He did live and you did great job. I've trusted you with that and now I'm trusting you to keep it to yourself.

The boy's sincere but curiously adult smile told Marcus he'd placed his trust wisely.

Back in his apartment, Marcus unpacked. The discs acquired from Ralph Peer were added to his record collection. Deposited among the works of Copeland, Milhaud, Ravel, and Stravinsky, Marcus suspected they would soon be joined by the likes Armstrong, Ellington, and Coleman Hawkins. Put into a simple silver frame at a Back Bay workshop, the sketch of Marcus and Langston Hughes executed by Elmer Campbell assumed pride of place in Marcus's small living room. And there was the other piece of art Marcus had acquired during the investigation, in a New Orleans back alley. Art which, whether he wished to or not, he'd always keep close to his heart.

In the metal filing cabinet containing his professional papers, Marcus placed not one but two notarized copies of death certificates for Gabriel Gibbs. The first he had acquired from the Orleans Parish Medical Examiner. The second, from New York City's Bureau of Vital Statistics, had been filled out and signed in Marcus's hand. The signature of one of America's leading literary lights witnessed the document. Behind the scenes, the strength of the Fenno family name had persuaded the bureau to overlook the document's glaring irregularities.

Two other objects were more problematic. The photos showing Gabriel Gibbs. One obtained from Sam Gibbs, the other from E.J. Bellocq. These, Marcus stowed away in another cabinet while he considered what to put in his report. A decision on their ultimate deposition could wait until after that…and possibly longer.

Over the following days, Marcus took many long walks as he settled back into life in Boston, resumed his medical practice, and reflected upon the adventures of the past month. The case of Gabriel Gibbs was extraordinary but, in the main, prosaic. Gabriel had died in New Orleans. He had not come back from the dead. Rebekah Gibbs, with ingenuity, audacity, and talent, successfully posed as her late brother to achieve his dream. Part of Marcus lamented that he again failed to find evidence of a life, and afterlife, of wonders.

Or had he? Mysteries remained. What was the ultimate origin of the silver trumpet figuring so prominently in the tale? Rebekah's story, and William Blackmon's, revealed its provenance only as far back as Colonel Scobie and his enigmatic wife. Marcus wished he had examined it before Rebekah departed. Perhaps the instrument possessed unusual properties. Who was the man Marcus met in New Orleans that, presumably, gave him the tattoo which later saved his life? What, really, happened that night in the bayou? And who was the woman Rebekah encountered in Harlem, warning her away the night of the deadly boardinghouse fire?

To Marcus's knowledge, the ASPR never issued a report on Gabriel Gibbs. Perhaps Fenno's account proved too wild and confused even for them. Or, just maybe, he learned something about grieving for a lost loved one.

These ideas and others swirled in Marcus's head as he pondered the report he must soon write. He found that Hughes' parting words loomed large in his thoughts.

Epilogue

Boston; October 11, 1929

Marcus sat in the same Beacon Hill mansion, in the same room, even the same chair, where his investigation had begun six weeks earlier. Maintaining emphasis on the report's unofficial and clandestine nature, Walter Franklin Prince had again insisted on meeting privately at his house rather than at BSPR headquarters.

Across from him, for the better part of an hour, Prince had carefully perused Marcus's report. In all that time he had not commented or even looked at Marcus. Indeed, the research director's only reaction as he read were occasional deep, throaty noises that were very nearly grunts. Nervously, Marcus wondered what that portended. Again, he scanned the bookshelves while waiting for his companion to finish.

At last, Prince sat the folder down beside him. A moment of heavy silence passed between them before he began. "I'm disappointed. I expected better from you, Dr. Roads." Prince chastised.

It didn't seem like an opportune moment to remind his host to call him Marcus. "I'm unhappy with the report as well," the physician admitted. He could do no better, he explained to Prince. But he couldn't tell the man why.

Minutes later, he exited Prince's mansion. Marcus thought it unlikely he would see its inside again. He knew the report he'd handed the BSPR's leader was a chimera of half-truths, obfuscations, and deliberate falsehoods. But, for many reasons, he found himself unable or unwilling to do otherwise. To Marcus's mind, only the report's opening sentence told the unmitigated truth, "The Gabriel Gibbs shot at the Savoy Ballrom is the same Gabriel Gibbs born in Mississippi and killed in New Orleans…in every way that matters."

AUTHOR NOTES

The story of weaving together the various people, locations, and events (both historical and fictitious) comprising *Gabriel's Trumpet* could take up a book of its own (granted, one few people would care to read). Below, I have summarized a few aspects of this process either because I think readers may actually find them interesting or because I believe a specific deviation from the historical record deserves to be pointed out and put into context.

Gates County: The fictional Gates County is an amalgam of other Delta counties in northwest Mississippi. Its two largest communities, however, have additional stories to tell. Pilate's Point owes an obvious debt to Natchez, Mississippi and the former's Underbluff is a serviceable doppelganger of the latter's Under-the-Hill.

In contrast, the name of Gates County's largest settlement, Terraplane, is an homage. Whether directly referenced or not, bluesman Robert Johnson looms behind any tale about a roots musician with alleged supernatural dealings. Naming the town "Terraplane," the title of one of Johnson's best known songs, is my acknowledgement of his silent presence in stories such as *Gabriel's Trumpet*. Johnson scholarship has come a long way in recent decades. For readers curious about Johnson's real life (no less impressive than the myths which have grown up around him), I recommend Elijah Wald's biography/critical analysis

Escaping the Delta: Robert Johnson and the Invention of the Blues (Amistad, 2004).

Historical Figures: *Gabriel's Trumpet* makes extensive use of actual individuals in bringing the world of the 1920s to life. These range from the universally known, like Langston Hughes, to niche figures like Ralph Peer. With one major and two minor exceptions, I have endeavored to keep their portrayal and behavior within the parameters of what we know about them (even Willie "The Lion" Smith's distinctive quirk of referring to himself in the third person).

The major exception is New Orleans photographer E.J. Bellocq. While contemporaries portray Bellocq as odd, taciturn, and sometimes antagonistic in his dealings with others, those accounts stop well short of the disturbing and ominous figure I created to lend tension and atmosphere to Marcus Road's visit to Bellocq's studio. His ghoulish habit of photographing murder victims is entirely my creation. In contrast, his aesthetically impressive photos documenting the lives of Storyville's inhabitants are very real and an invaluable window into the lives of people largely ignored by the broader society in which they lived.

While all the other events and accounts referenced by Charles Fort in this story can be found in Fort's writings (even the object which fell from the sky in Marcus's hometown of Marblehead, Massachusetts), I created the three examples of possible genuine resurrection he presents in order to advance the story's narrative.

Finally, I have no idea what Dr. Eugene Roberts' black bag contained. I selected injectable morphine, as opposed to the ether mask preferred by Marcus Roads, as an opportunity to showcase differing techniques of medical practice in 1929.

Supernatural Investigation in the 1920s: While Marcus Roads and Theodore Fenno are my creations, the backstory for their rivalry and dueling investigations is rooted in history. This includes both the ASPR and BSPR as well as the other individuals named as part of both organizations. The *Scientific American* contest and the investigation into Margery/Mina

240

Crandon really happened and the fallout from that investigation did result in the BSPR splitting from the ASPR. For an enthralling historical account of the Margery Investigation, I strongly recommend David Jaher's *The Witch of Lyme Street* (Broadway Books. 2016).

Although it is well beyond the timeframe covered by *Gabriel's Trumpet*, readers may be interested to know that, after time's passage had healed wounds resulting from the Margery case (and the death of Walter Franklin Prince sapped much of the Boston Society's vitality), the ASPR reabsorbed the BSPR in 1941.

Terminology: Accuracy is a virtue in writing historical fiction, but it is not the only virtue. "Harlem Renaissance" is a retronym. At the time, the phenomenon was known as "The New Negro Movement." Not only is that a term I feel awkward using but it lacks the punch of "Harlem Renaissance." For those reasons, *Gabriel's Trumpet* embraces the anachronistic term.

SOURCES

The resources listed below provide a scholarly examination of many topics treated in this book. Because new information constantly comes to light and data is open to interpretation and reinterpretation, I cannot not vouch for all the information and interpretations these works offer, but all are useful sources for readers desiring a deeper look into these subjects. While most of the resources target a general audience, a few are academic in orientation. Likewise, while many are available as eBooks or otherwise easily and inexpensively available, a handful are obscure and not easy on the wallet. Many of these works have been through multiple printing or are reprints of older books. An attempt has been made to reference the most recent easily available edition.

Charles Fort
Fort, Charles. *The Complete Books of Charles Fort* (Dover Publications, 2013).
Steinmeyer, Jim. *Charles Fort: The Man Who Invented the Supernatural* (TarcherPerigree, 2016).

Jazz, General 1920s
Hadlock, Richard. *Jazz Masters of the 20s* (Da Capo, 1988).
Schuller, Gunther. *Early Jazz: Its Roots and Musical Development* (Oxford University Press, 1986).
Stewart, Rex. *Jazz Masters of the 30s* (De Capo, 1982).

Jazz, Location Specific

Charters, Samuel. *Trumpet around the Corner: The Story of New Orleans Jazz* (University Press of Mississippi, 2008).

McCoy, David B. *The 1920s: Early Jazz and the Harlem Renaissance* (Spare Change Press, 2014, eBook only).

Schaal, Hans-Jurgen. *Jazz: New York in the Roaring Twenties* (Taschen, 2013).

Stokes, W. Royal. *The Jazz Scene: An Informal History from New Orleans to 1990* (Oxford University Press, 1993).

The Harlem Renaissance and New York City

Ferguson, Jeffery B. *The Harlem Renaissance: A Brief History With Documents* (Bedford/St. Martin's, 2007).

Huggins, Nathan Irvin. *Voices from the Harlem Renaissance* (Oxford University Press, 1995).

Lankevich, George J. *New York City: A Short History* (NYU Press, 2002).

Rampersad, Arnold. *The Life of Langston Hughes: Vol 1: 1902-1941, I, Too, Sing America* (Oxford University Press, 2002).

Mississippi Delta

Bond, Bradley G. *Mississippi: A Documentary History* (University Press of Mississippi, 2005).

Cobb, James C. *The Most Southern Place on Earth: The Mississippi Delta and the Roots of Regional Identity* (Oxford University Press, 1994).

Mitchell, Dennis J. *A New History of Mississippi* (University Press of Mississippi, 2014).

Williams, Dianne. *Mississippi Folk and the Tales They Tell: Myths, Legends and Bald-Faced Lies* (The History Press, 2014).

New Orleans and Storyville

Everett, Peter. *Bellocq's Women.* (Jonathan Cape, 2000).

Garvey, Joan B. and Widmer, Mary Lou. *Beautiful Crescent: A History of New Orleans* (Pelican Publishing, 2012).

Krist, Gary: *Empire of Sin: A Story of Sex, Jazz, Murder, and the Battle for Modern New Orleans* (Broadway Books, 2015).

Landau, Emily Epstein: *Spectacular Wickedness: Sex, Race, and*

Memory in Storyville, New Orleans (LSU Press, 2013).

Spiritualism, General

Alison, Lydia W. "The American Society for Psychical Research." Originally Published in the *Journal of the American Society for Psychical Research*, Volume LII, January 1958, Number 1. Available online by survivalafterdeath.info at http://www.survivalafterdeath.info/articles/allison/aspr.htm
Aykroyd, Peter and Narth, Angela. *A History of Ghosts: The True Story of Seances, Mediums, Ghosts, and Ghostbusters* (Rodale, 2009).
Leonard, Todd. *Talking to the Other Side: A History of Modern Spiritualism and Mediumship: A Study of the Religion, Science, Philosophy and Mediums that Encompass this American-Made Religion* (iUniverse Inc., 2005).

Spiritualism, The "Margery" Case

Jaher, David. *The Witch of Lime Street: Séance, Seduction, and Houdini in the Spirit World* (Broadway Books. 2016).

Vuodun (Voodoo)

Filan, Kinaz. *The New Orleans Voodoo Handbook* (Destiny Books, 2011).
Star, Riley: *Voodoo: Voodoo History, Beliefs, Elements, Strains or Schools, Practices, Myths and Facts. An Introductory Guide* (NRB Publishing, 2016).
Turlington, Shannon R. *The Complete Idiot's Guide ® to Voodoo* (Alpha, 2001).

DID YOU ENJOY WHAT YOU JUST READ?

If you enjoyed this book, *please* review it on Amazon and GoodReads!

It's the best way to support the author!

For fantastic fiction, in-depth articles by your favourite authors, open submissions, and more, please...

VISIT OUR WEBSITE
18thwall.com/

LIKE US ON FACEBOOK
facebook.com/18thwall/

FOLLOW US ON TWITTER
@18thWall

We'd love to hear from you!
You help make these books possible.

Sockhops & Seances

Curated by Nicole Petit

Kara Dennison's "Son of the Wolf"
From Nicole Petit's New Collection, Sockhops & Seances

Think back, if you will, to the Werewolf. The centerpiece of Shoreside Amusements, a wooden coaster that has been experienced by parents, children, and eventually those children's children. A staple of Port Buckroe's summer life. Tacky, but beloved nonetheless. A thrill ride that's more giggle than scream, from the fading painted maw of the mascot to the signs declaring *You survived the Werewolf's bite!* as you exit the ride.

If you asked visitors how highly they rated the Werewolf, it might receive a good-natured shrug at best. It was like asking what they thought of the restrooms or the hot dog stand. It was there, of course. What's there to think?

Year after year, that was the way of it: an unspoken, passive approval of the old coaster, ridden regularly but not enthusiastically. A first "big kids' ride" for children, something a little less threatening when the grandparents were in town. But certainly nothing special.

Of course, you know the tried-and-true way to make people care about something: replace it.

"The wolf will roar in agony when the final support is placed. His spirit will be released to ravage the town unchecked, no longer fed by the screams of his prey."

Lily squinted her eyes shut. "They're building a new roller coaster, Heck, not digging up a graveyard. Don't turn this into one of your things."

Lily's twin sister was well past it being "one of her things," apparently.

"The fall of the Werewolf and the rise of the interloper will bring seven centuries of suffering to Port Buckroe. Our only hope is scrapping the replacement and destroying the parts."

"Why seven?"

"The screams of the victims will ring out for…what?"

"Why seven?" Lily repeated. "Is that symbolic, or did it come to you in a dream?"

Heck tensed her shoulders; Lily could imagine her sour face.

"The ways of the spirits are not to be questioned."

"Ah. Of course they're not."

Lily knew the real reason for the outbursts, which she'd spouted to anyone in earshot as soon as the ride closed: Heck was attached, but didn't want to admit to being sixteen and in love with a "kiddie ride."

"The screams will not be of delight, mark my words." Heck peered in their shared vanity mirror, attempting to straighten out her eyeliner. So far she'd only managed to thicken both eyes' worth significantly. In one or two more rounds, it would go from vampy to comical.

"Don't let dad hear you talking like that. He's already nervous about the opening."

Heck frowned at her reflection. "And well he should be. To think, one of my own flesh and blood would be the one to bring such ruin upon my hometown."

This had, unfortunately for Lily, been Heck's mood ever since their father landed the new coaster project. He'd built a few carnival rides before and presented some hypothetical designs to liven up the park, but nothing had taken until Mel Bloom got bold and said the S word: "steel."

There had been a steel kiddie coaster running successfully in Ohio since '52, and rumor had it California was aiming to have one up and running before 1960. If Shoreside could squeak theirs in before then, it would be one for the record books: the world's first tubular steel roller coaster, right in unassuming little Port Buckroe.

The good news was the park wanted it. The bad news was there was only so much space, and they couldn't afford to buy out enough land for Bloom's design *and* actually build it. Something had to go. There was one obvious choice, of course: out with the old coaster, in with the new.

As soon as he heard, he immediately began reworking the ride, knowing that his new creation might be seen as an interloper or even a "Werewolf-Killer." Sure enough, that was the name the daily papers gave it. To appease them, Shoreside named the new attraction Son of the Wolf, pitching it as a "worthy successor" to the original. For extra goodwill, Bloom even invited the Werewolf's original designer to collaborate with him on the redesign.

248

But despite all the goodwill, all the hand-shaking, and all the promises that Son of the Wolf would be every bit as good as the mainstay whose patch it was invading, the locals were cross. And none was crosser than Helen Bloom, one of the designer's own daughters.

Lily, on the other hand, was fine with the whole thing. If anything, she was excited. She'd never been a fan of amusement park rides, but her father's work on the new coaster had gone some way to changing her mind. Seeing the calculations and blueprints laid out on the kitchen table were soothing in a way. There was something nice, something reassuring, about knowing that the thrills were actually controlled by checked and double-checked numbers. As amusements, they bored her; as perfectly functioning machines, she was slowly becoming enamored.

"So I take it you won't be going to the test ride tonight?"

Heck whipped her head around, glaring at her sister through over-lined eyes. "I will, actually. But I won't be riding, naturally."

"Really. I…assumed you'd be protesting via your absence." Lily barely stopped herself from saying she'd *hoped.*

"Well, I shall be protesting via my presence. Someone should be on hand when the dam breaks. And if no one else is willing to see the truth of this catastrophe, then I will have to be on hand to make that truth known."

Lily winced. "Please don't."

Heck went back to her makeup, leaving Lily with a mental image of her sister crashing the gathering late that night, swishing and wailing like some movie mystic. Fortunately, the two were to a point where no one who knew them well confused them, so the antics of one would rarely reflect on the other in any permanent way.

Still. This was about their *dad.*

She put the thought aside for the rest of the day, eventually walking to Shoreside in the afternoon.

The beach was only a few blocks from their house, and the scorch of summer wouldn't set in for another few weeks. Neither would the Shoreside tourists: most visitors could only stare curiously at the fence around the park as they drove past, as the gates wouldn't open until a good two weeks from then. They could, however, wonder at the two metal hills that poked above the fence, more like a latticework sea-monster than a werewolf. Where the massive, intricate criss-cross of wood beams had once stood, there was a streamlined curve of steel, supported with just more than the bare minimum of supports for safety.

Lily stopped a block from the beach to stare across at the Son of the Wolf—the top bits of it, anyway—with vicarious pride. She remembered the early stages, the sudden alterations, the sleepless nights sitting up at the kitchen table watching her dad attempt to wrangle numbers into working order. And there it was now, a hair's breadth from its world premiere.

"I don't care what anyone says, I like it."

The voice by Lily's ear surprised her. She flinched, but caught herself when she saw the speaker. It was Brian Callahan from her history class. Not someone she knew particularly well, but vocal enough that she'd learned his name.

"Mm. Me, too." She beamed, looking back at the coaster.

"I mean, sure. Hendricks built some of the most iconic rides on the East Coast, but everything has its time, you know?"

Lily peered at Brian out the corner of her eye. She genuinely couldn't tell if he was being sarcastic or not. His expression remained impassive.

"Erm...Hendricks?"

"Yeah, you know. Carl Hendricks. Built the Werewolf. And the Skull-Rattler in Jersey."

"Oh."

"He did the Beachside Specter down in Florida, too. Both of those are still up and running just fine." Brian sniffed. "I don't know about this whole steel thing. It's fine for the kiddie rides, but what's it gonna feel like to actually ride? You won't get the same sounds, neither."

Lily smiled awkwardly. "Well, you know. We don't know yet, do we?"

www.ingramcontent.com/pod-product-compliance
Lightning Source LLC
Chambersburg PA
CBHW051528280626
47161CB00022B/2853